Middle East peace? It must be a mirage. But for Joe Dekel, "certified paranoid," one-time novelist and Israel's only religious anarchist, the quest for peace between old enemies leads to a maze of intrigue among old friends . . . Sent by his newspaper's editor to cover an Israeli-Palestinian Peace Conference in New York, Dekel is waylaid by an earnest young American Jew who informs him he is Joe Dekel's "Silencer," assigned by a maverick right-wing blacklister to keep unwelcome pro-Palestinian literature from being published in the United States.

Truth or fantasy? Led to a secret rendezvous in a downtown office block, Dekel finds not his youthful informant but a wrinkled old man with a bludgeoned head, who denounces him as a traitor, then dies . . .

Who is manipulating whom? The "Silencer" has disappeared. The dead man is the alleged blacklister, Murray Waiskopf. Is someone setting Joe Dekel up? True to his vocation of making the wrong moves for the right reasons, Joe follows the twisted trail of clues, into a labyrinth of abduction and violence, hints of spy scandals and bizarre alliances between American Christian fundamentalists and Jewish zealots, against the background of Palestinian rebellion and the schisms of modern Israel. Will Joe Dekel ever find out what the eccentric FBI Agent Oral Kool is after? Will he fall foul of peace activist Dorothy Morgenthal's deadly nunchaku sticks? Is Joe Dekel really being Silenced, or is he just falling prey to the shadows of his own frustrations and fears?

From New York to the schizoid city, Jerusalem, from the West Bank to the Church of the Living Christ in Utah, Joe and his wife, the stubborn and determined Anat, are jerked along the tangled path of deceptions in a political thriller which charts the forbidden zones of the Israeli-Palestinian feud.

From the critically acclaimed author of the *Blok* Trilogy comes a novel which combines comedy and tragedy mixed with the devastating anarchic clarity which is uniquely Louvish.

On *City of Blok*

"All mediterranean life is here . . . yet the author achieves an articulate account with commendable prose . . . Buy the book and enjoy, but then place it on a high bookshelf out of reach of your children, unless they are studying for a degree in obscene expletives."

Jewish Gazette

"Louvish's novels juxtapose recent Israeli history with grotesque fantasy, rather like a Jewish *One Hundred Years of Solitude* . . . Louvish is rather more frenzied than Philip Roth – but no less humorous – but, unlike Roth he excels as a political satirist in the school of Heller and Vonnegut . . . No writer has captured better the minutiae of present-day Jerusalem . . . *City of Blok* is especially powerful when it finally differentiates between its proliferating Babel of voices . . . His commitment to a saner world is clear. On one level this makes reading Louvish particularly terrifying. For he has probably anticipated better than anyone outside Israel further madness to come."

BRYAN CHEYETTE, *Times Literary Supplement*

"Original and anarchic . . . *City of Blok* is an ambitious book. It would not have achieved its objectives, as it does, had its anarchic purposefulness not been supported by literary skills. The fabric of the prose is admirable . . . Above all, it is Louvish's passion – his fulminating anger – that elevates *City of Blok* to excellence. The sections condemning the martial spirit and, in particular, the last part of the book, which bewails that abominable and criminal adventure, The Lebanon War, are no less than brilliant."

MORIS FARHI, *Jewish Quarterly*

"Louvish writes like a fire in a munitions dump: explosive and breathtaking . . . probably a Booker Prize winner."

New Musical Express

"Louvish comes into his own as a satirist rather than stand-up comedian, with an enviable gift for making hardened Zionists and PLO leaders squirm."

JONATHAN KEATES, *Observer*

"Simon Louvish is a real comic writer, one who makes jokes about life and death, love and fear, intellect and emotion. He is a proper satirist (which is good news for those of us who get fed up with the parochial sketches by literary groupies masquerading as such, for Swifts read sparrows), and he is a born storyteller."

GILLIAN REYNOLDS, *Punch*

On *The Therapy of Avram Blok*

"The book succeeds as the hilarious wail of a stand-up comic delivering punch-lines from the rubble. Mr Louvish has enough combustible talent to earn the comparisons with Joseph Heller, Kurt Vonnegut and Swift that have come his way."

New York Times Book Review

"A great fizzing parcel-bomb of a book . . . guaranteed to offend and enrage, to make all save the most effete and illiterate roar and whoop and weep with laughter"   *Punch*

"So ambitious, so assured, so brilliantly brought off . . . sheer unstoppable verve . . . irresistible"   *Daily Telegraph*

"This great sack of a novel, bulging with allegory, fantasy and black humour"   *Guardian*

"Highly intelligent and very funny . . . demonstrably talented"
Financial Times

"If they gave Nobel prizes for books of unflagging energy, this would certainly be a contender"

CLANCY SIGAL, *Kaleidoscope*

"He writes with the power of an old testament prophet in the style of a modern absurdist – and arrives on the literary scene with the force of a hurricane."

Kansas City Star

"Read it at your peril . . ."   *Jewish Chonicle*

THE SILENCER

THE SILENCER

Another Levantine Tale

SIMON LOUVISH

INTERLINK BOOKS

An imprint of Interlink Publishing Group, Inc.

NEW YORK

First Emerging Voices edition published 1993 by

INTERLINK BOOKS
An imprint of Interlink Publishing Group, Inc.
99 Seventh Avenue
Brooklyn, New York 11215

Originally published in Great Britain by Bloomsbury
Publishing Ltd.

Library of Congress Cataloging-in-Publication Data
Louvish, Simon.
    The silencer: another Levantine tale / Simon Louvish.—1st
emerging voices ed.
        p.   cm.
    ISBN 1–56656–116–7—ISBN 1–56656–108–6 (pbk.)
    I. Title.
PR6062.0785S57   1993
833′.914—dc20
                                                    92–24536
                                                    CIP

Printed and bound in the United States of America

10 9 8 7 6 5 4 3 2 1

For Abbas

We lived through the real thing!

1

MAN HAT ON

February, 1989

A CERTIFIED PARANOID, Son of my People, I suspected for some time I had a Silencer but had no real proof until he turned up, creeping up on me like a bad dream, whispering his existence in my ear. In this case it was he, not I, who was Daniel in the lions' den, as he had gatecrashed the Special Conference on Jewish-Palestinian Peace in the guise of a human being. Correction, a journalist, flying the colors of some obscure ethnic rag in New Jersey. They proliferate, I am told, out there over the Hudson, espousing views ranging from a little left of Isaiah to far right of Attila the Hun.

My People! And my Cousins, the Palestinian Enemy, crowding into the New York University hall like lemmings who have misplaced the ocean. Hawking, spitting, muttering and grumbling about precedence, they take their place in the Aaron Spelling Lecture Hall. Outside, the mock Greek temple building's pediment is inscribed with noble, historical names: Homer, Herodotus, Sophocles, Plato, Aristotle, Demosthenes, Cicero, Virgil. But inside we are unable to field more than Yochai Magen-David, ex-Chief of Military Intelligence and converted ex-guru of the anti-Arab crusade, now a spear carrier for Israeli-Palestinian Peace; Daoud Abu-Naim, Deputy Speaker of the Palestine National Congress and one of the twelve right arms of Chairman Yassir Arafat; Eliyahu Saltsman, Member of the Israeli Parliament, the Knesset, for the Citizens Rights Party which espouses dialogue with the Palestine Liberation Organization, Reserve Sergeant Major and Professor of Human Ecology at Tel Aviv University; Akram Ibn Ghallallah, deposed Mayor of Ramallah, on the Israeli occupied West Bank; Yirmiyahu Dubcek, Industrialist and founder of the Israeli-

3

Palestinian Center for Reconciliation; Hatem Abu Riad, ex-terrorist newly converted to pigeonhood; Howard Battalion-Gold, ex-President of the World Jewish Congress and convertee to the Great Historical Compromise which the Conference was called to proclaim. Haloes shone above everyone, none so brightly as above the gray-white head of Dorothy Morgenthal, Conference Organizer, a tough leather-hide mother-of-four and ex-wife of three who had cut her teeth on the Civil Rights movement of the 1960s and had, only three weeks before, bearded, so to speak, Chairman Arafat himself in a hotel room in Stockholm and prized out of him his first unequivocal declaration of recognition of the State of Israel. It was breakfast time, she had revealed to me over a late Bagel Nosh down in the East Village, and the Chairman had wheeled into his presence the morning slops he had become addicted to since the Beirut siege of 1982: A large bowl of salad topped with cornflakes washed down with hot tea, which the Chairman stirred vigorously with a wooden spoon, then adding two spoonfuls of honey. Matching bowls were offered to each of the four American Jewish delegates who had come to Sweden to persuade the Chairman not to shirk his decisive Peace Initiative at his coming United Nations address due three days thence at Geneva.

"I was the only one who ate the concoction," she told me, biting through baked dough and cream cheese, "while my colleagues simply picked at it, very timidly. Then I called for more. He gave me half his. I said to him: Can't we do the same with the land? He laughed, and told me I reminded him of his own mother. I concealed my unease."

Of such trifles are historic moments conceived. But I liked Dorothy. She reminded me of my own mother, but I didn't tell her this. Some analogies I am not yet ready to take. When my editor, Nahum Lauterman, manipulator extraordinary, asked me to abandon my usual TV column and take the next El Al flight out of Tel Aviv, Israel, to Jew York to cover the Jewish-

4

Palestinian Conference I did my usual Moses act: But I am slow of speech, and of a slow tongue, and cleft palate. See, no mole upon the right cheek, no gap between the teeth. I am definitely not the Mahdi, the Expected One. But he pooh-poohed my fears. Get your head out from between your legs, Joe Dekel, he said, using the *shem hamephorash*, the Explicit Name, in a vain attempt to appropriate my soul. Peace! he said, the great Salaam, the *sulha*, the reconciliation of mortal enemies which alone can end the hundred years' war in this benighted sliver of shit both sides call our homeland. I can't have you, one of the nation's ace journalists, sitting at home and driveling about *Dynasty* and *Are You Being Served?* Here is a First Class ticket to New York, son of a bitch, see how I mollycoddle my Chosen Ones? Now get out there and make good!

So here I am, not even bothering to hide my hattie, the emblematic skullcap or *kipa* of the Faithful and Devout, as I usually do on jaunts abroad, to avoid being accosted in the streets and subways and underwhelmed by declarations of sympathy and support for policies I hate and revile. But here in Manhattan, I thought, there should be safety in numbers. As in the Homeland, I should be inconspicuous in the melting pot, the other promised and promoted land . . .

There is no doubt the times demand action. It has become too difficult to hide, even in one's own four walls. Too damaging to the self, the self's esteem, to crawl under the bed, the armchair, the sofa, to barricade the door, seal up the windows, put on blindfolds and earplugs and switch off the sounds of battle, insurrection, pain, anguish, the anger and frustration of the oppressed, the loutish bays of the oppressor, the thud of wooden clubs against flesh and bone, the clattering fire of "plastic" bullets and "live" rounds, the teeming babbles and strangled protests of thousands rounded up into detention camps, prisons and police cells.

The times, they are a-changing, Bob Dylan sang, twenty

5

million years ago, but he did not have this in mind. Since December 1987 the Palestinian *intifada*, or insurrection, in the West Bank and the Gaza Strip, has been a fact of life shattering official conceptions, overturning moribund expectations, killing myths, destroying shibboleths: The "liberal occupation," "the creation of facts," "the wholeness of Israel," "time is on our side." Myths of the primitiveness of our enemies: And lo, the natives are not happy to be hewers of wood, drawers of water, passive, quiescent, *untermenschen* shaken occasionally by "outside incitement" leading to acts of mindless terror. Suddenly they are an organized force, united in voice and action, demanding rights, refusing collaboration, facing armored cars and armed soldiers with rocks in slings and petrol bombs made out of milk and soda-pop bottles.

How are the mighty fallen. And yet, not so fast. For are we not too victims, Davids, not Goliaths, charred remnants of holocausts, bona fide wretched of the earth, a card-carrying oppressed people, having by circumstance to bite and scratch to survive? Spewed out by the world's nations, have we not, by our blood, and the sweat of our brow (not to speak of diaspora donations and United States aid), carved out for ourselves a home in our ancient homeland, readied ourselves to defend it, our lives, our women and children, by all means, sadly, in a savage, ruthless world? And so, in our eyes, the children of stones, no longer mute victims, are transmuted, by our own fears, into slavering Nazis, riding on gray unseen tanks, their slingshots deadly arrows aimed at the heart of our will to fight on . . .

"We fucked ourselves up completely," I told Dorothy, as she demolished a Bagel Nosh salad. "We used to be Ari Ben-Canaan, Paul Newman, with blond hairs on our chest. Today we're back to being Janusz Korcak, following the kiddies into the gas chamber. All our tanks and guns and warplanes are will-o'-the-wisps, ghosts that have failed to frighten our enemies. We're back in the ghetto again."

"Nebesch," she said. "I weep for the bastards who run your country. Rabin, Peres, Shamir. Who do they think they're fooling? Don't tell me: The diaspora, mainly America's Jews. Well, let me tell you, they have not lobotomized all of us. We can still smell a turd under our face, even if they call it a rose."

I knew the feeling. The same happened to me long ago, but never so strongly as over the Lebanon War of 1982. The sense of the terminal collapse of the myth under napalm, in the reek of burnt corpses and mass graves. The lies, the perfidy, the total collapse of all moral values, the plunge into the abyss of stupidity and deceit. The tanks that punched into refugee camps and cities, the planes that bombed apartment buildings. And at the finale, the hands washing themselves clean of the Sabra and Shatilla massacre. I wrote a novel, trying to encompass that madness, a work of fiction, about the aftermath. A thriller, based loosely on an old friend who had become embroiled in the shadowy world of spy-counterspy and had vanished into the oblivion of censored reports and gossip. It was called *The Death of Moishe-Ganef*. And therein lies the curious root of my present tale, the first echoes of my Silencer's whisper . . .

And behold, in the abyss post-Lebanon we found there were depths which we had not yet begun to plumb! The ten thousand clubs ordered by the army from a carpenter in Tel Aviv, which his Arab workers refused, to his surprised chagrin, to produce, the Defense Forces' gravel-shooting truck, the Ministerial order to break bones and heads, the children inexplicably dead of gunshot wounds . . . *Intifada* time, and out of the pit, out of the deepest despair, nevertheless, new moves, the desperate attempt to crawl up and out, at long last, towards the impossible, forbidden discourse, now raising its hesitant head . . .

Yochai Magen-David makes the keynote speech. He praises a historical breakthrough: When Chairman Arafat recognized Israel at Geneva, everything in the Middle East changed. The historic roles of compromiser and rejector had switched. The

PLO was now a partner for dialogue, whatever the government of Israel might say. Private persons must step in now where the government fears to tread. He himself, who had once accused the Palestinians of planning genocide, was recanting his old ideas in public. He beat his breast physically, producing a somewhat hollow sound, which nevertheless earned him applause. He called for a change of heart, of mind, of policy. He saw light at the end of the tunnel. Then he sat down, and was heard to demand a hamburger should be brought to the podium. Dorothy Morgenthal, at his left, calmed him with a hand at his neck, fingers poised over the pressure points.

Daoud Abu-Naim, deputy to Yassir Arafat, spoke next, praising his predecessor. We have all got much to learn from each other. We meet to build a bridge over a chasm of misunderstanding and hatred. For decades we have killed and maimed and destroyed each other. Now the time has come to speak of brotherhood. The brotherhood of the Jews, who have suffered so much in the past, and of the Palestinians, who are suffering now. Peace, in the Holy Land, between equals, for our children, and for all humanity.

I joined the applause. After all, here was a bona fide terrorist, the slavering Arab beast of our propaganda, a baby killer from our worst nightmares, cooing and stroking our ruffled feathers. Here at least was something new. Perhaps, after all, there is hope, Joe Dekel? You never know until you've tried . . .

As when I wrote my book, and sent out the manuscript. My friend in Tel Aviv, Yigal Zayit, the publisher, published it in the Holy Tongue. He put on it a cover with an exploding truck and a portrait of the Ayatollah Khomeini. I favored a naked girl with open legs, but he decided to stick with the text. Then we sent the manuscript to a string of New York houses. No result. What else could we expect? My next-door neighbor, the veteran author Bardak, laughed in my face to hear my woes. "To die in New York," he said. "It is our destiny. Who wants to read your gloomy prognoses? And anyway . . ." He edged away towards his German motorbike, with sidecar, *circa* '42, disappearing in a wodge of nods and winks, hints of enemy action, boycotts, blacklists. I have heard all this before. My friends are all convinced their world fame is blocked by sinister forces: Powerful right-wing lobbies, ultra-Zionist zealots, market forces, the Illuminati. I am as paranoid as the next liberal bleeding heart in this country. I look under my bed, my pillow, my car chassis, every day, for booby traps, bombs, blood, lice, frogs, the plague of the first, second and third born. We have been taught from birth to fear our enemies. But we were not warned how they might so proliferate. We have become like Chico Marx's grandfather, who put the cheese in a-mousetraps, and brought his own mice with him. "In Each Generation, They Rise Upon Us To Destroy Us, And In Each Generation, The Lord Blessed Be He Saves Us From Their Hand." And if not the Lord, the Israel Defense Forces. Many people have now confused the two. So I just continued to send out my manuscript, filing away the rising tide of rejections, counting my modest local gains. Living my life with Anat, the lady I live and love with, in the few moments she could tear from her professional devotion as an organizer for the Arts of the City. We now have a modest apartment in the white areas of town, in Rehavia, away from the ultra-orthodox neighborhood near which we lived before, whose youthful zealots took to slashing the tires of our beloved beach buggy, Alexander, in protest at our abandoned lifestyle, i.e. Anat's perambulation in summer in bare-armed and bare-legged clothing, anathema to God's Own Troops. At least in our present apartment in the secular section we can put our feet up and joyously curse the bizarre antics of our people as seen on our TV. The never-ending Wars of the Rabbis, the Yogi Kibbutz, the Saga of the Stolen Brazilian Baby, the Jewish Sioux Chief arriving for his Bar Mitzvah, not to speak of the repeated saga of our election process, the ur-satire of our election broadcasts: The mumbling

Rabbis, the Cult of the Lubavitch, the pro-Transfer Party, the battle of the pigmy giants; Likud versus Labor, the two Golems who hate each other but are unable to tear the Aleph off each other's foreheads to render one or the other *Met* – Dead, and so have ended up in the sweaty contraceptive embrace of another National "Unity" government. And, amid all this, the *intifada*, appearing, like an inevitable superimposition on a censored screen that can't quite be cleared of the rolling bad news.

"In all this," said Anat, "you want to worry about whether they're going to publish your little book in New York? Just be thankful they've decided not to call you up to batter ten-year-old kids to death with a club."

She was right, as usual. I have no sense of proportion. My own life, and that of the Universe, seem to me to be interchangeable. It is a personality defect, intensified by four decades of life on Our Soil. I have to have things that are tangible to prove to me existence is. I have been reduced by the grotesqueness of my surroundings to a pre-Kantian mode of being. I cannot accept synthetic judgements a priori. Only my self, my friends, my VCR, my personal computer and television screen, my hi-fi, my fridge, my blender. Everything else, the Nation, the State, the Government, the Financial Recovery Plan, can only function as potentialities. Apart from God. My own private vision. No salesmen or delegates need apply. This particular issue is now closed to discussion. Does anyone want to buy a used soul?

The Conference's first session broke up, amid an optimistic glow. Mortal enemies had sat together and yodeled. The lion and the lamb, et cetera, though it was more like a reunion of geriatric vultures, who have nothing left but each other to feed on. The Israeli journalists, my colleagues who had flown with me across the oceans, were already getting bored. "So who cares about meeting with the PLO?" said Milek Stuckman from *M*—, "they are uninteresting people who dress very badly, smell of garlic and use terrible aftershaves." He should know, having won the World Halitosis Championship fifteen times running, against stiff opposition. But my colleague, Amnon E—, who is a decent scribbler, was impressed, and said it was "a good show. Anything is better than Algiers . . ." he added, rolling his eyes towards the ceiling. Dorothy Morgenthal, visibly relieved, motioned to us and said: "We're going out to get Yochai his hamburger. God save me from ex-generals and ministers, they can't tie their own shoelaces. There used to be a Chock-Full-O'Nuts on the corner. If not, it'll have to be Grandma's Cafe."

I said I would join them and sat down to gather my notes together. I was not sure whether I could take either option. I was not quite up to listening to Yochai and Abu-Naim beating each other again into the ground with which side had murdered more of the other's secret agents in 1959. Newly-found brotherhood between enemies is fine in principle, but the practice can get a bit queasy. It's not only nuts they can be chock full o'. As I stayed behind, the hall thinning out and the security men filing in to check if anyone had left anything lethal, I felt a presence at my right elbow, and glanced up to see a willowy American youth with a wispy moustache and a knitted skullcap. They cannot be escaped, and I cursed the day I decided to drop my usual policy of dispensing with my own hattie outside the Holy Land, not that even that precaution might have saved me here. The youth wore a tag marked "PRESS: THE NEW JERSEY JEWISH COURIER."

"You're Joe Dekel," he said. "I've seen your picture."

"I haven't made a movie since Stroheim," I said, alarm choking me. Had they posted my monicker on the U.S. Mail Wanted section? Or on twenty-foot-high posters, as of the Ayatollah Khomeini, stuck on the side of the Empire State Building? Paranoia can only go so far. But he went on: "I know all about you. I've read your book, the English manuscript. Unfortunately I can't read Hebrew. I really enjoy the way you write. But you wonder how I know. I'm not really a journalist. Do I work for a literary agent or publisher? No. Can I see through walls? Not really. Have you guessed yet? I'm your official Silencer. I work with the people who make sure your kind of book won't be published in the United States. In Israel, that's your privilege. Sweden? We don't mind. San Marino? Be our guest. But the United States, that's a problem. I think we should talk outside. Do you have a moment? I'm sorry, I didn't tell you my name . . ."

For a Silencer he was incredibly gabby as he hopped, skipped and jumped at my side, down the swathe of Uptown Broadway, past the Barnard Bookforum and Ollie's Noodle Shop And Grill on 116th Street. It was a familiar February, with the aftermath of snow lying in cold muddy pits at every street corner. The sky a gray steel canopy, locking in the old apartment blocks. Green-grocers kept their merchandise behind icicle-licked glass.

"Didi Schaeffer," he introduced himself; "a good Jew. What-ever that means, nowadays. I used to think it was a simple matter. You went to shul. You *benched*. You demonstrated for Israel. Your parents gave to the UJA. If your heart told you, you went to Israel. You worked on kibbutz. You kissed the Western Wall. I grew up, like my father, with the little blue and white tin. Pennies for the Jewish National Fund. When I was able to put in a dime, I was proud."

"Inflation," I said. "It hits all of us."

"Then I found it wasn't that easy. The Six-Day War. Israel was encircled. The Arabs were threatening to drive the Jews into the sea. I was thirteen years old. Just that month Bar Mitzvah. I was scared to death. It was as if the knife was being held at my own throat. But what could I do? I was just a kid. When Israel was saved, I cried all day with joy. I made up my mind I would do what I could to see the Jews were never in such danger again.

"Why didn't I go to Israel, you're saying?" I was saying absolutely nothing. "I went, when I was seventeen, and loved it. But my parents weren't keen. The usual story, they wanted me to make good, be a doctor, a lawyer, get into real estate and all that stuff. They sent me to college, on a business course. Go to Israel later, if you want, they said. I got involved with the Jewish student groups there. Then whoops, the 1973 War. Yom Kippur. Israel is attacked by the Arabs again. Demonstrations, fund raising, the whole shtik. It was at that point I met Murray Waiskopf. You heard the name? I didn't expect you did."

We were still standing on the corner of 116th Street, marooned by a huge pool of freezing glop thrown at our legs by passing cars. I moved down the street in the direction of Riverside Drive. He followed me, geysering like Old Faithful. It was a punishment by the God of my enemies for my presumption in talking Peace with the Infidel. If I closed my eyes, would he vanish, like Hamlet's father's ghost, at Elsinore? I cursed the moment I had left my earplugs at the Beacon Hotel.

"Murray Waiskopf," he repeated. "He had been a big macher in the United Jewish Appeal. For thirty years he had been a publisher. Then he had retired to devote himself full time to a new project, for which he was recruiting staff. He was going to open an independent office loosely affiliated to the Anti-Slander League. It would have its own personnel and facilities and would be strictly unofficial and deniable. The Anti-Slander League collects and publishes information about anti-Semitic and anti-Zionist activities in the United States. Nazi groups, white supremacists, Arab lobbies and propagandists. But Murray's office was going to deal with a new, growing problem – the Jewish and Israeli defeatists."

At last, he was getting round to Joe Dekel. I uncurled my ears and turned to listen.

"You know, a lot of people talk too much," he said. We had crossed over Riverside Drive. We leaned against the stone fence looking down on the park, the busy freeway beyond, and the gray smudged swirl of the Hudson. New Jersey was hidden in fog. The park was covered in slush and deserted. In the autumn, I remembered, squirrels gambolled here in hundreds, rushing up and practically spitting on any human hand that failed to hold out a crumb. "People babble," he said, "they don't hold their peace. You know what I mean? They don't wait and reflect about the effects of what they're saying. They think they have a right to their opinion. Which they have, but do they think of the others? Do they consider what ammunition they're giving to those who want to cut their throats? It all boils down to how you look at the situation Jews are in today, and whether it's different from how it's been through the ages. Yes, we have a Jewish state. Yes, it has an army, and tanks, and aircraft, and missiles. And most of us feel we have to have that, we know the Holocaust is not a myth. But does it make us any more loved, or even tolerated, in the world? That's the basic question. We lost a third of our numbers in Europe. Our strongest presence is in the United States. Because we're strong here, people think we're all-powerful. They think we run the world, the press, TV, the Pentagon. In fact we are on a knife's edge. We hold on to threads that can be cut tomorrow. The bottom line is, nobody wants the Jews, except the Jews. And some of them are doubtful."

"Self-haters." I got a word in edgeways. "I was a founder member."

"I know," he said. "It's in my file. I know all there is to know about you. Your maverick view of religion. Your leftist ties with the *Matspen* movement – the Jerusalem Group, ultra-Trotskyites. A Socialist Middle East, with all the trimmings. You're an ex-Intelligence Officer in *Tsahal*.* You used to write the political column, for *H—*, before you gave up and started doing your regular TV column. Then in the Lebanon War you reactivated yourself – anti-government articles, letters, demonstrations. Ad-Hoc Committee Against The War In Lebanon. End The Occupation. Support For Conscientious Objectors. The Red Line. The Twenty-First Year. And now you're meeting the PLO. It's illegal by Israeli law. You could get three years' jail or a fine."

*The Israel Defense Forces.

15

"And I would meet people like you in jail," I said. "*Gush Emunim*. Right-wing terrorists. Killers of Arabs without a license. Missionaries for Blood and Fire. On second thoughts, I'd be safe. I think they pardoned the last batch of you just the other day."

"You're not listening," he said. "Why am I telling you this? I'm working for an office that isn't there. The Waiskopf Project doesn't exist. Nobody keeps files on dissident Jews and Israelis. Nobody boycotts leftist Israeli films, plays, books, et cetera. It's a paranoid myth. A blood libel. There is no McCarthy-style blacklist preventing people like you from being heard, seen, published in the United States. Do you hear me? It's all your rabid imagination."

"You don't exist," I told him. "You're a ghost. We're not standing here, freezing our balls off. We're actually floating in a jar of pickled cucumbers."

"You better believe it," he said. "What are you going to do? Go about foaming at the mouth, crying that the Jews are after you? Forget it. You just can't fight shadows. Not that we have it all our own way. Only a month ago Murray was told to fuck off by a big macher at Harper & Row. We had a problem with a book about Israeli arms sales. But they're going to publish anyway."

"There's hope for me yet."

"Don't count on it. Your book's as easy to kill off as a fly. Who wants it anyway? Unpublished novels. Stack 'em up, they'll reach right up to Mars. You wouldn't sell a thousand copies. There are four million Jews in New York City, but they don't want to read depressing Israeli novels. They want to keep their dreams, their hopes intact. They have a right to have a bit of *naches*."

"*Schlaff, mein kinderlech, schlaff . . .*" I yodeled. We stood together, in the smudgy winter, dripping stalactites of nostalgia. The cold, however, was penetrating to my bones, my intestines,

16

my marrow. And there was the cozy image of my conference colleagues, sitting in the warmth of Grandma's Cafe (the Chock-Full-O'Nuts, I had noticed as we passed, had closed, and been replaced by a Tofutti emporium), chatting about President Bush and Irangate and swapping tabbouleh recipes.

"So why are you telling me all this?" The penny finally dropped. I had the dreadful insight that I had a defector on my hands. Would I have to take him in and feed him, bring him lokshen soup and pastrami sandwiches while I tried to find him a secure sanctuary, preferably not in Brooklyn. Perhaps the *intifada* youths might shelter him, in a basement in Beit-Ur-E-Tahta, brown up his face and dress him in a kafiyya and old torn schmutters . . . Fantasies swirled, ebbed, faded.

"I won't tell you now," he said. "How can I trust you? I really liked your book. You have a point there. Some people these days are out of control. But you have to see the other side. You think you can just kiss Yassir Arafat and the frog will turn into a prince. You think a thousand years of hate can turn into love with a gesture. So maybe Murray Waiskopf is holding his pinkie in a hole in a crumbling dike. The world is going to pot, everything's changing, and nothing can stay as it used to be. You know that, I know that, and Murray Waiskopf knows that. But there are a lot of new problems . . . Or rather some very very old ones, with a new, frightening face . . ."

He took my arm and dragged me back across the road, down and up 114th Street, as if suddenly aware of our isolation in the slush and keen to meld us back among the crowd. Past the Papyrus Bookstore, my favorite storehouse of progressive verbiage, and up by the Tamarind Seed Health Shop towards the entrance to the subway. He took a small notebook out of his pants pocket and wheezed: "Do you have a pen?" scribbling down an address and thrusting a torn-out folded page at me. "Meet me there, tomorrow evening, six o'clock, sharp. Ring bell C three times. Don't fuck me up. This is important. It's

17

definitely to your advantage." Then without further palaver he hopped, skipped and jumped out of my body space and rushed down the steps of the subway, taking my pen with him, leaving me snorting and gargling on the sidewalk, shaking my head, picking my nose, tearing out small tufts of my hair, clearing my throat, slipping and sliding on ice . . .

The revelation that all my paranoias are true caused me severe breathing problems. Once you know something like this you know you have to do something about it. You can no longer lie back on your bed, making paper planes, twiddling your thumbs, watching the daytime soaps, knitting. You have to get off your butt and move.

But move where? In the Beacon Hotel, movement can only be cyclical. Half the hotel seems tenanted by old ladies who have already died but still wander stiffly, through the corridors, up and down the elevators, complaining about the cold though the steam has been turned up in the building to 156 degrees. Outside, you freeze, like an Arctic Lot's wife. Inside, you lie nude as a *Playboy* spread, pouring sweat into the bedclothes. My life is lived, as usual, in extremes.

I did not confide, at this stage, in Dorothy Morgenthal. Some things, in fact most things, one does not confide to one's mother or her vicars upon earth. She was in good fettle at Grandma's Cafe, as I staggered in after my brief encounter, finding her explaining to Daoud Abu-Naim the meaning of a bagel with a shmeer. Yochai Magen-David was purring, having had his hamburger, and Hatem Abu-Riad, the ex-terrorist, was slurping his second chocolate milk shake. Akram, the ex-Mayor of Ramallah, whom I met years ago before my kind military authorities grabbed him from home one day at three in the morning, dragged him away from his wife and children, and dumped him in a helicopter at the Allenby Bridge into Jordan, shooing him across at riflepoint, greeted me like a long-lost brother, as is his wont, and asked me to mediate in the current dispute concerning the evening's entertainment. Should it be a new off-

Broadway play about Nicaragua, or a held-over screening of *Roger Rabbit*, which the PLO delegates had not yet seen, as they had been too busy running the revolution to see it when it had passed through Tunis. The fraternal needs of the culturally starved official comrades swayed the decision towards the leporine saga. I cried off, saying my life was enough of a cartoon, and I had seen the film in Israel.

"You can see films in Israel," said Daoud, mournfully, "while I, who was born in Jerusalem, cannot even breathe the air of my homeland."

He was right. I was an unadulterated schmuck, stooge, lackey of the Zionist bourgeoisie. I made my farewells, consumed with guilt, and returned to the Beacon Hotel as Dorothy Morgenthal led the PLO into the subway downtown in the direction of Steven Spielberg. But the heat in my hotel room was unbearable, and the tenants in the neighboring apartment room were noisily beating each other to a pulp. I donned my Arctic gear and exeunt, reflecting on the diverse means of relaxation available to the wanderer such as I in different parts of the world. In England, the luxury of snooker or anything on Channel Four or BBC2. In France, the outdoor cafés and the stupefying nonchalant beauty of the passing *jeunes filles*. In Germany, staying in your hotel room and blowing your own brains out. But here and now, just the commonplace homicidal neighbors, versus the frostbite of the Manhattan streets.

I hied myself to the 100 Percent Charcoaled Burger Joint on the corner of 76th and Broadway. The friendly warm pungent clatter. Any onion rings? Any fries? Try our Jumbo Platter Hawaiianburger. Nothing here is done by halves. I ordered a Texasburger with a Greek salad and sat back contemplating my life. I blamed Nahum Lauterman, my editor, for everything. My present predicament, the state of my psyche, of the world, the galaxy, the universe. After all, he was the original know-all, the man who knows where all the bodies are buried. I put him in my unemigrating book, as the manipulative journalist who got me involved in the internecine wars of the intelligence service. But four years ago he was a mere correspondent, albeit the paper's expert on West Bank affairs and one of the country's foremost crusading reporters, defender of the weak, proponent of human rights, scourge of corrupt politicians and businessmen, exposer of all the nation's worst scandals, the man with the X-ray eyes. Small wonder he was pushed up the ladder of promotion to be finally isolated and castrated as the paper's executive editor.

"Be my eyes and ears, Joe," he pleaded with me, waving his stick, groping for the light, "bring me the news from elsewhere. Tell me what's happening as I grapple my Ouija board and fend off breakfast invitations from the Prime Minister and other criminals." Now that he was at the top, he indeed saw nothing, cut off by the mountain fog from the battlefield, where schmucks like me crawled and scrabbled for scraps in the junkyard of everyday terrors. The growing repression and unstoppable brutalization of ourselves and our Palestinian victims, the shot six-year-old boys, the blood in the dust of villages, the crunch of breaking bones and ideals, the visage of Mister Hyde emerging from Doctor Jekyll in all our bathroom mirrors.

And Anat's betrayal, too, of my lust for the quiet life, as she backed up Nahum's call to arms: "Go, do it, Joe. Take part. Show them you're not neutral. I'll look after your City for you. Go to the Peace Conference, honey. It'll do you good to take your mind, for a while, out of the time warp."

My beloved, the lily among the thorns, not that she does not grow her own prickles . . . The *sine qua non* of our besieged lives . . .

Yes, escape the warp. But like the Old Man of the Sea, it is carried with me, everywhere. And now I have Didi Schaeffer to thank for driving that nail right in my skull.

What should I do? I unfolded the note he had scribbled for me, carefully avoiding the Greek salad. The address was 1— 29th

Street. Not a part of the town I knew at all. Hardly, if I remembered rightly, a residential area. But who knows? People live in warrens, caves, niches, bolt-holes all over the city. Not to speak of those who inhabit the streets forlornly, even in this Siberian weather, staggering about wrapped in old rugs and festering woolsacks, rattling cold coins in paper cups and begging for anything you might throw their way. I could even glimpse them through the icicle glass of the restaurant, frosty ghostlike shapes hovering to accost sated leaving diners. "Any spare change sir? Thank you." Their manner had changed over the years. As they proliferated, they became gentler, politer, more and more subservient, if more insistent. Was this President Bush's "kinder, gentler America"? Somehow I'm inclined to doubt it.

I paid my dues and walked down towards the subway entrance on 72nd. Tomorrow evening at six o'clock stretched ahead beyond a wasteland of frustrating limbo, the snow versus the Beacon Sahara. Patience was never one of my virtues. Entering the subway, I descended into the underground warmth of the crowds. A black man, on the opposite platform, was singing "Yesterday," unaccompanied, bending with his outstretched hat. His voice was throaty, timbrous, trembling. "All my troubles seemed so far away . . ." His memories were e punged by the clatter of the number 3 train carrying its human cargo all the way from Harlem to Flatbush. People hung on, puffing little balls of steam. A sign before me said: "ACCIDENT? CALL 495–HURT." A middle-class black mother smiled from another advertisement: *Roaches showed up at our dinner party for my husband's boss. It won't happen again, thanks to COMBAT."* I should sell that to some of our gung-ho ex-generals.

Exit at 34th Street, Penn Station. Madison Square Garden, Macy's, A&S, the works. Dragging down 34th Street, in the shadow of the Empire State Building, its spire utterly hidden in the clouds so one could not see whether there was a giant ape up there or not. I sent the poor mythical beast fraternal greetings, as I ploughed my way east. The address was between Lexington and Third Avenue, in a block so nondescript it looked as if it were due for demolition by dawn. A dingy, gray fifteen stories, with warehouses on the ground floor. The entrance door was closed. The bell marked C was in a row of ground-floor buzzers. I hesitated on the brink. There was nothing to indicate what lay within, though I could see, nose pressed to the glass doorway, a dismal board with office names. Should I press C? Or just go away, come back tomorrow at the appointed time? I stood back looking up at the building. No lighted windows, no signs of life.

What the hell. I pressed bell C. Just once, not three times. I did not really want to queer my pitch. At the end of the day, I did want to hear Didi Schaeffer's tale of Paranoia in Jewland. This trip downtown was obviously redundant. A complete waste of time. I was just about to step away when there was a response. The doorway buzzer sounded, and the intercom coughed and rasped. The buzzing went on, insistently inviting. I pushed the door open and stepped in.

This was not according to plan at all. Not even according to impulse. My entire life is a series of accidents, which I have always been able to avoid only by total immobility. The moment I rise from my armchair, exit the womb of my house, I am doomed. I sighed and looked at the board. Amalgamated Rubber Products. Nishawan Trading. Fogolsen Inc. Mishkin and Mishkin. Doberman Brothers. Leisure and Leather. Floors one thru sixteen (thirteen as usual was absent). But for the ground floor, no names. I slithered carefully along the corridor, lit by a gloomy half-watt night bulb. The doors on either side were not numbered. But the third on the left was very slightly ajar. I stood to one side and pushed it gently. It gave an inch or so and then stopped. Something seemed wedged against it. I had no doubt what it was. The instinct of a gory imagination, fed by a thousand torn paperbacks with lurid covers and contents. Inevitably, I pushed against the door.

He was a small, black-haired and wrinkled faced old man, his black silk skullcap almost nailed to his head by the force of whatever blunt instrument had caved his skull in full force. One hand was stretched to the door knob, the other flung out towards the buzzer and intercom phone which was dangling free. His face and baggy suit were caked with blood. He was still alive. His hand scrabbled towards me, pulling at my sleeve.

The dying man's last words. In the best tradition, I bent forward, brought my face up, my ear to his lips. The light from a close streetlamp shone through the room's window to cast its glow on the disheveled, ransacked room, his face and mine. His eyes widened.

"You're Joe Dekel," he rasped. "I've seen your picture . . . You turn against your own people . . ." He coughed blood, retching. "You ought to be ashamed." He gasped some more, then pulled harder on my sleeve, bringing his mouth closer to my ear. Hebrew words seemed to trickle out: "*Soneh Amcho* . . ."

He fell back, breathing sharply, bubbles of blood frothing on his lips. His head shook, his body trembled. He fell back, pushing me, with his last movement, away, relinquishing his hold.

The sound of New York rattled through the window. Far sirens, taxi horns, the swish of tires screeching through slush.

Wot, no "Rosebud"?

The dying man's curse: *Soneh Amcho.* "Hater of your people." Well, they're not easy to love. Particularly in their present Master Race phase. It's not easy to love the pinch-faced generals, the sad sack politicians, the madcap settlers shooting Arab teenagers in the back in the name of self-preservation and God. On the other hand, there are some of the people I do have a soft spot for: A number of bleeding hearts like me, the conscience-stricken, protesters and no-sayers, refusalists and conscientious objectors, though they too can be a pain. Self-righteousness is our national sickness, left to right, across the board. Others of "my people" I quite like: My grocer, my local garageniks, assorted cheerful kebab stall owners, a bus driver or two, various ordinary people of all walks of life in their domestic and non-lethal mode. If we are what we eat, and if we are fed shit, by our leaders, day in day out, what can you expect?

The corpse room became lighter as my pupils widened to take in its sparse confusion. There were a couple of filing cabinets, knocked to the floor, their spilled contents, old contracts and account books, for what appeared to be schmutter business. Tails of men's shirts and underpants. There was, on the bare desk, a telephone. I picked it up, using my handkerchief as the movies had taught me. It was connected. I dialled for the operator. New York Telephone, can ah help yah? Give me the police, quoth Dekel. I had no choice. The man might still be battered back by science into the world of the living. He who saves one soul in Israel as if saves the entire world, the Sages say. Against my better, coward's judgement. I stood outside in the freezing street until three squad cars came racing up, sirens blaring. Catapulting me into the movie. Wot, no Cagney and Lacey? Just cops imitating actors imitating cops et cetera. The Chinese boxes of the modern world.

I sat in a dingy office of the 20-something Precinct, with peeling walls and an obligatory bare lightbulb and posters advertising the Sixty-Seventh Annual Police Benevolent Ball, and offering business courses and medical insurance at a reduced rate. The heating system was inactive. A policeman in an Alaskan parka typed my statement with one finger. Time went click, clack, click. My interlocutor was a florid pug-faced Irishman who introduced himself as Detective Flynn, and was a dead ringer for Charles Durning, who played the cop in the movie *Dog Day Afternoon*, in which Al Pacino holds up a bank to get money for his friend who needs a sex-change operation. I did not need a sex-change operation, but there my detachment ended. Detective Flynn, dressed in a massive fur coat which must have been culled from seven brown grizzlies, laid the dead man's wallet on the table and flashed the corpse's driver's license at me.

"Murray Waiskopf. Know the fella?"

He didn't like the story I told him. Didi Schaeffer, Silencers, blacklist offices and afternoon assignations. I didn't like it much either, but I had no choice but to tell the truth, mad as it seemed, since there was no other possible trajectory which could have led me to the dead man's malediction.

"Jewish politics," he said. "Can you believe it. I spent three years in Crown Heights. When it comes to politics I pass completely, but down there you get to learn things you never imagined you'd need to know. Now let's see if I remember this right: The Hassidim of Galicia wear shoes without laces and gray socks. The Belzer and the Vizhnitz wear white socks and a kaftan with back pockets. Some of these people wear a kind of cravat round their middle, to separate the heart from the groin. When you have them in groups going at each other with iron bars, you better know how to tell 'em apart. But in normal times you get zero crime from 'em. No mugging, no drugs; nuttin'. How do you explain it?"

I tried to tell him about God, and the Messiah's imminence in their eyes, and the thin line between faith and intolerance, but the one-fingered cop could not keep up with us. We ignored him and entered into animated discussion about the Lubavitcher Rabbi. Four hours later, I exited the police station, aware that my brains had been picked but I had been given no shred of information to enlighten me about my own problem. Allowed to walk the streets until further notice, a police car took me back to the Beacon Hotel, to make sure I had told at least the truth of my whereabouts. One of the long-dead old ladies latched on to my escort, urging him to investigate the owners of the hotel for bugging her room with hidden microphones. "My husband was Don Corleone," she said. "They want to know where I hid his diaries."

"Yes, mam," the cop said politely. "I'll get on to it first thing in the morning."

Three a.m. The heat was tolerably low, having been turned down to one hundred Fahrenheit. I could even achieve some semblance of sleep, for ten minutes, until the refuse collection trucks rumbled up below to do their duty. They seemed to be relieving the lower cellars of hell of a million Zaybars packages. Murray Waiskopf appeared to me in a vision. He was wearing a gray striped kaftan and furry streimel hat of the *Toldot Aharon* yeshiva, the spearhead of zealot Sabbath guardians in my embattled Holy City. He was coming out of the Beit Agron Cinémathèque, which had been targeted for showing the *Rocky Horror Picture Show* repeatedly on Friday nights, eve of Sabbath, covered in rice, and holding the bloody severed head of Didi Schaeffer, whom he had caught red-handed watching the show. The left eye of my Silencer closed at me in an almighty wink. He clamped his lips and shook his head warningly. Helicopters hovered overhead.

27

Where does one stand, in all this confusion? When I wrote my book, I dealt with fiction. Dead bodies tumbled out of closets, police morgues, hotel rooms, off the conveyer belt of imagination. There is a balm, creating mayhem in your living room, on the pure white of the page, shutting out for as long as possible the genuine sounds of live rounds being loosed off to keep the rebelling natives at bay. Don't fire till you see the whites of their flags! And nevertheless, no surrender. The stubborn undaunted sacrifice of the sansculottes, the dispossessed, the constant offering of live bodies to be shot, beaten, broken, imprisoned, day after day, rank after rank, until the jails and detention camps are full, and still they come, defying our own image of them as weak-willed puppets of incitement. And the indomitable stupidity of the defenders of Law and Order, our Law and our Order, elevating to state policy the apocryphal claim of the Jerusalem policeman arraigned once for brutality against a demonstrator: Honored Judge, he simply ran into my truncheon with his head, and then repeated the offense thirty-five times.

Soneh Amcho. The dying man's curse. On the second day of the Israeli-Palestinian Peace Conference, historians of both sides maneuvered painfully round the garbage piles of received myths. Yossi S—, member of Knesset for the Civil Rights Party and ex-Labor member, made an impassioned speech about the dead children on either side. We need to offer our children a better future than bullets or petrol bombs. Who could disagree? Nevertheless, I could hear the rustle of Murray Waiskopf crawling along under the seats. Was he really the nemesis of Didi Schaeffer's story, the Gag Man, the man with strings everywhere, or was the young punk just trying to string me along, telling me what my psyche wants to hear, selling me lokshen, trapping me into that meeting for some reason I can't fathom? But if so, why the corpse at the unappointed time? The dead man who also knew my name, and saw into the depths of my perfidious soul?

The Peace Festival droned on. It was becoming routine. Ancient enemies slumped together on the podium, welded by tedium. Such is peacemaking, it lacks the macho clout and thrill of bullets, commando camouflage, massed armored columns stomping the desert. My journalist colleagues are already twisting in their seats, reading the weekend imported Hebrew newspapers, or the paperback of their choice. *The Bonfire Of The Vanities*. Indeed. Milek Stuckman snores, his head thrown back like a fish out of water, gasping for air. The man whose arm he has slumped on to I recognize as one of the security guards assigned by Yassir Arafat to the delegate Abu-Naim. The man glowers, as the dandruff of Zionist Imperialism drops on to his dapper jacket.

Lunch, I lacklusterly join the delegates at the Golden Lotus Chinese Restaurant. Daoud Abu-Naim holds forth before the journalists about his Enchanted Vision of Peace. Open borders, small children carrying flowers, Arab and Jew sitting together sipping arak in gardens, selling kettles to each other. What about Damascus? What about Jerusalem? What about the settlers? What about the Ayatollah Khomeini? Aaah, Daoud's eyelids close, slowly, as he clings to his inner rapture. Yochai Magen-David reveals to everyone his prognosis for the Soviet Union, Europe, China. He sees a multi-polar world, whose next aim has to be the rescuing of Africa and South Asia. He has become converted, it appears, to the defunct ideal of the world state proposed by Bertrand Russell. The nation state, he claims loudly, to the Chinese waiters, if to no one else, is the stupidest idea invented by Man since the divine right of kings. All the PLO delegates droop their eyelids, shovel in the won tons. I am unable to corner Dorothy Morgenthal about my piddling personal problems. She has enough on her plate, what with Roger Rabbit and grandiose plans for world order.

Should I, nevertheless, despite my night excursion, keep that afternoon assignation? The police would no doubt slaver at the sight of Dekel returning to the scene of the crime. Would Didi Schaeffer turn up? Would he be able to enlighten Detective Flynn about the white socks of the Belzer Hassidim? Thinking of that particular devil, he materialized, in his fur-clad Irish bulk, barreling in to the back of the Conference Hall towards the end of the afternoon session. He had with him another plain-clothes, raincoated, baby-faced man, clipped at the neck by a bow tie. Catching his eye, I sidled out, as applause closed the session, and joined the duo in the bright winter sun under the statue of the University's Alma Mater. A bronze, nonchalant dame, she had a book in one hand and a scale in the other.

"This is Agent Kool, with a K, of the FBI," Flynn said to me. By now I would believe anything. The baby-faced man extended a hand in the limp manner described by W.C. Fields as a "hearty handshake." "Agent Kool would like to hear your story."

"Let's walk," said my first live G-man. He proceeded in a tall and gangling way, like a triffid, to ambulate across Amsterdam Avenue towards Morningside Park. We halted by the statue of Carl Schurtz – "A Defender of Liberty and Friend of Human Rights." Agent Kool took a long hard look at the obscure granite visage to make sure he could not cite it for some federal violation. Detective Flynn leaned over the stone and looked down at the narrow strip of green, still flecked with snow and slush. A black man, wrapped in the Sunday *Times*, took his cue to roll off the stone bench below the statue and tottered off in the direction of the Cathedral of Saint John the Divine.

"Pollard," said Agent Kool.

I was not quite sure just how I was expected to respond. Should I scream, foam at the mouth, cry Eureka and throw my scarf in the air? Or was it a word association game? Bollard. Dullard. Pollen. Pillock.

"I assume you know the name?" Detective Flynn puffed steam over Morningside Park, looking out towards Harlem.

"Pollard, the Israeli spy?" I said. He gave me a smile, as if I had won some jackpot, a bag of sweets perhaps, or a plastic rattle. Naturally I was reasonably familiar with this quintessential scandal of our times. An officer in U.S. Naval Intelligence, Pollard, it was claimed, had offered his services to Israeli Intelligence, which had milked him for several years of thousands of documents pertaining to Arab states' capabilities, according to Pollard's confessions, but to everything under the sun, according to the U.S. prosecution. When found out, the spy tried to shelter in the Israeli Embassy in Washington, but was evicted from there into the waiting hands of Agent Kool's colleagues. It was a major outrage which struck at the heart of American Jews' fears of vulnerability to charges of double loyalties. My government had hurriedly claimed the entire operation was unauthorized and disbanded the espionage unit which had carried out this vile, once in a lifetime provocation. Allegations of other Israeli spies in the United States were rife, but no one else was discovered. Pollard was sentenced to life imprisonment by an American judge. His plea in mitigation that he loved Israel and had been led astray by "the infection of a foreign ideology" – Zionism – did not count for him for much. He was a textbook case of a man who had swallowed the myth whole and been consumed by its acid realities. Many people felt he had been betrayed and sold down the river by the very people he had idolized and served. I could have warned him, but no one listens to me. Perhaps it's true, I need no Silencer, my words just disappear into the void, by the natural course of human deafness, apathy and disinclination . . .

"You know Lewis Carroll?" said Agent Kool. I gave up trying to follow his train, which was pulling out from stations I didn't even know were on the map. "*The Snark:* 'They sought it with thimbles, they sought it with care, they pursued it with forks and hope; they threatened its life with a railway share, they charmed it with smiles and soap.' We never believed Pollard was a one-off. We searched high and low for other Israeli agents. We put the armed forces through the ringer. For five months we hunted Jews more thoroughly than Martin Bormann. Oh, there was a deal of wailing and gnashing of teeth before we had to back away, for a while. For the Snark was a Boojum, you see."

"I'm afraid not," I said. "But what has this got to do with Murray Waiskopf?" I was not sure I wished to know the answer. Writing fictions about secret services is one thing, getting entangled in their real life fantasies quite another. It would be no exaggeration to say that under my façade of everyday panic I was becoming really alarmed. But Agent Kool didn't answer my question.

"Your friend Didi Schaeffer," he said instead, "is in Israel. Or at least that's what the grapevine tells us. If you met him yesterday he must have slipped back in for some reason. He has been living for the past year and a half in a religious settlement on the West Bank. Land of his fathers. And God gave it to Abraham, for his seed, and his seed's seed after him. I am told you are a religious Jew, Mr. Dekel. Isn't that what you all believe?"

"Not all of us see God's word as a real-estate contract," I said. "There are spiritual dimensions. Our Snarks, too, sometimes end up as Boojums."

"Lewis Carroll; I really liked that man's style." Agent Kool shook his head admiringly. "Some say he was a pervert who enjoyed undressing little girls, but in my view that's a canard. I believe he was just an enthusiast for photography. But that was a more innocent age. Today nobody can get away with anything. No one knows what to believe. The crisis of faith. Your friends turn out to be your enemies. Your enemies turn out to be your best friends. I think what you folks are doing in there is OK. Peace on earth, goodwill to all men. I have to tell you, Mr. Dekel, I have no interest in your arguments with your fellow Jews. My job is solely to investigate federal crimes, uphold the law and protect American citizens of whatever color, religion or race. There is no evidence as yet that the killing of Mr. Wais-kopf comes within my remit. Detective Flynn is so far in complete charge. But if you ever need me –" He held out a card, which flipped suddenly into view between his fingers. "Didi Schaeffer's residence is in the town of Amiel, half-way between Tel Aviv and Nablus. I understand it's a thriving community. But then, life is full of surprises. Have a good day." He turned, and, trailing the Irish policeman, floated back towards the University, leaving me to grope in my fog.

"They're setting me up for something, that's for sure," I told Dorothy Morgenthal, "but I only wish I knew what." We were sitting in her apartment on West 82nd pondering the echoes of the McNeil-Lehrer show. Daoud Abu-Naim had appeared in split screen with the Israel Deputy Minister for Defense speaking from Israel, much to the latter's annoyance. "We do not think there is any point in talking to the terrorists of the PLO," he said firmly. "You're talking to one now," said Daoud. "Why don't we just meet personally for a cup of coffee?" "Is this on split screen?" said the Deputy, cottoning on. No, it's on split personality.

All in all, Dorothy had reason to feel pleased with the impact of the University Conference, though she appeared exhausted at acting Henry Kissinger to two groups of recalcitrant orientals, two collections of egos large enough to flatten the Empire State Building. All the more reason for her to give me scant thanks for my embroiling her in my petty personal murder. The books lining her apartment walls leaned out at me warningly, a biography of Golda Meir poised ominously above my head.

"Why are you doing this to me?" she lamented, stretched out over two armchairs with a mug of rosehip tea. The cry of the Jew through the ages. We had first met one year before at a Peace Now convoy of bleeding hearts heading into the West Bank at the peak of the early months of the *intifada*, to express their solidarity with Palestinians faced with the army's repression. It was Lauterman's first attempt to draw me out of my shell since he took office as my paper's working supremo. "There's a delegation of progressive American Jews," he said. "That's news for a start, isn't it?" My heart sank, as I saw this wispy

34

gray-haired woman, accompanied by two skullcapless Reform Rabbis cramming into Peace Now's station wagons. They sang old homeland songs, as we punched out of Jerusalem, south, along the Bethlehem Road, to Hebron. But before we got to the bountiful city on the mountain, Al Khalil, the Jewish settlers of the new town of Kiryat Arba, stapled by *force majeure* on to the Arab city, had formed their own barricade, with the army standing by tentatively. The settlers smashed the windows of the front vehicle with iron bars, and wagged their beards and assault rifles fiercely. Eli B—, who was a Reserve Lieutenant Colonel as well as a certified pigeon, tried to order them back, wielding the Voice of Authority, but they spat in his face, shouting: "Traitor! Arab-lover! Impalement is too good for you!" I became worried that matters might escalate from this normal, everyday bonhomie to something more nasty. The army, as is its wont, was reluctant to interfere in our people's internal squabbles. But Dorothy Morgenthal surged forward, cutting her way through the mêlée. As if to the manner born, she began plucking the iron bars from the settlers' hands. "Give me this," she said, in a broad Brooklyn twang which stirred something in the depths of the beasts. "I'm taking these back to New York," she said. "People should know what's going on here." She loaded the iron bars on to the nonplussed Reform Rabbis. "Let's go," she said. "We have a date in Hebron."

I never knew, until my present U.S. visit, whether Dorothy Morgenthal had really tried the incredulity of Lod Airport Security with a consignment of iron assault bars. But now she admitted she had left them behind, in the custody of a police inspector to whom she had complained about the incident. I told her they might well have been pressed into further service for interrogation procedures. Waste not, want not, in our embattled country. Where else could they invent a vehicle that gathers up the pebbles thrown by demonstrators and shoots them back at them from a high-velocity nozzle? In Alaska, the whole insurrection might have petered out for lack of fuel, but in our biblical landscape, stones are one thing we're not short of.

Her view of the escalating repression was refreshing to me. "I'm not having it," she said simply. "That's how we got civil rights in this country. Hundreds of thousands of people said we're not having it. It took a hell of a lot of sacrifice, by the blacks, as it is now, by the Palestinians. And for what? Things we now take for granted: The right to sit anywhere you like on the bus, the right to vote, a job, simple security. In twenty years people will look back and say, why the fuss? All that shooting and killing, to stop what was so obviously right, a people determining their own future, flying their own flag, electing their government, lousy or good, that's not my business. If as a Jew and a woman and a human being I can't fight for that, then I'm a lousy Jew and a lousy human and not much of a woman either."

A far cry from the dying man's curse. *Soneh Amcho*. I suppose, as the BBC would say, both views are valid. But what am I to say, with my brains battered by midnight grillings and FBI flimflam? Where can I plug in all these loose connections, flying about in the wind? I tried to grab hold of them in Dorothy's apartment, letting the herbal tea soothe my gullet, as we moved from the overt to the covert. "It doesn't make sense. Why should Agent Kool, assuming he is not just a figment of the Zeitgeist, babble on to me about Pollard, scaring my pants off, implying a connection with Waiskopf but not stating it, then give me this guff about Didi Schaeffer? If he's here when he's not supposed to, given his behavior with me, surely he would be a prime suspect? But they don't seem concerned about him at all. They know much more than they're letting on to me. But why should they tell me anything at all? Unless I'm a sort of bait they're using . . ."

"I never liked Raymond Chandler," Dorothy said, "those plots that you could never make out. The fear and loathing of women. Hammett was the same, but more violent. The macho left, God, how they wound me up! Though I was partial to the *femme fatale*. If men don't respect us, at least they should be scared of a bullet in the kishkas. But I can't see how I can help you with this mess you've stirred up. Except to advise you to keep your nose out of any more trouble. I've heard of Murray Waiskopf in my time, but this blacklist of yours, it's sheer hearsay. Sure, we get pressure all the time, from the Lobby: AIPAC, shmaipac, the Anti-Slander League, but that's all on the table. Now and again, we get old-fashioned smear campaigns. I went to a UJA meeting once, where they were passing round a photograph of a well-known liberal-left Israeli politician, dressed in bondage gear, getting the full Madame treatment. I thought it was an airbrushed forgery, but you never can tell. In the past people lost their jobs, got intimidated into silence. Sometimes more than the usual moral blackmail, you know the stuff, don't rock the boat, you're putting us straight back into the gas chamber. Old hat. But this stuff with Pollard, that's dangerous. That's taboo. That strikes right at the pupik. If American Jews feel Israel is lying to them about spying on the U.S., then the shit will really hit the fan. I don't have to tell you, it's what happens here counts more than what goes on in Jerusalem. The strategic relationship, the big bucks, the armament deals, the Pentagon scams, Irangate and points east. Everything is so tangled. Whatever foile shtik Waiskopf was involved in, you don't want your dick, pardon the unfeminine expression, caught in that mangle."

Assuredly not. And yet the threads of that medusa seem to have slipped round my ankle. Obsessive questions: Why had Didi Schaeffer blown his cover, such as it was, by approaching me at the Conference? What was he doing at the Conference in the first place? Keeping an eye, for Waiskopf or others? Should I simply walk away? Conniving at what I have been told, true or false, amounts to my own silencing, does it not? Just what have we stumbled into?

"God save me from Israeli journalists," sighed Dorothy. "You used to be so good and cuddly. You went to the Government Press Office and printed straight what they told you. You banged the drum and tooted the horn in all the right places. Now you're all slavering for scoops, tales of woe, exposés. I like it, but can't you keep a sense of proportion? Start with the little, easy things, like Middle East Peace. Then let's get on to the really tough stuff, U.S. Imperialism, the Pentagon, major espionage. You think the Anti-Slander League is any less lost than you are in that morass? Boy, you have another think coming."

I looked at her beseechingly, over my depleted rosehip tea. Thumping my tail on the floor.

"OK," she sighed again. "Against my better judgement. Do you want to meet a hundred-year-old man? This one is quite a phenomenon. His name is Nederlander Schatz. I know you've never heard of him, he keeps in the background, but he knows whatever there is to know from the inside about the wars of the Jews. Ned was born three years after Ben-Gurion. He knew all the founders of Israel personally, and punched Menachem Begin in the face once, in Poland, in 1935. I'm thinking of him because he actually called me, out of the blue, just before the Conference. Difficult to tell whether he was just keeping tabs, in his dotage, or flying a kite for somebody. But this man might just have some answers for you. He has his fingers in every conceivable pie. I'll call him. We might go over directly. He never sleeps any more, and lives on yogurt. I don't know why I'm doing this for you. But I don't like to see you stuck this way. I can read you, Joseph. You pretend you care about nothing, but it eats you up inside. The drive for justice. It's a Jewish disease. Like Tay Sachs. It's genetic. I should talk. Look at all the mutations we've been getting."

She made the phone call. There seemed to be a response. We took a cab across town, coasting through the deserted Central

Park, Dorothy falling asleep by my side, the driver regaling me with all the rapes and murders that had occurred in the Park since the New Year. "Ya'd think, in da winter, da place wad be empty, but yooman beens, dey just never learn." Tell me about it, brother.

The hundred-year-old man lived in an upmarket apartment block on the Upper East Side, at 69th Street. He lived alone, and opened his door to us, ushering us inside with all the vigor of a ninety year old. His face looked like a papyrus on which the history of the century had been written but had already faded. He heard my story with a great deal of relish, cackling like a demented chicken. He especially enjoyed my description of Detective Flynn's knowledge of Hassidic footwear.

"Eh! You have to keep the goyim on their toes," he said, "especially the Catholics. You have to be nimble and keep 'em guessin'. Be yourself! That always has 'em flummoxed. That's what I can't stand about these guys from *Commentary*, Norman P. and all his cohorts. They think if they just play down-the-line Reaganites, Wall Street will just kiss their ass. But Wall Street just pisses on them from its uncircumcised Wasp heights. Boy, I have seen it all, I can tell you. There's nothing you can surprise me with. Spies! I cut my teeth on spy work. I was with the Jewish Underground, NILY, in the First World War. *Netsach Israel Lo Yeshaker!** We spied on the Turks for the British. We were hand-in-glove, too, with the Arab Nationalists, we had many things in common. I met Lawrence of Arabia several times. He was a small, stocky man with a long face, not a bit like Peter O'Toole. But I felt he was one hundred per cent genuine. He was an Arabist *and* a Zionist. Can you imagine that? Not many people remember that we had common interests from the start. Rid the Middle East of Colonialism! All that European master race nonsense. After that we got it in spades. But the Arabs

*The Eternity of Israel Will Not Lie.

39

screwed it all up. They thought the Nazis would help 'em get rid of the hated British. The mufti of Jerusalem, he went to meet Hitler. It was a godsend to our propaganda. Still today they try to tar the Arabs with that pro-Nazi brush. But I don't have to teach you how to suck eggs. You want to know about this mess today.

"Power, my boy! It's the oldest story. You know what year I was born? 1889. The same year of Adolf Hitler. He thought he could force the world to fit into his own crazy vision. But millions of people paid the price and what's left of him? The spit and bile of history. But the Germans were not a vile or vicious people. A bit too thorough for their own good. Nu, it's difficult to say this to a Jew. But at my age, you tend to see a pattern. Power, my boy, power and dreams. Maybe some dreams shouldn't have power. Not that I'm making analogies some of our enemies like to make. That's nonsense. I tell you, if there really were all-powerful Elders of Zion, they would be fighting each other. Like our great Rabbis, who love to scratch each other's eyes out. We Jews can agree together on nothin'. It's our strength, but also our weakness. Today, after the State of Israel was created with blood and fire and terrible sacrifice, and I did my share, let nobody tell you otherwise, today, people want to play the Power game. The Game of Nations. A chessboard on which we keep dreaming that the pawn will become a queen. But a pawn is a pawn. He has to use cunning. His very destiny is to be swept off the board. Better not to play chess at all. But in the Power game, you are forced to. Now listen. You mentioned the Anti-Slander League. Well, let me tell you, boy, I founded that organization, back in 1924. We had the Ku Klux Klan, and the American Defense Society, and the provocations of Henry Ford. He had a newspaper, the *Dearborn Independent*, which reprinted *The Protocols of The Elders of Zion. The Jewish Peril*. In fact, it was the *Christian Science Monitor* no less, that first brought that up, in 1920. America was panicking about Communism. And Communism meant Jews. Later we had a whole package of lunatics, anti-Semites and rabble-rousers. Father Coughlin, the Black Legion, the Silver Shirts, all sorts of Christian fundamentalists. Some of them became openly pro-Nazi. So we had a real problem. Some of us thought we needed a special organization to keep tabs on all these hatred squadrons. To lobby the government, and alert our own people. That's how the Anti-Slander League was born. It was purely concerned with American issues. Later on, in the forties, all that changed. The Holocaust was all our worst nightmares come true. Israel might be our only salvation. We fought for her. Damn hard. It was life or death, for every Jew in the world. We had a new enemy, the Arab Nationalists. They wanted the Jewish state stopped. Pretty soon they got their act together; they worked with the British, the French, the State Department. So we began keeping tabs on them too. And that meant we worked with the government of Israel. So the nature of our activity changed. Other lobbies were formed. We made new partners. The Power game came into play.

"You see what I'm telling you, it all became complicated. Before, we were community oriented. Now we became foreign policy oriented. And when you touch that scum, you get dirty. All sorts of deals start to be made, which have nothin' to do with your original aims. You want the U.S. government to scratch your back, you scratch theirs. You get involved in Central America. You get some Ollie North, who is selling this in Guatemala to buy that to use in Honduras to send God knows what to Iran. Where are the moral principles? You have hung them up in the closet. You play *realpolitik*, than which there's nothin' as unreal. You lose sight of any sense of direction. The Israelis have some big strategic thing with Iran, as a bulwark against the Arab world. Khomeini comes and talks like Hitler in spades, but the strategy is still there. In Nicaragua, some big shit family that supported Somoza is Jewish. The Sandinistas kick

41

them out. The next thing I know people are phoning me asking for my support for the Contras and to denounce the Sandinistas as anti-Semites. Listen, I tell them, I've been a progressive Democrat since 1920! You want to help a band of fascist assassins, go ahead! I'm just sorry I saw the day!"

He was getting excited, and leaning forward in his chair, tapping the formica table in front of him with his plastic spectacle case. His room was even more book lined than Dorothy Morgenthal's, with serried ranks of old and new volumes of encyclopedias, year books, Hebrew Talmuds and anthologies, complete works of Jewish dignitaries so obscure they had dropped out of the Israeli school curriculum. Bashevis Singer in the original Yiddish, bound volumes of the serializations. And, wherever there was any residual wallspace, framed photographs of Nederlander Schatz himself, with Chayim Weizmann, David Ben-Gurion, Golda Meir, Franklin Roosevelt, Winston Churchill, Joseph Stalin, Khruschev, Charles de Gaulle, Einstein, Sigmund Freud, Judge Brandeis, Justice Felix Frankfurter and all.

"Now I'm hearing that Murray Waiskopf is dead and his murder might have something to do with these politics." He had regathered his bones in his armchair, and put his glasses case in his pocket. "I know Murray Waiskopf very well. A good organizer. But he was a little extreme. Now they'll tell you all sorts of things about American Jews but let me tell you no one knows shit. American Jews aren't against what you're trying to do at your Conference. They think the present Israeli policy is knuckle-headed. They don't trust Yassir Arafat and who can blame them. But if these PLO peace offers are a bluff, let's test 'em. We gain nothin' by just saying No. Let's draw 'em into a negotiation, and if they are genuine let's go for a deal. Nobody in America, except the assholes of *Commentary*, wants to keep the West Bank and Gaza. Those people, they hated the Jews, they want to be on their own. A strong Israel has nothin' to fear. But a strong Israel, mind you, not a squabbling Babel. But what can we do, you have a democracy there. The Israeli people will decide, not Ned Schatz and Dorothy Morgenthal, and not Murray Waiskopf either. They are the people who have to do the fightin' an' dyin'.''

He turned to me. "This blacklist of Murray's that you're talking about. It's kids' stuff. Small potatoes. He had a phone, and he rang round his friends. Some guys, you know, they don't like anyone to have an opinion that's different from their own. So you were one of his victims. Tough shit. Just hang in there. You'll get your say. This killing, it's something else entirely. I can just tell you this. Murray Waiskopf had his finger in all sorts of pies. This kid, this Didi Schaeffer, he was his errand boy and gofer. About a year ago, I heard, he decided to up stakes and go to be a pioneer in Israel. Can I complain? They need soldiers. Peace Now or Peace Tomorrow, they'll always need soldiers. It's the way of the world. The bottom line is you gotta defend yourself. The problem is how not to turn into a heel doing it. That's a knack they'll just have to learn. I don't have to tell you. You may look at me like some kind of Mel Brooks joke but I've been around and I've seen what I've seen. Now, Murray Waiskopf . . ."

But at precisely that moment the lights went off in the apartment. A choked-off "Oh shit," from Ned Schatz. And in the ensuing silence, a definite click of the lock at the apartment's front door. The hundred-year-old man cried out: "Who's that? Is that the Super? Henry?" Then his dry rasp reached out to my ear. "Just where you're sittin' there's a drawer with a gun in it. It's loaded with two shells." I swung off my seat as silently as possible and scrabbled for the desk drawer. The room was pitch-dark, I lost touch with Dorothy, seated across the way from me under the bookshelves. The dry breathing of the old man was the only orienting feature, a harsh squeaking bubble around which the universe swirled. I could sense, however, that there was a fourth presence in the room. Hopefully a stray cat. My hand touched a cold metal object which I slowly drew from the drawer.

"Lights, goddamn it, lights," growled the old man. I lunged towards him, clamped my hand over his mouth and dragged him out of his chair to the floor. He fought like an alley cat, but subsided when I whispered my name in his ear. I still could not guess the whereabouts of Dorothy, but hoped that she too had found a cushion to crawl under. Something was knocked off a shelf.

"Whoever's there," I called out, "identify yourself. I am armed. Please give your name, rank and number." I moved sideways, tensing for the possible consequences of giving away my position. But this was one movie cliché that did not material-ize, yet. Nevertheless, there was someone there. Above me, I could make out the square of a window, obscured by its secured blinds. Very thin wisps of grayishness peeked between closed slats. I released the old man and inched up, groping for the pulley or string. I found it, and pulled the slats open. A sullen New York gray oozed between them. There were two shapes ahead of me. One smallish and familiar, bent over a handbag, the other rather large, its head covered with a hood.

"Who the fuck . . ." rasped the old man. A flash and an explosion came from the large figure's midriff. I literally felt the zing of the bullet coming between the old man and me. The sudden flash was blinding. I fumbled for the trigger of the object in my hand but couldn't find it. There was a sudden, barely human cry from ahead of me, something shrill, like *"A Sa Fa —!"* Then a clunk, as something solid hit something slightly less solid. The large figure disappeared.

A scrabble of sound from the doorway heralded two torches shining light into the room. Two heavy voices, calling out: "Mr. Schatz, you OK?" "Goddamn it, someone shot somebody . . ." Heavy boots clattered up. The torch shone in my face and a

44

hand with a club seemed to rise to strike above it.

"Not him, Henry!" rasped the old man. "I'm OK, fellah's over there!"

The torches swung, revealing an astonishing tableau. On the floor, by an overturned coffee table, the intruding hulk lay, gray hood still in place above a black suit and rumpled tie. Standing above him, Dorothy Morgenthal held her handbag in her left hand, clutching, in her right, the top half of two wooden nunchaku assault sticks connected by a thick chain. The lower stick dangled wistfully from the chain, as if yearning for another crack.

"Oh my Gad," said Dorothy Morgenthal. The old man burst out in a cackle, not unlike a wooden rattle, wielded by a manic child.

On the third day of the Palestinian-Israeli Peace Conference, delegates began discussing the details of peace plans that floated for the moment on purple clouds of fabulous wishful thinking. How much territory the lion would have, how much the lamb. In which factory the swords would be rendered into ploughshares and would union rates be paid there. This little boy who would lead them, would he be Jewish or Arab, or some kind of ethnic hermaphrodite?

As my editor, Nahum Lauterman, may his cattle sicken, and his kine succumb, emphasized to me when tearing me away from my TV womb and dispatching me across the oceans, via the tribulations of Lod Airport Security's queries – "Have you packed these bags yourself? Did anyone give you a bomb in the last twenty-four hours? Are you a registered terrorist? You realize I have to ask you these questions. After all, you're flying, not me." Absolutely true, my friends. "Peace!" Lauterman held forth, "between Israel and Palestine! Two peoples, battered to a pulp by history, finally realize their destinies must lie together. It's ironic that they, not us, have been the first to wake from the nightmare. We shouldn't have taken the sleeping pills. But nevertheless, Joe! The wings of history! Be my seeing eye, gladden an old man's heart, I implore you, bring me back the good news!"

But brought down to earth, before I could do this, in Detective Flynn's office, again. My second visit to his decrepit kingdom. "We must stop meeting this way," he says. I am surrounded by funny people, but I am less and less amused. Flynn looked, shaking his head, from Dorothy Morgenthal to me and down to the array of *objets d'art* his officers had placed on

46

his desk: Dorothy's nunchaku sticks, the hooded intruder's gun, a neat little Beretta automatic, plus the thing I had pulled out of Ned Schatz's drawer, a carved replica of an Uzzi machine pistol, with "Compliments of Moshe Dayan" embossed on it. The real gun, it turned out, had been in the other drawer. The hundred-year-old man had cackled in amusement. "Israelis, eh? If you ain't good with guns, what are you good for?" Indeed. My cousin Meir, I could answer, does ace embroidery. I have a school-friend who did wonders in the lingerie trade. It is all a question of stereotyping.

The rapid appearance of the security guards at Schatz's apartment was due, we found out, to a buzzer installed in every chair and bed in his home. Nevertheless, he thanked Dorothy Morgenthal effusively for saving his life. Detective Flynn was less appreciative.

"This is a lethal weapon," he told her. "It's illegal in New York State. Where on earth did you get it?"

She had received it, she said, from a Black Power client in the days she had practiced law in Chicago. It gave her confidence on the subway, she said, apologizing for the impropriety. She had taken it along on impulse, given the prospective cab ride back across Central Park post-midnight. "You remember that cab that broke down, and nobody found the bodies till three weeks later, in the Pond?" But Detective Flynn looked weary, and offered no more tales of Hassidic footwear. He told me to my face he was sure to blazes I knew much more than I'd let on about this whole affair. Me and that FBI agent, Kool. "I never trust a man who quotes poetry," he said to me. A man after my own heart. "Any more surprises?" he asked. "Secret assignations? Spies in bedrooms? Bodies falling out of closets? When does your Peace Conference end?"

"I don't see what this has to do with Middle East politics." Dorothy looked aggrieved. "Surely we're dealing with a simple burglary?"

Oh yeah? He was having none of that. Like Inspector Clouseau, he ticked off the facts. Fact: All the lights go out in a secured building, and instantaneously an intruder slips in with a key. Fact: He is clean of any identification, just a pillowslip hood and a wad of ten-dollar bills. (A brief glimpse under the hood had shown us the nondescript mid-Atlantic face, with a rugged jaw and a thankfully thick skull, as the ambulancemen carted Dorothy's stunned victim off to the casualty ward.) Fact: Two prominent Jews targeted in twenty-four hours. Fact: The coincidental Peace Conference. Fact: Joe Dekel at both locations.

Conclusion: Joe Dekel=Trouble. He kicked us out of the police station. "God, I hate politics. Piss off, Mr. Dekel. Go back to Israel. I have enough nightmares in this town."

Wot? Not even a material witness? Eat your heart out Hamilton Burger. And not even an offer of a squad car to chauffeur us back to terra firma. We hailed a yellow cab on Third Avenue. I dropped off at the Beacon Hotel and let Dorothy proceed home to 82nd Street. She did not want to speak, and waved at me wanly. She had been warned charges might be preferred and was probably regretting her rash cruise into my sea of troubles, as if she hadn't enough storms of her own. I rose guiltily but thankfully alone in the hotel elevator. No dead ladies to complain of the cold. Fumbling with my key, a momentary frisson of fear that I might find a dead body in my room, on the bed, preferably not my own. But the bed was empty, the room untouched, though heated, as expected, to infernal levels. I slept, and dreamed of demons with pitchforks, and badges for the Anti-Slander League. I had been libeling hell, it appears, in articles suggesting that it was no place to live. I was misinterpreting the inclemency of the climate and the excruciating agonies suffered by its inhabitants as a deliberate state policy, rather than the inevitable consequences of attacks by external enemies. I was sentenced to be impaled and roasted, while listening to recordings of old Abba Eban speeches. Through the sulphurous flames, Dorothy Morgenthal struggled to rescue me, flailing her nunchaku sticks, encumbered by a chain of Palestinian and Israeli peace activists fastened gibbering to her left ankle.

In the morning, the death of Murray Waiskopf finally joined the news that's fit to print. On page ten of the City's organ:

Retired Community Leader Battered To Death On East Side: Mr. Murray Waiskopf, once a prominent publisher and leading member of Jewish community groups such as B'nai B'rith and the United Jewish Appeal, was found dead early yesterday morning in a building on East 29th Street. He had been struck on the head by a blunt instrument. Police Inspector Lucius Clay said cleaning staff had found the body in the early hours of Tuesday morning when they entered a ground-floor office used for storing old files by a trading company, Mishkin and Mishkin. Mrs. Dolores Santiago, who manages the firm, was too distraught to speak to reporters. Inspector Clay said the police are pursuing the theory that Mr. Waiskopf had disturbed an intruder, but cannot provide any reason, as yet, why Mr. Waiskopf should have been in the building. Mr. Waiskopf was a widower, who left three children. His eldest son, a prominent Brooklyn banker, said: "We are all shocked and devastated by our father's death by violence. He was the kindest man that ever lived."

Is that it? You'd think we were still in Russia. Arthur Ochs Sulzberger, please copy. Of course, I was glad they left Joe Dekel out of it. Not to speak of Detective Flynn, Agent Kool, Didi Schaeffer, Unca Scrooge McDuck and all. But the truth, Goddamnit?? And who the hell is Dolores Santiago? Someone's pouring on the oil, and my money is on my Snark-loving G-man. But what can I do? I dragged myself uptown, hoping to relax in the harmony of Peace Conference Day Number Three.

But no balm at all here, with shit flying in all directions over the issue of Jerusalem. The oldest Talmudic saw: Two take hold of a prayer shawl. One says she is all mine, the other says she is all mine. Much merry elucidation ensues. Myself, I am in favor of internationalization, under a Fijian flag. Come to think of it, Fiji had a military coup, did it not, quite recently, by Christianized fanatics. So I am totally lost. Perhaps we should sell the Holy City to private enterprise, to the Disney Corporation for example. A mighty theme park, with all of us replaced by audioanimatronics, with plastic hearts and a taped loop of patter. So what would be the difference? I sink back in my seat, exhausted, ticking off my list of unanswered questions to myself while Dorothy Morgenthal, on the podium, tries to arm-wrestle Israelis and Palestinians into some coherent narrative. A changed figure, in my eyes, after the Ned Schatz incident. Is that matronly demeanor just a front? Any moment I expect her to flail out either side, mace Yochai Magen-David and scalp Daoud Abu-Naim's smooth pate with a kitchen knife or tomahawk. Pay attention, oriental pascudniaks! But I have my own problems:

a) Why did my Silencer make himself known to me?

b) Why did Agent Kool feed me lokshen? If he and Flynn accepted any part of my story, why their lack of interest in Didi Schaeffer?

c) Moreover, if, to their knowledge, said Didi was in Israel, why did his sudden presence on 116th Street and his assignation with me not even make them mildly curious? Surely he would be a prime suspect? Unless they knew he was not. Ergo, they, not me, knew far more than they were ready to hint.

d) Why did Agent Kool babble on about Pollard? Not to speak of Lewis Carroll. A broad hint to me about other Israeli spies in the U.S., and Murray Waiskopf's involvement. That's not small potatoes.

e) Who was the man in Nederlander Schatz's apartment? Would he have shot all of us if Madame Kung Fu hadn't got him first? What was the Mel Brooks joke going to tell me before he was so rudely interrupted?

f) How did I get entangled in this? I, a mild-mannered TV critic who only wants to sit moping at home, in his womb, cracking sunflower seeds and cursing the government from his armchair?

None of this makes sense. It is like a contrived scenario, the first draft of an abandoned screenplay. Real life is not like this, is it, as I contemplate Milek Stuckman dropping dandruff on to the chaffing PLO? Irishman Flynn is right. I should go back to my country. New York is too cold and dangerous for me. I should get back to the balm of my sunny homeland, where combat troops chase little children down alleyways, and enemies who preach peace are imprisoned without trial, where babes in arms are shot in the head for breaking a curfew, and an ex-terrorist and an alcoholic wield brute power in the name of Peace and Sobriety.

It is no longer a question of preserving sanity. We have to reclaim it, in the lost and found. I have a vague memory of what it looks like. Or was it that fuzzy thing, with blue pom-poms? Nothing but a dead childhood remains. The streets of a smaller, cozier Jerusalem, divided by its high sandbagged walls from its Looking Glass image on the other side. An awareness of community, unwracked by prosperity, the modest world of a common fate and experience. Before the flood of imperial *folie de grandeur*, Greater Israels and Strategic Alliances. I think of Anat, and our discussions about starting a family, seeing as we had finally tied the official knot in our relationship, to please her old folks and mine. The lectures she had to abide by from Rabbis' wives about menstruation and how to please your husband in bed. Making babies is not only a duty, she was told. There can be pleasure involved. Who would have believed it. Anyway, we signed the dotted line, broke the wine glass and were embraced by all our relatives. My father was glad for a few hours, at least, that he had come to Palestine from Germany, instead of mourning a lost arcadia we all know lies buried deep in blood. My mother made a tshoolent Joshua Nkomo would have drowned in. My eldest sister, Sarah, flew in from Norway, where she is straightening out the fiords for NATO, or something such, and I even had to grit my teeth at the advent of my brother-in-law, Elisha, who had dragged my other sister into the Kingdom of Judaea and was now a "moderate," eager to prove to the world that he did not want to kill all the Arabs, only those who did not accept our dominion. A good old Jewish family, we had our inbuilt UNIFIL forces to hold us apart. But what next? The outlook is not rosy. Conception, gestation, parturition, the growth of the mysterious embryo in the womb, sucking its thumb, dreaming of a continuing good time, to be interrupted by birth into – what? At the end of the day, what has any offspring of mine to look forward to, apart from an early place at the American Embassy in the queue for a green card?

All over the world, people want change, subject populations are tired of being treated like dogs, salivating at the clang of bells. The old-fashioned, stubborn cry for democracy. Russia responds. Even China. Countries as dazed as Poland and Hungary are clamoring to rejoin the human race. Millions of people want to control their own lives and blast their own brains out with their own choice of values, quality or dross. People want to schmooze on the beach, lick ice cream, fuck without fear. And we, we're merrily marching in the other direction, waving our iron flags of blood and fire, terror and prejudice . . . Can one sue one's own government, for malpractice, malfeasance, malicious damage and reckless endangerment of its citizens, making one's life a misery, a one-way ticket to Palookaville?

Nevertheless, I had only planned my present escape as a short visit. New York in February I could pass on. Three days, and back in time for the private atavisms of my Sabbath weekend. Back in the cage, with a few cashew nuts thrown through the bars, a couple of cuddles from my wife, and the occasional glimpse of British TV series that are less than thirty years old. Relatives used to send food parcels to the Holy Land. Now we only take video cassettes. BBC and Channel Four preferred. We are picky. Our expectations have risen. We want the best, but we know enough by now not to expect it. Any scrag-end is welcome.

But could I just leave, like that, in the middle of the movie, with barely the first reel unfurled? Just climb aboard the plane with the identity of Dorothy Morgenthal's nunchaku victim unrevealed? Uncertain whether my Silencer was still lurking for me over here, or over there? With Murray Waiskopf's killer unknown? Could I bear the suspense? And what would happen to Dorothy? Although she seemed better able to defend herself than I was. This was her city, not mine.

I could not think straight in the Conference ambience of tugging emotions, impassioned appeals for brotherhood and goodwill. I walked out, casting a friendly grin at Milek Stuckman, who looked physically sickened by the bonhomie emerging notwithstanding. It was snowing again, on the Alma Mater and the mock heroic Greek pediments. Outside the gates of the University the homeless converged, in padded sacking and boots thrust into boots, caps over shawls. "It's a cold winter, man. Help me stay alive." They have eschewed euphemisms. I found myself unloading dollar bills. A tall, raggedy middle-aged man grabbed my arm.

"What's your name, son?"

"Joe Dekel."

"I'm Francis Luther King. God bless you."

I wriggled free and crossed the road, heading for the strip of the Morningside Park, looking like a forest of Christmas trees. The statue of Carl Schurtz, Defender of Liberty and Friend of Human Rights. Who the fuck was he? Before I could reach him two men appeared out of the swirl of the snow and grabbed my arms from either side.

"Come on, gentlemen, I've run out of cash."

"We take credit cards," one of them rasped. They were not dressed in rags, but in dingy raincoats not unlike Agent Kool's. But their eyes did not look like eyes that had ever considered scanning a line of Lewis Carroll. A car drew up, a long black Caddy limousine, with smoked windows. I was bundled inside, in the back, by a man who was large and whose rugged jaw jutted. A hospital bandage was wrapped round the top of his head. He reached out and clapped handcuffs on me.

"I'll give you my name, rank and number later," he said hoarsely. "Asshole." And then he clubbed my right temple.

I fell into a dark valley. If it was the valley of the shadow of death, it certainly was a familiar one, peopled by familiar ghosts and demons. Old army buddies crawled through the underbrush, looking for the nearest latrine. Here and there were black lumps of napalmed casualties, rubbish of old wars and skirmishes. Dead cows, broken-down tractors, bullet-marked statues of men with one arm or one leg. My schooltime friend Moishe-Ganef, who became a burglar for state security, was being led blindfold across stone terraces by several figures in camouflage jackets, who waved to me, hooting old Boy Scout tunes. As I moved through these distractions, weighed down by a heaviness like a mental ball and chain, I passed through a glade of pine trees into a clearing, occupied by a long, festive table laid out for the Passover *seder*. There were about forty chairs surrounding the table, which was groaning under the weight of tureens of chicken soup and plates of roast chicken and hard-boiled eggs, but all were empty, except for the chair at the further end of the table, upon which, on a pile of cushions, a figure in a black fez reposed. He was swathed in sheets, which came up to his eyebrows, which were a bedraggled, bushy gray. As I came closer I saw the sheets were stained, shockingly, with excrement and urine, a puddle of piss spreading under the table and sinking slowly into the ground. Columns of black ants scattered away from the saturated earth, climbing up the table legs, on to the white tablecloth, devouring the ceremonial *matsoh shmura* and carrying it off in crumbs in triumphant columns back towards dry ground.

"The beasts of the earth," said the swaddled figure, in a mellow, resonating baritone, "the fowl of the air, everything that creepeth upon the earth. Only Man remains to be formed. Do you have any suggestions?"

The figure belched, and a black stain formed on the sheet below its eyebrows, which I saw were moulting. The entire construction, table, soup tureens, clearing, valley, was disintegrating before my eyes, accompanied by a familiar stench I recognized, from the good old days of the Six-Day War, as that of massed rotting corpses. The whole universe was shaking. I became aware of a sweating hand. I fixed it with my gaze, trying to move its fingers. It moved and cuffed me on the face.

"He's comin' round," said a voice floating in a jar of formaldehyde.

"You shoulda brought the ampules," said another.

"It wuz you that had 'em," said the first, gratingly.

OK, fellas, I confess, it was my responsibility. I fucked up, once again. I mumbled.

"Shut up," said the second voice. "Just lie there quietly and you won't get your skull broke."

It seemed a good offer. I subsided. I was lying hunched on the back seat of the limousine, which seemed to be moving at a fair lick, somewhere. The windows were too dark for me to glimpse anything.

"The Colonel wants to do that himself," said the second voice, which came from the passenger by the driver. "The Colonel hates Jews, and he especially hates double-crossin' Mow-sad agents."

"I am not a Mow-sad agent," I grunted, despite myself. Some calumnies cannot be ignored. Double crossin' – ehh. That I can live with. Sometimes life's path does get crooked. One has to defend oneself, against income tax officials, the army call-up, customs men, rabid anti-Semitic colonels, whoever they might be.

"Shut up, Jewboy," said the bandaged man, who obviously harbored a personal grudge, apart from his failure to bring the ampules. He raised his hand and cuffed me again.

"Don't knock him out again." The driver spoke for the first time, in a voice surprisingly mellow, not unlike Richard Nixon in his prime, when he was assuring the American people he was not a crook. "We're getting there." This used to be, I remember from London visits, the slogan of British Rail. I am full of useless information at the wrong time. They used to serve terrible sandwiches, but Anat, who had visited the UK recently, said the cuisine had improved. As for colonels, I have never liked them. Their salaries are lousy, most of them will never be generals, and they always think they can run the business better than anybody else. In my homeland you find them everywhere, in the plasterwork, in redundant businesses, political parties and all communal cookie-jars. Right to left, they proliferate, breeding endlessly by promotion and parthenogenesis.

My mind is wandering, I am not giving sufficient attention to the matter at hand: Joe Dekel, survival of. The situation was unpromising. With three thugs around me, and my hands, I now realized, handcuffed behind my back. Luckily I could move my tongue, over my swollen lips. What a luxury. The perennial question: What would Philip Marlowe have done?

How can one charm a Jew-hating colonel? Sing selected Christian hymns? "Nearer, my God to thee"? "When the roll is called up yonder"? A limited repertoire. Should I prattle on about my collection of small arms and World War II handguns? I have a Parabellum, used by an Irgun hit squad against British squaddies in the late forties. A Nazi Luger, bona fide loot from the Libyan Campaigns. I have a Karl-Gustav, taken off a dead Syrian NCO in the Six-Day War. On second thoughts, this would only confirm these people's prejudice of my Mow-sad affiliation. Anat always castigated me on my delight in the instruments of what I most hated. "It's like living with Lee Van Cleef," she said. I was devastated. I was aiming for Clint Eastwood. The Man With No Name. Otherwise known as Blondie. "What can I do?" I protested. "I am a bundle of contradictions. I am a Man Of My Time." Come back, Middle Ages, all is forgiven. After all, Torquemada meant well . . .

My mind had wandered again. I came to with a start, realizing the car had bucked and turned right, over the bump of some gateway. My three abductors had fallen silent. I twisted my head, glimpsed white trees dimly through the smoked windows. Two minutes later, the limousine stopped. Hands (not across the ocean) grabbed me and dragged me out, into what passed for bright sunlight. It was like an entrance into Father Christmas land. On top of a snow-caked hill, with picturesquely coated trees, an old, many gabled three-story wooden house, in the colonial style. It had the creaky look of a prop in a ghost film, the sort of place Granmaw Sarah hung out in, two hundred years after her death. The wooden porch, the scattered sticks of furniture, even the rocking chair, flecked with snow. The two thugs dragged my rubbery legs up the steps to the porch, as the driver with Richard Nixon's voice rapped on the scuffed main door.

There were no signs of life. The windows on either side of the door were shuttered. Five empty milk bottles were standing by a large rusty tray filled with what looked like congealed Catlit. At any moment I expected Natalie Wood to breeze out and ask in erotic Deep South tones: "Is that you, Bubber?"

The mellow driver knocked again. My handmaid, he with the bandaged head, was trembling from tip to toe.

"What the fuck is goin' on, Harold? Where is he? Ain't you got the right address?"

"There is no mistake," said mellow Harold. "Just hold your horses a minute." He stepped down from the porch, walked around the left corner of the house, cupping his hands: "Yo! Anybody there?" His voice echoed across the white glade, stretching down the hill in both directions, into a larger wooded area. The roofs of houses peeked up over the treetops. Further off, the tops of taller buildings, apartment houses, billboards.

The men on either side of me were increasingly nervous. But they still held on to my handcuffed arms.

The second formaldehyde voice spoke up: "This is shit, Harold! There ain't nobody home!"

What a bunch of schlemiels. I began to perk up. This situation had possibilities it had not had five minutes earlier. The unpredictable might turn in my favor. As if in answer to my desires and prayers, the screech of tires came from the driveway and two black saloon cars topped with snow raced up, disgorging black-coated figures. A megaphone blared: "THIS IS THE STATE POLICE AND FEDERAL AGENTS . . . PLEASE COME FORWARD WITH YOUR HANDS VISIBLE . . ."

No invisible hands need apply. I had seen this movie before. I only had a split second before a gun was held to my head and "a hostage situation developed." Hold your fire, men! It's only Joe Dekel. Oh, OK then, fire at will. My two minders had relaxed their grasp on my limbs. I had already tested my legs on the steps. I leapt down them and ran down the snowy lawn, my hands still cuffed behind my back. My brains still scrambled, I cried out: "Don't shoot! Foreign press!" Home habits die hard. I hopped, skipped and jumped down the hill, avoiding trees and a sign tacked to one which I swore blind read "NO SPEED-ING. AUTHORS WALKING." Squirrels chipmunks leered at me from their hibernation. Cheshire cats puffed in my face. I tripped and rolled down the hill, landing headfirst in a snow-drift. I scrabbled with my legs but my body refused to move. There was a deathly silence. No tweet of birds, no shots, no backfires. Then a voice spoke up above me:

But oh, beamish nephew, beware of the day,
If your Snark be a Boojum, for then
You will softly and suddenly vanish away,
And never be met with again.

I managed to free my head from the snow and looked up. Upside down, looking up at me from the direction of China, Agent Kool, chewing the cud under his bow tie, bedraggled raincoat snow-flecked.

"Giddiyup there, Mr. Joseph Dekel," he said. "You have an appointment with an El Al check-in desk in less than twenty-four hours. I am taking you into protective custody until then. You are not safe running loose."

Boy, ain't that the truth now. I surrendered into the arms of the Law.

In *The Trial*, by Franz Kafka, another neurotic Jew, a man from the Styx begs admittance to The Law from the doorkeeper who will not let him in although the door is open. After the man has sat his whole life on a stool by the door through which he may not pass, the doorkeeper reveals to him, at the point of his death, that that door was meant for him alone, and he, the doorkeeper, was now going to shut it.

I meet people like that all the time.

I am not quite on my deathbed, in protective custody, but there are several corpses of roaches, keeping me company, which may well have emulated K's supplicant. I feel like Eichmann, in his glass cage. Except that I am not facing Justice in Jerusalem, but only the seedy walls of an apartment hotel room somewhere in Queens, overlooking Queen's Boulevard, *en route* to the Van Wyck Expressway and twenty minutes' drive to zap Joe Dekel into an airport packing case at JFK and Hi Yo Silver. My doorkeeper is a gorilla with a shoulder holster who has either had his larynx removed or is auditioning for the silent remake of *The Godfather*. He plays nursemaid and keeps me away from the window, lest I be shot, I presume, from one of the million cars zooming by on the freeway. I tell a lie, he has uttered two words: "Coffee? Sugar?" He did not know the word for Milk, no drawback, since there was none in the icebox. The room is utterly bare, apart from the dead bugs, refusing, like my companion, to identify itself to Man nor God.

One phone call allowed to Dorothy Morgenthal, whom I asked to inform Anat, in Jerusalem, that I was out of circulation only temporarily. Dorothy offered, on my behalf, to call a practicing lawyer she knew, who had defended Daniel Ellsberg,

Eldridge Cleaver, The Weathermen, and Nixon's Attorney General, John Mitchell. I assured her I would rather not join that hall of fame, and, given the situation, had no serious objection to being shooed through El Al first thing the following morning. I told her I was co-operating with the FBI and was expecting my free award of a fedora, a tommy-gun and a signed portrait of J. Edgar Hoover imminently. My out-of-town jaunt was not yet news fit to print, and she agreed, reluctantly, to stall any of my colleagues who might have woken up sufficiently in the Aaron Spelling Hall to note my sudden disappearance. That had been, in fact, the last session of the Peace Conference, which had ended, Dorothy revealed, in a burst of enthusiasm and an exchange of addresses all round. Golden visions of the plough-share factories and the little boy caressing the beasts. *Sic transit, gorier Mondays*. At least I had enough material to justify my expenses, and anyway I had a date with my local Jerusalem synagogue in a couple of days, eve of Sabbath, to resume my atavisms. Not to speak of Anat, my beloved among the thorns, who would certainly notice my absence on the weekend, though on weekdays she has her own bed of nails to distract her at the Jerusalem Municipality's Department of the Fine (and less fine) Arts.

What else could I do? Strategic withdrawal was the only option. No one was going to tell me what was going on, anyway. My two original abductors had been captured, but the mellow driver had got away. Whoever was watching me on Kool's behalf at the University had managed to note the limousine's number, and the forces of Law and Order had moved in as soon as they could. This at least was the Official Version. The house on the hill was indeed empty. The "Colonel," whoever he may be – Agent Kool wasn't telling – was absent. Had he been fore-warned? And how? And by whom? Everybody was stum. Kool only revealed the house itself was an abandoned property which had belonged to a now bankrupt publisher, who had disclaimed all knowledge of the use to which his house might have been put. The location was in Westchester County, not far from the world-renowned penitentiary of Sing Sing. Now who would have believed that? A stone's throw from Spencer Tracy and all I got was a headful of snow and an earful of slush.

Agent Kool in person typed out my statement of the events as I saw them, a document not unlike that of a hooked fish trying to make out the nature and mores of angling. I signed the script. No TV rights were mentioned. A most un-American shroud of reticence upon the whole shmeer. Wot, no District Attorneys flashing subpoenas, all the razzmatazz of Federal Law Enforcement, charges of white slavery, violation of civil rights and constitutional liberties? And what about Murray Waiskopf and the hundred-year-old Jew?

"Na," said Agent Kool, proving that he was not as alienated from Jewish affairs as he pretended, as he brought me a takeout Szechuan, certainly more than Kafka's supplicant was granted. "We'll ask you for a further deposition from your homeland, as and if. Meanwhile, we're holding these people and investigating. It's out of your hands. Of course, you can shout and yell, talk to newspapers, print your story. But if you want my advice, take it easy. There are serious problems here you don't want to get tied up with. A good journalist is judged by what he doesn't publish as much as by what he does. I can't blame you if you want to dig, but it's rocky ground. Spy and Counterspy. Who needs it? You and I know most of the stuff that gets traded is noise and dud information. People kill and get killed and risk life imprisonment for out-of-date back-up data the other side has already. The Stealth Bomber, SDI, it's obsolete before the hardware leaves the launch pad. So just keep ploughing your own furrow. Trust me, it's the best for you. Leave the rough stuff for the professionals. Go on shaking hands with the PLO. Look after your own little corner, before it goes up in smoke. We can't be hurt by our war games, we're too powerful. It's other people who get hurt in the crossfire."

Indeed. I shovel up the little dried roach corpses, adding them to a bag of rubbish which my silent Godfather hands to another clone by the door, free hand poised at his shoulder holster. Outside, the rush-hour traffic congeals, grinds to a halt on the Expressway, a three-lane metallic centipede yearning for its daily escape. In Orson Welles's version of Franz's *The Trial* the gargantuan genius suggested to his actor, Anthony Perkins, the key to playing the eternal victim: Joseph K. is guilty. There are no innocent bystanders any more. All Snarks are Boojums. Or is that the perfect excuse for mass villainy?

Dorothy: "Are you sure you're all right, Joe?"

"I can handle it."

I am an old, ragged whore. The ebb and flow of the traumas of my battered country, the blistering, jagged, sandy winds of circumstance have carved their marks on my soul. How could anything inhuman be strange to me? My bodyguards devouring their fried rice. But Agent Kool relented a little on his harsh judgement of my uselessness in the global game. Nudging me, as I tucked into the garlic pork with baby corns: "If you feel the need, if you can't sit still out there, go see that man of yours, Didi Schaeffer. He is definitely now in Israel, in the town of Amiel, on the West Bank. You might find it an interesting encounter. Officially we're not going to touch him. It's not our turf, or so we're told." He sighed, spearing a baby corn with a white plastic fork. "The Middle East. I tell you, my friend, it could all have been so different. There are a lot of good people there. I know. I've been there, I've sat in cafés, and watched the world go by. The grace of living. My theory is, at heart, it's all simple. People just don't allow themselves to like each other any more. No individuals, only causes. Don't you think that's the real tragedy?"

2

IS REAL?

OUT OF THE FREEZER, into the fire. Back to my Homeland, the Land of the Promise, the Covenant between God and Abraham, the celestial Give and Take, the Milk and the Honey, the battleground of faiths, the field of so much bluff and blather, the tragicomedy of our age. Ersatz Yisrael! The sun-kissed land, blessed by God with so much attention. So why don't you leave us alone? The old saw. Choose someone else for a change. I have my own personal relationship with the Old Progenitor, which I shall keep to myself. Everyone should have a peculiarity. With some it's a boil, a wooden leg, a stamp collection or an ideology. With me it's my attitude to the Creator. I believe it's solely my business. It binds no other soul or group. My left-wing bleeding-heart peers have learned to leave me alone on this. Even Anat has given up trying to convince me of the vacuum at the center of existence. Bashevis Singer defined it once to my satisfaction: Nevertheless, there is something there. Somebody had to decide to set off the Big Bang, even if He regretted it henceforth. Whether He wants me to commit the 613 *mitsvot* of Judaism is quite another matter. I have compromised on 235, or thereabouts. Anat tells me this is illogical. But there is no logic in Faith. It is simply a personal decision. It does not mean you mortgage your reason or your emotions to rabbis, priests, mullahs, the Maharishi, Bhagwan, or any other shmendrick. The name of the game is free will, not slavery.

That's quite enough of that.

Back to my home, safe in the confines of "white" Rehavia, away from the apartment within a stone's throw of the religious area of Mea Shearim, when all the stones came in my direction.

Back to my one and only Anat, whose bare limbs used to raise the ire of my neighbors so they took to slashing the bare tires of my car, Alexander, the famous Austin beach buggy. Back to my gun collection, so heavily disapproved of by my peace-loving friends. Back to my rejection slips, the myriad letters from the Golden Land, saying: *"We have read your offer*, The Death of Moishe-Ganef, *with interest, but unfortunately the market does not take kindly to the mix of thrills, comedy and politics. The particular ethnic specificity of the book does limit its appeal still further."* Ethnic specificity, my ass! They're lucky I didn't turn up in full streimel and kaftan, with white or gray socks, on their doorstep, collecting for the Shnipishocker Rebbe. Was this an ear that my newly revealed Silencer or his dead boss had whispered into? Or just the normal, unsolicited brush-off? New paranoias in the land where paranoia is life's blood, no aberration, but the breathed air, the miasma spreading from ourselves to our enemies and back again, firmed up in our national newspapers' headlines:

ARAFAT: THE MOSSAD WANTS TO MURDER ME. The leader of the PLO made this allegation yesterday in Cairo, at a news conference arranged for Israeli correspondents attending the meeting between Foreign Minister Arens and Soviet FM Shevardnadze, who had also met Arafat the same day. "They have a plan called 'The Best Hit,' to assassinate me," said the PLO leader. Arafat emphasized he was not worried by the "negative image" he has with Prime Minister Shamir: "They call me a terrorist and I call them 'the Israeli Junta.' I am more concerned whether the ordinary person in Israel sees me in a negative way. At any rate, peace is only made between enemies, not between friends. We have a hysterical (not historical) opportunity to make peace now."

The Chairman's making Israeli jokes now, God help us. My colleagues are lucky they didn't get offered the famous cornflakes *mit tchai.* Our own New York meeting gets the usual treatment. The usual mix of apathy, hype or abuse. My favorite right-wing columnist, A— A—, writes trenchantly about "KISS- ING AMALEK'S ASS." Peace means War. Love means Hate. We are all dupes, et cetera. We have plunged a knife in the Nation's back. And I thought I was plunging it in its heart. Some people's ass and face must be transposed.

And here is the rest of the news, as out there, beyond the "green line," the old border between Israel and the Hashemite Kingdom of Jordan, the war of Arab and Jew proceeds with its slingshots, Arafat Cocktails and Galil assault rifles. A genetic regression to the original core of our dispute in this land, before all the global games: RENEWED VIOLENCE OF UPRISING. A ten- year-old child has been shot in Tulkarm by the army. A soldier has been knifed on Mount Zion. Another soldier has been missing, feared kidnapped, for three weeks. The army has dyna- mited the homes of the families of three Palestinian Arabs who petrol bombed a Jewish settler's car. West Bank settlers have demanded the sacking of our Defense Minister for being too soft on the Arabs. The "*sicarii,*" a new group of ultra-right Jewish would-be terrorists, named after the zealot assassins of the first century AD, have threatened to kill a pop star who made an appearance at a leftist rally against the Occupation. The moneylenders of Nablus are against the *intifada* because the organizers of the Uprising want them to raise the rate of the Jordanian dinar to three shekels and one agora for purchase, and three shekels-two to sell. It's good to know we still have allies among the natives.

My country, right or left. In Cairo, Arafat, according to the report, stretched his hand out to the TV correspondent, Ehud Y—, who did not take it, saying: "I respect the laws of my state." And what about the state of the laws, gottenyu? I rest my case. But my case refuses to rest . . .

Late February, hoping for the balm of March. It had been a

hard winter, leading up to my New York excursion: Temperatures had dropped below freezing, solar heaters burst, crops were ruined, streets deserted. Frost had clung to the battlements of the Old City walls, freezing the balls off the patrolling Border Police guards and garnishing the thrown stones with ice. Anat and I had huddled, cocooned in our central heating, viewing the world through the warped peephole of our TV. The checkered balm of *Dynasty, Are You Being Served?* and the massed choirs, on the rival Amman channel, belting out the Jordanian National Anthem at the end of each day's transmission. God Save His Majesty the King. The hegemony of dwarves . . .

Anat behind me, in the bathroom mirror, elbows me aside in the toothbrushing war. She had listened to my bizarre tale of New York, all *noir* and Yiddisher Damon Runyon, with characteristic sang-froid. Anat is amazed that I am able to walk the streets without falling over my shoelaces or braining myself on a lamppost, and she has read my book, so she believes nothing I say unless I have photographs, but nevertheless, I see she is concerned. We live in an uncertain world. It has ever been thus, since our first bout in Safad of 1972, when we met in the aftermath of civil rights demonstrations (the case of Ikrit and Bir'am), and crossed swords over my demonstrative hattie. Ah! the heyday of bucolic Trotskyism, before the ice picks and the Empire's decline: The Yom Kippur War, Lebanon, Permanent War instead of permanent revolution. God! In those days you could actually climb aboard an aircraft without having your groin felt by an airline official, not like nowadays, when you abandon hope automatically and are unutterably relieved when the only menace comes from the proximity of the ultra-orthodox passengers complaining to the stewardesses about the shrink-wrapped *glatt kosher* meals. My zealous co-religionists always suspect, on El Al in particular, that they are being served pigmeat as part of a secular Zionist conspiracy to condemn their souls to limbo. In so stormy a world, who can be surprised at bodies tumbling at one's feet in New York City? Or being kidnapped to Sing Sing? Nevertheless Anat says softly, having rinsed out her toothpaste: "Take care, Joseph. Don't mix fact with fantasy. It's difficult enough in this country." Adding the commonplace Israeli advice: "Keep a small head, a small head, Joe." She used to rush around, like the rest of us, insisting that the world be transformed immediately, in the name of Justice, by six o'clock the next morning. No longer. We have all been whittled down.

That Friday I arrived back, we settled down for the Sabbath. The air raid siren that notifies the advent of the Lord's day, rather than the Syrian Army. And then the city folds in on itself, curls up in its cozy ball, purrs itself asleep, apart from the bolt-holes of secular youth's discos, where, I am told, everything is happening these days. But I take the old-fashioned road, pulling my shades down, retreating into my atavism, pursuing my private chitchat with God. The words, feloniously appropriated by all the forces of darkness in this state: "*I believe, in complete faith, in the coming of the Messiah, and even if he is tardy, I shall wait for him every day till he comes . . .*" Too many of my compatriots have already booked him in for their personal version of apocalypse. They see him coming in full combat gear, with tear gas grenades and pouches. A Messenger of Wrath. (Amazing, in that case, that they feel so hostile to Mohammad, after all the embodiment of that concept . . .) For the zealots the Messiah is the incarnation of all their petty desires for power and mastery over others. A club-footed *pied noir*. No wonder false messiahs queue, round the block, in every quarter of my redivided city, at every ice-cream kiosk and bus stop, vying with the bewildered tourists wandering under armed guard around its strike-bound Arab quarters, clicking their cameras at the shuttered souvenir shops, wondering why every day seems a holiday . . . "Wow, these people are really devout, Seymour! When do they ever do business?"

When, indeed. But no peace for the tormented. No sooner is the Sabbath over, according to the official timing, the phone rings. What a surprise. It's my editor, Nahum Lauterman, calling from Tel Aviv. He has just returned from Cairo, hobnobbing with our old enemy, now known as Camp David partner. "President Mubarak asked me what's going on here," he said cheerfully. "Why are we so afraid of talking to an adversary who can hardly make a cup of tea, let alone war? What's with your government, he asked me. Have they gone mad? The whole world sees them defeated by children with stones. Can't they read what's written on the wall? I told him they are using special blind units with kerosene cans to make sure it's all washed off. So how was New York? I hear it went OK."

"An entertainment from start to finish," I replied. I was not sure if I wanted to confide in Lauterman. But on the other hand, he knew of short cuts to answers I could not avoid seeking. "Some very strange things happened to me on the way to the Peace Conference," I told him.

"Strange things are always happening in New York," he said; "the last time I was there there was a grape-catching championship, to see who could catch the most grapes in his mouth that were being thrown off the Empire State Building. A Chinese contestant ruptured his stomach and died."

"Are you coming to Jerusalem tomorrow?" I cut him short.

"No way," he countered. "I never leave civilization if I can help it."

"All right, I'll come to Tel Aviv," I told him.

An onerous act, but unavoidable. Tel Aviv, like death and taxes, is always with us. Lauterman moved there a couple of years back, from Jerusalem. He said he didn't want his kids to grow up in a place where they assumed a Jew was genetically fitted with a little cap and pin. I suggested he gave them tomahawks and teach them scalping, but some people are strange. I find Tel Aviv too noisy and hasslebound, a Meditteranean city without the bonus of not being in Israel. If I am going to be among my people, I might as well take them in their most virulent form, as a sort of inoculation.

The usual hazard of the service taxi. I would have driven to Tel Aviv in Alexander, but Anat had a prior claim on the car to track down Art in some outlying hamlet in the hills. So, the *sherut* taxi. Inevitably, there is some altercation. This time it was a woman who offered the driver a one-shekel note in lieu of a coin. "Lady, I can't take this," he grated, "it ain't legal tender no more." "All right, I'll look for a *djouk*," said the patient lady, rummaging in her purse for the tiny silver gobs dubbed "cockroaches" by the populace. But nothing can be resolved so easily. A passenger in the middle seat rebukes the driver: "You should take the note. It's still legal. I take them all the time in my shop. It's an offense not to." A third passenger, a strapping lout with a hairy chest bursting through his shirt, laughs and waves towards the driver. "See, you've committed a crime! Let's call the police." The driver has no sense of humor. He begins swerving the taxi dangerously down the bustling Jaffa Road, as trucks and buses hoot nervously. "Whadyoumean, a crime? What police? What's with this country? In my own taxi, you threaten me? You want to get out and walk?" "Don't get anxious, it's just a joke, mister." "What joke? What crime? For one shekel? Arabs kill Jews and nothing happens. I ask for one shekel and I'm on the Most Wanted list?" He hurls the taxi wildly down the terraced hill towards the coastal plain at 75 mph. I close my eyes, and pretend I am winging my way 38,000 feet above the ocean. I am perfectly safe. The *glatt kosher* meal is coming. We are merely experiencing a little turbulence. The Captain has switched on the Fasten Seat Belts sign.

Tel Aviv, the Central Bus Station. Who says we don't belong in the East? Exhaust fumes, shopping bags, elbows. The hummus sold in the falafel stalls here was shown in a medical study to have three hundred times the amount of bacteria than is acceptable to the human brain. There has long been a school of thought that our troubles here are biological, a sort of mass cafard brought on by the heat. Now, at last, scientific evidence. But I suspend my judgement.

My newspaper's Tel Aviv office is in the commercial area, in the most unattractive part of the city. Vans and trucks raise choking dust in narrow, bustling and congested streets. In summer it's pure hell, and even in the balm of winter it's not my idea of serenity. The office is, ironically, across the street from a nondescript block which is known to be a Ministry of Defense Unit involved in Information Retrieval, a sort of neo-Mossad tumor. Was it here they sat and sifted through the thousands of documents the spy Pollard vacuumed up in Washington? We used to play games, from our windows, pretending to photograph the people coming in and out of the building, till a discreet phone call caused Lauterman to call us in and ask us not to annoy the natives. He stood in his office now, overlooking the landscape of moving vans unloading office equipment. The raucous cries of workmen having filing cabinets dropped on their heads. He closed the window, shutting out the cries of pain, and listened to my story, playing all the while with a brass sphinx paperweight he had brought out of Egypt.

"That's not a bad story," he said, when I had finished. "Did you hear what happened to Fishelsohn in Manila? He had to share a taxi with the PLO rep, who had once been an engineer for a Popular Democratic Front bomb unit. They were going from the city center to some villa for a South-East Asia Peace beano when they were stopped and kidnapped by an urban unit of the Communist insurgents. They were about to be shot as Imperialist stooges, but the guerrillas found a portrait of Arafat in the Palestinian's wallet. They were given fifty dollars each as compensation for their trouble and released on the spot."

"I shall carry the Chairman close to my heart always," I assured him, "but what do you make of all this stew? The

Anti-Slander League, Pollard, the FBI, Murray Waiskopf? Any inside clues?"

"Joe," he said, giving me the fatherly look, though he was two years my junior, "you and I, we go back a long way together. When we met, when was it, 'sixty-nine? You'd just started on your work for the paper, and I was demobilized from the army magazine and was taken on as a reporter. The first years of the Occupation. The heyday of Golda Meir. 'Who are these Palestinians? I've never met any.' A neat and closed orthodoxy. Now it's all blowing in the wind. The great victory of 1967. The ship was sailing. The Americans came on board. Everybody admired us, except the Third World, that bunch of wogs, who cared? Everybody deserves an imperial hubris. Ours just happened to last half an hour. The warning signs of arrogance and presumption. The Yom Kippur War. Menachem Begin. Lebanon. No more invincibility. And then, to twist the knife, *intifada*. Some people just can't take it, Joe. They want that half-hour back, to stretch for ever. They want the smart Jew, who pisses on everyone. Pollard? Psccht! We can put a hundred Pollards there, or none, if the mood suits us. We have the best intelligence service in the world. Aren't there a zillion paperback books out there, to prove it? Everybody knows we're the best. We may have gone down the tubes in the morality stakes, but in military power, hi-tech, spook stuff, we are the unchallenged champions. We even export our expertise to Guatemala and El Salvador and Colombia and other bulwarks of freedom. But you and I know it's all crap. We know the machine is creaking with overload and stress, the spies are burnt out, on the defensive, fighting for their jobs and careers. The war of all against all. Remember, Joe Lebanonization? We're far from private armies and cantonal fiefdoms, yet, but the mentality is already there. The army knows it can't defeat the Uprising. The intelligence services know they're falling behind. What's the use of knowing the private names of the Soviet politburo's mistresses if your country trembles at a kid with a stone? Hubris, Joe. Infallibility dies hard. All sorts of projects and alliances set up when we were riding on the crest of the wave can now be liabilities when we're on the street, with everyone else. Take a look . . ."

He opened the window again, and squinted, but shook his head. "We can't see it from here. You know it well, the Ministry of Defense radar tower. That concrete prick that hangs over the city. Its satellite dishes can sniff out a cough in the Iraqi secret service canteen. But it can't tell you what's going to happen tomorrow in Kafr Tushtush, just down the road. Teenagers with aerosol cans are determining the fate of this whole mighty machine, this Supergolem with feet of clay."

"This still doesn't explain," I said, "why two shmendricks in New York want to stop me publishing a mildly subversive book, or why one of them gets his head bashed in, or why an FBI agent keeps quoting Lewis Carroll at me."

He sat down and looked at his sphinx, as if this shoddy little tourist souvenir had the answers, like its original. "Why don't you go to Amiel then?" he said, trying to look inscrutable, but only succeeding in appearing constipated. "Go and check out this 'Silencer' of yours. This globe-trotting Didi Schaeffer. If you don't get any verbal mileage out of him, at least you can sell him a Frequent Flyer voucher. I could give you my Special Press pass for the West Bank, but it might be a red rag to the bullshitters. Your own topknot should get you by the Faithful, though I'd hide it from the hostile tribes. Come to think of it, I'd welcome a little digging out there on the growing settler backlash. If your 'Silencer' wants to make with the mouth a bit, sound him out on the new Jewish Underground. Any angle on the mysterious *sicarii*? What about the plans for 'Free Judaea'? I'm planning a major series on the subject. Amnon E— has been doing some legwork. The Right-Wing Revolt. The OAS phase. Go, nose around a little among the Godfearing. Meanwhile, I'll see if I raise any sparks on your Manhattan Melodrama. I'll dig a bit in the manure pit. So how's Anat? Don't forget to give her my love. Any gleam of a family budding? A man has to look to the future, even here, in the pressure cooker. It's a gamble, you never know how the next generation turns out. They want my younger daughter to kiss the Torah in her class every morning, but she refused. I went to see the teacher. She said, well, the Americans kiss the flag, isn't that the same thing? I should have told her to kiss my ass instead. But I try to immunize them, with the virus of progress. Give it a shot, boy, you never know, what the hell, you too might strike lucky!"

The West Bank. To some a bane, to others an endangered home, to yet others, the center of the universe, the nub of an ancestral promise. To me, a foreign country, tacked on to the heartland of Israel by means of rubber bands, tank grease, brute force, and the dreams of my *bêtes noires*, the settlers, who claim an infinite lease, signed by God. Genesis, Chapter 17, Verse 8. A genuine problem for me, as far as physical travel is involved. In "normal" times, before the *intifada*, one could move about with reasonable impunity, apart from sporadic burning tires, an occasional grenade, and permanent dagger looks from the suppressed. Today, it is all *stimmt verboten*, the press locked out by military order, lest they report that the Palestinian inhabitants no longer love us, and the solidarity patrols of the Peace Now movement, gathering information on human rights abuses, can only penetrate the area singly in Arab taxis, hoping to slide unseen among the familiar enemy through the army roadblocks. The only sure way through is, as Lauterman said, with beard and hattie, the stigmata of the resident Jewish settlers. And therein of course lies the rub. Having habitually refused to wear the skullcap in the Conquered Colonies, to avoid identification with my ideological sworn enemies, could I now afford to jettison it as the sole disguise to get me through the lines? The dilemma being, what if the rebellious inhabitants, spying my stigmata, decide to treat me with their usual mode of greeting to their zealous neighbors, of stones, petrol bombs or other solid objects such as sticks with nails or iron bars? With this in mind, no settler travels in the Occupied Areas unarmed. Often they shoot first to prevent the offense, or, for general purposes, at random, *pour encourager les autres*.

78

Well, I warned them but they wouldn't listen to me. I wrote all about it, in my *Moishe-Ganef*. My doubts, my skepticism, my reservations, as soon as the tanks had rolled in, 1967, about the grandiose certainties of the conquest, the efficacy of the clearing out of the "nests" of "saboteurs," the mass arrests, the intimidation, the harassment, the coercive network of total control. All the colonial methods that had lost France Algeria and Indochina, the Portuguese Africa, the British everywhere else. The "liberal occupation." Ah, the nostalgia! We brought in agricultural and industrial experts, shining and sweating with goodwill and enthusiasm, bringing the backward natives new forms of cultivation, advanced farming techniques, a better health service, and so on. But the ungrateful Arabs failed the test of our generosity, agitating repeatedly for political rights, self-determination and other subversive concepts, instilled in them by terrorists and Commies. Nevertheless, for twenty years, it worked. Despite the agitation, the people co-operated in their daily lives with our administration, applying to its offices for permits and licenses, generally keeping the peace, outbreaks of nationalist verve notwithstanding. Or so it seemed, until December 1987, when something snapped, and the shit finally hit the fan.

The West Bank: 3,500 square miles, a blip so small on the global map it might be a fly speck to be brushed away. Two hours' drive north to south (petrol bombs permitting), seventy minutes west to east (ditto). Despite the offers of Israeli progress, an effective time warp of brown, rolling terraced hills, dotted with villages that might be snoozing in an eternal siesta. At the best of times, sheep grazing lethargically across the hillsides, women and men bent over green fields, little boys selling fruit by the roadside, teenagers by watermelon stalls, an old man in traditional robes smoking under an olive tree. The Bibleland of American Jewish fantasy, except that it is peopled with real people, with real desires, not audioanimatronic robots.

To these places came people like my brother-in-law Elisha, all agog with Biblical excitement. Genetic place names inscribed on his retinas: Hebron, the Tomb of the Patriarchs, the afterglow of the presence of Abraham, Sh'chem, where he could nose out, like an ethnographic Sherlock Holmes, the footsteps of Abraham, Jacob and Joshua, to name but a meager few. Beit El, Anatot, Gilgal, Shiloh, Jericho, Giveah, Beit Lehem. There was no shortage of markers. No matter that by now there were people living there, with their own ancestral lodestones: Al Khalil, Beitin, Anata, Sinjil. Usurpers, strangers, latecomers. My brother-in-law and his friends were interested in ontological, not political rights.

God walked here! Forget about Jesus, and Mohammad, who just flew in for a quickie at Mount Moriah, then moved on. At first the settlers came by stealth, setting up small units, a few tents, a caravan and mobile water tanker. Then they took to turning up, in army trucks, in the dead of night, to hammer the tent pegs into the ground and assert their presence by daybreak, creating ersatz "fortress and watchtower" villages, as if the British were still in the land. Then, when Menachem Begin became Prime Minister, they came in great numbers, singing and dancing, with iced containers of soft drinks and sandwiches, and several Cabinet Ministers in tow. "This soil, to which we have returned after two thousand years of exile . . ." My brother-in-law Elisha always cried. One saw him on the television news, the tears flowing down the black-bearded cheeks as potent a pull for the TV cameras as aniseed is for dogs.

The West Bank. A pin-sharp blue-skied pre-spring day, the breeze fresh and sweet, flicking my face through Alexander's rolled-down windows. Security requires windows to be shut here, so the army never fails to advise, in case of hostile missiles at close quarters. A commercial company, I saw in my evening paper, is now marketing special wire mesh protection to be fitted over the windows of private cars. "The Answer To The *Intifada*,

Can be installed and removed within minutes: Enables the motorist to travel with protection in the Necessary Areas Only." It's a good thing they don't advise you to use it in your backyard. The neighbors might get weird ideas. Of course, the settlers here already use it regularly, they never leave home without it. It is part of the Quality of Life and Freedom they sought, having bussed themselves all the way from Brooklyn to live behind their barbed wire and ammunition belts. Zionism, to paraphrase old Karl, repeats itself first as tragedy, then as farce, and then as God knows what.

To minimize my time in hostile country I drove first towards the coast and turned through Kfar Saba towards the old "green line," flashing my hattie at the first army roadblock, which waved me by, then whipping it off rapidly as I passed through Kalkilya, the Arab town immediately beyond the defunct, but mentally redrawn border. Inching by the shuttered shops and closed cafés, nodding my head vacantly at the little knots of youths sitting silently on railings, mumbling Good Morning, "*marhaba*," and generally trying to give the air of an imbecile who has lost his way. If looks could kill. The town basked in its ominous silence, an air of pride in its buttoned-up ambience of non-cooperation.

I was glad I had not taken the gun, my prize World War II Luger. I had considered the idea, took it out of its glass case in the study and put a box of shells beside it. Anat came in, giving me a look which expressed our seventeen years of living together, the war weariness of stalemated arguments, the entire history of the Jewish people in capsule. I put the gun back. But I did hold up, determinedly, the Pink Floyd at Stonehenge cassette.

"You cannot sever me from my roots," I told my wife. She left the room without comment. Next week we use Apache smoke signals. After our brief reunion and day and a half of rest following my return from protective custody, Anat has been too busy with the Municipality's current crop of exhibitions for any

81

more in-depth consultations. In fact, she has been busy all year. The Uprising, occurring in the State of Israel's fortieth year, exacerbated the outbreak of Exhibitions and Festivals, which have proliferated like locusts. The Arts, Music, Theater, Cinema, Sanitation, Basket Weaving, Origami, Folk Dancing. We have been celebrating our anniversary with a growing manic depressive compulsion. Ersatz tent cities of 1950s' immigration camps spread over the Tel Aviv Exhibition Gardens, complete with young Moroccan girls washing clothes in old tin basins, babies bathed in wooden tubs, recreated standpipes, old men lolling on piles of blankets, while white-coated men and women, in a special hut, sprayed incomers with disinfectant. The good old days! Anat had no part of that horror, but she was fully engaged preparing a "Jerusalem in Miniature" exhibit, due to open at the coming Independence Day celebrations, April, six weeks ahead.

But I had no time to play my Pink Floyd cassette before the town of Amiel loomed before me, *sans* watchtower or surrounding fence, an unexpectedly large conglomerate of gleaming white stonework and fresh black asphalt roads, with an arched gate cheerfully announcing "WELCOME TO AMIEL" in Hebrew, English and French. I whipped my hattie back on as a bag of khaki rags rose off a folding chair to meet me, dragging his pouches and M16 carbine on the newly tarred road. "Yes, honey," he said, "what can I do for you?" His eyes were bloated with fatigue. A smart, white-shirted local with beard and hattie and matching rifle sauntered over.

"I'm looking for Didi Schaeffer," I told the local. "I was with friends of his in New York, who wanted me to pass on a message."

"You're a friend of Didi?" he asked.

"We met in the winter," I told him. Why tell a lie when small truths can prevail?

"He's at the plantation," said the smart local. "Straight down the road, past the synagogue, turn right at the post office, half a mile, left again, past the school."

We greeted each other with laconic waves. My people, right or left. We communicate in codes, like Kwakiul Indians. I was instantly co-opted into the clan. Israeli license plate, hattie, New York, pass friend. I pressed Alexander up the road. Neat, one- and two-story houses, freshly built, with little gardens in front. Larger blocks of apartment houses with terraces and rows of saplings in front. Young women wheeling laughing offspring in carriages. Children gamboling with hoses. A strange pyramidal synagogue, built perhaps by an architect who was someone's brother-in-law. An odd monument at a road junction, all white-painted twisted girders. Signifying, perhaps, the coils of the Jewish soul, or Menachem Begin's brainscan. The whole giving a fresh feel of uncrowded spaces, peaking at the top of a rolling hill, overlooking the surrounding landscape, the brown hills, the stone terraces. The air clear and sparkling. A genuinely pleasant place to bring up your family, far from the urban sprawl, car exhausts, pollution. The Quality of the Environment. Hey, boy, which side are you on?

I turned right at the post office, half a mile, past a school playground with two dozen tiny tots happily yammering, most with *kipas* and sidecurls. A couple of buildings further on, the fringe of cultivated fields. I stopped the car and got out. Ploughed earth stretched ahead, and I ambled up a gravel path towards some huts by rows and rows of some crop protected under plastic wraps. Do I know a beetroot from a kohlrabi? Just about, but there it stops. At a corner of the field, a number of Arab workers were handling bundles and loading crates on to a truck. Two white-shirted, skullcapped settlers were standing by, giving instructions, one a short, thin individual, the other a beefy giant with a massive black beard. I walked up.

"Good morning."

"Good morning," they answered, diffidently. The thin man

looked at me curiously. The giant barely threw me a glance. He was perturbed by something his workers were doing. "Hey, Farid, take it easy there, you'll smash the side . . ." He spoke Hebrew with an American accent.

"I'm looking for Didi Schaeffer," I said to the settlers. "I met him in New York, and then I saw some friends of his who asked me to give him a message."

"What's the message?" asked the giant, without taking his eyes off his errant laborer.

"I have to speak to Didi Schaeffer himself," I said, "it was a personal matter."

"You're a liar," said the giant. "Hey, Farid, for God's sake!"

"Pardon me?" I said. I was not sure whether he had addressed me or the Arab.

"You're a liar," he said. "I'm Didi Schaeffer, and I've never seen you before in my life."

Oi vei. Perhaps I should have brought the gun after all. This man was built along the lines of Eric Campbell in the old Chaplin movies. He was about eight feet tall and had arms like tree trunks descending from mountainous shoulders. His eyes were very small, and could hardly be seen without a periscope by a normal-sized person.

But at least I had my hattie. Advertised as a fellow practitioner, I would not be pulped without due process. I scratched my head, drawing attention to my security badge.

"Well, that's something . . ." I shook my head in puzzlement. "The fellow I met . . . he introduced himself as . . . this is very strange . . ."

"Who sent you?" he asked in English. "Was it Murray Waiskopf?"

Was he genuine, or just playing ignorant? I took a step back, just in case. "Murray Waiskopf is dead," I said. "Haven't you been told? He was found with his head bashed in, in an office on East 29th Street. It happened one week ago, last Monday."

"Let's go talk," he said. "Mottke, keep an eye on Farid. The crates break before they get to the stockroom. Everything spills. The food rots. Tell him I'm getting really pissed off." The thin man waved. The giant grabbed me by the arm, off the field. "You've got wheels? Let's go."

We parked at the outer perimeter of the settlement, where the asphalt road petered out at the side of a partly fenced hill. Old olive trees grew on one part of the slope, but on the other a brown gash in the earth signified a grove that had been up-rooted. That particular part was fenced in. Between the trees and the non-trees we walked along a crumbling terrace, over-looking the plain.

"You see," said the giant, as if mouthing rehearsed words, "on a clear day like this you see right through to the coast. An artillery battery from this hill can bombard Ramat Gan and Tel Aviv proper. That would wake up Peace Now from their beds." He turned his head down to me so I saw a flicker of eyelashes. "I know you. You're that writer, Joe Dekel. You're the worst kind of Jew, a religious traitor. But that's the way things are with the Jews. We love other people but we hate ourselves. It's a sickness. The exile disease. The answer is, to come home and tell every-one else: Kiss my asshole, baby. For thousands of years, they killed the Jew, tore his guts out, disemboweled his women, battered his babies' heads against the wall. Now let someone else suffer for a while."

"David Opatoshu, in *Exodus*," I identified the quote. "I re-member when I first saw the film, in 1960. That Eva Marie Saint, she made me go weak at the knees. Who was the actress who played Jordana?"

"You're a joker," he said. "But there are no jokes here, unless it's all you leftist half-Jews. You want to give away the half that you've already given up, the half that makes us what we are. I know, I was like you, a long time ago. I was a secular Zionist. But that whole trip, being like everybody else, of course, it ends up castration. I heard a story about Egyptian peasants once, in the villages of Upper Egypt, who fuck the earth that the Nile overflows in. The Nile flooding leaves the soil a smooth, wet suction. The men put their cocks in and get off on the earth. It's an image I like."

"It wouldn't work in this soil," I observed, looking at the dry rocks and gravel.

"It's like in your book," he said, "you look down on every-thing. If anybody thinks something's sacred, you piss on it. Why bother wearing that 'hattie' of yours? Or go to the synagogue?

What does the Messiah mean to you? Or the Covenant? The basis of the Faith. The Land and the People. What for? You might as well take the *kippa* off and eat pork on Yom Kippur like the rest of them. What is a Jew to you?"

"I can't say," I said. "I'm waiting for the next coalition statement on the issue."

"We are a sick people," he said, shaking his head. "The Arabs don't go around asking Who is an Arab? They just come out with their stones and petrol bombs. They know who is a Jew, that's for sure. At least I respect them for their certainties, for their single-mindedness. They know what they want – Jews out of the Land of Israel. But you don't even listen to their authentic voice, because you're too busy sticking your tongue up Arafat's ass, licking up that poisoned honey." (Yucch!) "They know what you want to hear so they play you all the right tunes. Two states. Three states. Peace in our time. Dance, Jewboy, dance. Where have your brains gone, Dekel?"

I did not wish to engage the beefy giant in the Moral Debate of The Age, in this setting, at any rate not without at least a Kalashnikov to even the odds between us. I tried to steer him off that course, knowing I was entering as stormy if not more turbulent waters.

"If the man who came up to me in Manhattan wasn't you, then who was he? Do you have a brother?"

"We're triplets," he said. "Huey, Dewey and Louie. How do I know what you're talking about? You tell me Murray Waiskopf is dead. So, I used to work with the guy. He was a good Jew. He worked hard for his people. New York is no bed of roses for us either. We have Black Muslims there, Fatah propagandists, asshole Jews like you. You name it. A sea of troubles. So what's with you and Murray, and what's it got to do with me?"

"A man came up to me," I said, "and told me he was my Silencer. He said his name was Didi Schaeffer and he worked for a man named Murray Waiskopf who worked on blacklisting

Jewish subversives. He set up a meeting at a certain address for the next day. But I went there that night and found one dead man, who turned out to be Waiskopf. There was an obituary in the *New York Times*. I met some interesting policemen. But after that, it gets a bit strange."

"What's strange is your head, Dekel. You've been smoking too much hashish. What's this blacklist crap you're trying to sell me? So I worked with Murray on information. We monitored anti-Semites, Nazis, Black Muslims, Arabs. What's this gotta do with subversive Jews? We'd need a battalion to deal with you lot. Who cares? You're not that important."

"You said you read my book. How did you get it? I don't remember submitting to Murray Waiskopf."

"I read it here, in Hebrew. *Ivrit*, our native language. Remember? Are you surprised? I read books. I'm curious. You think we're non-human. You see us the way you say we see Arabs. You're paranoid. You take self-hate beyond psychosis. Now we've got to 'the Jews are after me.' They're trying to ban your book in America. Gevaldt, you're not going to be the number-one bestseller, *New York Times Book Review*, front page. Is that what this is all about?" He reached out and grabbed hold of my shirt at the neck, shaking me as if I was a recalcitrant pussycat. "Look! Look in front of you, you asshole! Look at the landscape, look at your heritage! Breathe the air! Isn't it wonderful? Is this God's land or isn't it, idiot? Isn't this worth dying for?"

"Uuurgh! buurg! duurg!" I answered. But he wasn't going to let go of my collar, and all my other shirts were in the wash, at Zisselmacher's Laundry.

"Two weeks ago one of our residents, one of my friends, Oded Handeman, you've never heard of him, how could you, he wasn't a stinking leftist, drove down that road with his wife and two kids, one aged five months. They came out of that village over there, you see it, it's called Kafr whatever – they threw a petrol bomb in the car, which exploded. They burnt my friend's wife and his baby, dead. The other child and my friend got away with first-degree burns, they'll look like shit to the end of their lives. And you're out there in New York – I know what you were doing there, I read the newspapers, I can even make out your name – I'm not blind, you were hobnobbing with the people who did that to my friend, your beautiful peace-loving Palestinians! They burn our children and when we go in there and show them what the price could be, and try to catch the murderers – the army comes in and pulls us out! Your IDF oppressors! They defend the Arabs but they don't defend us! And you're kissing Arafat in New York!"

He let go of my neck. I dropped three feet, hit ground and rolled, crouching, ready for anything. But his spasm of rage had subsided. He walked away a few paces, sat under a tree and smoothed his beard with his hands.

"I have a wife and two kids myself," he said, quietly. "We are going to live and die here. You can send your army to take us away, and you'll soon find out what we're made of. We've stopped running. There'll be no ovens here, and no black or white Nazis. Jew-haters, watch out."

I gathered my wits, at a sufficient distance, gauging my escape route to the car. There was nothing I could do about his friend's tragedy. The old chicken and egg syndrome. Who killed who first? The primal murder. The politics of the most recent atrocity, that *perpetuum mobile* of our agonies. This was not the place and time to air the argument of presence and provocation. At points of life and death, dialogue vanishes. I turned to go, clearing my throat to make sure it was still there. He just sat under the tree, breathing harshly, his small eyes closed, as if dozing. There seemed to be nothing further to say, but, like the schmuck I am, I said it anyway: "You know a man named Nederlander Schatz?"

He said nothing, but his lips moved in a sort of raspberry.

"Someone tried to kill him too. Do you know anything about a Jew-hating colonel who has the FBI on his tail?"

"You're looking for Jew-haters?" he said. "Look in the mirror. It's a needle in a haystack. Go away, Dekel. You're a madman. Don't infect me with your crazy fantasies about FBI agents and Israeli spies. We have enough problems here."

There was that sort of silence in which one hears a grenade pin drop.

"I didn't say anything about Israeli spies," I said quietly. He opened his piggy eyes and looked at me.

"You're a dead man, Dekel," he said. And closed his eyes again, leaning against the tree trunk. I walked away slowly, then faster, up the hill, climbed gratefully into Alexander and drove away, slamming through the gate past the slumped soldier, and back towards the pre-Occupation "green line" and more familiar fears . . .

A dead man wanders round Jerusalem. So what else is new? From the old houses of the Bukharan Quarter with their old wrought-iron shutters, to the quiet leafy solitude and spacious, partly hidden gardens of the Bethlehem Road, Dekel's genuine old Jerusalem takes shape under the disappearing contours of the "reunited" city. Nothing older than 1853. Don't give me those ancient battlements of the Turkish Emperor, the raucous side streets down which they whipped Jesus, the captured splendor of the mosques which hold us captive, the scuff-marks and bloodstains of the Crusades and that Wall, that barrier of tears, with its surroundings bulldozer-cleared for worshippers, prompting my mentor, Professor Yeshayahu Leibowitz, doyen of Jewish anarchists, to call it the biggest parking lot in the East.

Idolatry. Idolatry. Idolatry. The worship of old stones, of faded markers, of tombs, the entire excrescence built on the pristine structure of the Faith as she was. Thou shalt not make unto thee any graven image. Well, that puts paid to Anat's models of Jerusalem. But false Gods, they have always been a temptation. The state, with its flag, the blue and white schmutter. At least try the star-spangled banner, it has one more color. The banned Palestinian flag has four.

So what am I left with? A complete stalemate. The further I pry, the murkier it gets. The FBI, Agent Kool, the mysterious colonel, the bandaged thug laid low by Dorothy Morgenthal's oriental talents, the Anti-Slander League, the Waiskopf carcase. Capped now by two Didi Schaeffers, not to speak of his friend's dead child.

There is no answer to an opponent's agony, except surrender to his viewpoint, or withdrawal. If you had not parked yourself by force in their midst, you say. What about Jaffa, and Tel Aviv, they reply? One has to stop somewhere. One cannot continue reprising the horrors of the past, over and over, expanding the circle of despair. Somewhere one says Stop, enough. I believe our enemies may have reached that stage. We had reached it earlier in our history, but then we swerved away, into our hubris and nightmare. We descend into our own abattoir.

I could not face going back to Nahum Lauterman, right away. I sat at home and did my weekend piece on New York. None of the excitement, just the dull routine of bleeding hearts in search of Peace. How Eli Saltzman, Citizens Rights Party member and Reserve Sergeant Major, told Hatem Abu-Riad, ex-Fatah Brigade Commander, that they had faced each other over three hundred yards of rubble in the refugee camp of Ein el-Hilwe in the Lebanon War. I was trying to kill you and you were trying to kill me. Birds of a feather flock together. The realization that we were all links in one chain, or the famous Siamese Twins of Edward Said's phrase, aching for the surgeon's healing knife. I put in some words about Dorothy Morgenthal dragging her Israeli and Palestinian charges to Grandma's Cafe and to her favorite Jewish dairy restaurant on West 31st Street, featuring on the menu such oriental delights as gefilte fish dumplings in sour cream, borscht, potato latkes, pure cholesterol and tshoolent. The whole place filled with middle-aged Jewish men taking their mothers to lunch. I described their endearing confusions as the PLO's swarthy bodyguards sauntered in, sweeping the room with their suspicious stares. I made it sound funnier than it was at the time. You have to give the readers something to cackle about. They will not get it from the front page. To wit: Israel will not be moved by Soviet diplomacy aimed at bringing Israel and the PLO to negotiations. Prime Minister Shamir says (again) that the PLO's talk of peace is a "monumental deception." Defense Minister Rabin says he will talk to Palestinian leaders in the West Bank and Gaza, but not to the PLO. The only trouble is, they all refer him to Tunis, and he has locked up most of these leaders, anyway.

The delights of politics. Locally, municipal elections are due. A genuine test of the people's stand: right-wing moderation, right-wing centrism, or right-wing extremism. I shall vote for the incumbent Mayor, Old Sandpaper, not out of any love, but to keep my co-orthodoxees from turning the city into a combination of Beirut and Belfast. It's bad enough already, what with tear gas fired by police at Arab demonstrators wafting over to sting the eyeballs of the Jews of Abu Tor and Bak'a. At least they no longer tear gas the tourists, which they did once to a group of American ladies who protested against the random arrest of a teenager in the Old City bazaar.

I phoned Dorothy Morgenthal in New York. She asked me what was happening. I said: "The usual. Didi Schaeffer was not Didi Schaeffer. The real thing is King Kong with a skullcap. I still don't know what's going on." Nothing was happening at her end. She was basking in the unusual luxury of not having any Jews or Arabs to nanny. No ex-terrorists to be taken to see *Roger Rabbit* or fed ethnic coronaries. Would I phone so-and-so in Tel Aviv to find out why she hadn't been sent the latest Peace Now dossier on abuses of human rights? I said I would, teeth clamped tightly. Bleeding hearts, bleeding ulcers. Still, people do what they can. She had no news for me as far as my own impasse was concerned. Detective Flynn, the expert on Hassidic socks, had taken another statement from her, and then cut off contact. Nederlander Schatz had disappeared to a hideaway in the Virgin Islands, protected by an impenetrable force field of retired Mafia elders. Agent Kool had not bothered to quiz her, and in fact her tone suggested I had made him up out of my warped memories. She had, I am sure, watched Efrem Zimbalist, Junior in the first run of the late sixties G-men show, whereas I had only caught the flickering reruns on Hashemite Jordan TV.

"That man I hit in the face," she said, "apparently he was

93

released on bail. Can you believe it? I understand now why people wail about crime. Attempted murder, kidnapping, gurnischt. Somebody's got a proper lawyer. I think you were wrong to agree to hush your story up, Joseph, I just hope it's not your funeral. Speaking of which, there's a memorial to Murray Waiskopf next week. Everybody who is anybody will be there. The community is treating it as just another city crime. The man disturbed a burglar, end of story. I dug a bit, but nobody will talk about blacklists. The last time I made those sorts of allegations, at a UJA meeting two years ago, I was treated like the Hunchback of Notre Dame."

"I know the feeling," I said, ringing off. Aye, you lollop about, clinging to the deafening bells, gasping "Sanctuary! Sanctuary!" to no avail. Eking out your time dragging the sewers and posting up pasquinades about your enemies on every available wall and billboard. Like the famous *"peshkvilim"* of the ultra-orthodox, the ubiquitous wall posters denouncing rival rabbis, the secular world and anyone who gets in your way. "WOE TO THE HOLY CITY, DRAPED IN SACKCLOTH AND ASHES, OUR PURITY HAS BEEN BESMIRCHED IN THE MUD," et cetera. These cries of pain are in our blood.

In fact, Anat has gathered a collection of these posters for her Jerusalem exhibit, due to open at the Arts Center known as *Mishkenot Sha'ananim*, "The Abode of the Tranquil." I had no choice but to attend the opening. It was a Wednesday afternoon, usually my blue period, but nevertheless I thought it might take my mind off my troubles to hobnob with the prettiest farts in the city, apart from the Mayor, Old Sandpaper, who was not speaking to me since I had written an item about twenty-five story buildings appearing miraculously in the city, destroying its skyline, against the advice of planning commissions. Who is the Aladdin rubbing this lamp, I asked? Old Sandpaper had not been amused. "For twenty years I kept the peace in this city!" he raved at Anat. "And kept the fanatic right out. And look who attacks me!"

But he was ebullient at the exhibit, his white cowlick bobbing as he shepherded his usual gang of visiting American would-be donors round the show. The centerpiece being this massive papier mâché thing of Jerusalem in miniature, on several historical levels, mounted on sliding shelves. There was Canaanite Jerusalem, a sort of savage moonrock jabbing up to the sky, and David's City, as imagined by the archaeologists who had been excommunicated by the ultra-orthodox for disturbing Jewish bones in their work. As if the whole city, including their own seminaries, was not built on mounds of ancient graves. The dead outnumbering the living in this bivouac by several million to one. There was the Second Temple with which we are all so familiar, the Herodian Jerusalem of Jesus, Aelia Capitolina (wot, no pagan statue of Jupiter?), Byzantium, and there it gets a little blurred. Anat fought a savage war to expand the budget to include two full levels of the Moslem period, but what was approved was the Crusader era and the Ottoman renovation, with Suleiman's Walls. Some you win, some you lose. The Municipality giveth and the Municipality taketh away. Blessed is the Municipality, which preserveth us from civil war and environmental wimps.

The place was full of all the people I had sworn to avoid until the end of time, all the city's most sensitive souls. Woodcut wallahs, engravers, silver gewgaw craftsmen, sculptors and sculptresses, daubers of every school and gender. People who had brought the light of the Holy City to the darkest parts of Los Angeles and Miami. Dancers, poets, illuminators, lithographers, lesbians, laminators, quilt makers, water colorists, would-be Jewish Andy Warhols and Chagalls, cans of Campbell Soup, black-and-white photographers, collagists, impressionists, pointillists, vorticists, embryos in bottles, oozing about the polished floors of the exhibition rooms carrying paper cups of kiddush wine and Coca Cola. The dwarf painter Rumachansky, who does Van Gogh imitations despite being half his size and a millionth his talent, staggered forward and clutched my knees.

"Our very own Joe! It's good to see you back! I read your article about the Palestinians in New York. Keep up the good work!"

I hate being supported by people I can't stand. Now I know what Groucho Marx felt like. I moved him aside with my ankle. The bullish sculptor Kadishzon, who is not at all bad, threw his beefy arm around my shoulder, pinning me to a submission. "Joe! My brother! My father! My son! Isn't all this completely disgusting?"

"Absolutely," I agreed with him. "Kitschland *über alles*."

"I sympathize with Anat," he said, gesturing towards my other half, who was being pressed by Old Sandpaper towards a grizzled Chicagoan who was reputed to have ten million spare macaroons looking for a suitably ethnic home. "She does a terrific job. The Arab artists show. The *intifada* paintings. The poets competition. At least force the people to see what's under their nose. But the price to be paid . . ." he gestured towards the mini cities with a cup which had more than cola in it. "We are all going to be little puppets in a vast theme park. The Zionist Dream. The stuff of nightmares. God, I'm glad I don't drop acid any more."

Those were the days. Proud young Jews wandered round the Old City, seeing the True Being of the stones. Today it's only the embattled residents, brainwashed tourists, tax collectors and massed uniformed patrols who wander dazed in the strike-bound alleys. Twenty years of reunification and we are more divided than ever. Co-existence at its lowest biological level.

"Who needs acid, when every day is an unending hallucination?" Kadishzon asked, squeezing softly. "Did you read about the police pretending to be journalists, who leapt out and beat up kids? The soldiers firing marbles at demonstrators, or squirting tear gas from little vials into women's faces? And what about that general who led a hunt in four helicopters after a teenager who threw a stone? How can we fantasize, when in real life soldiers shoot at balloons which bear the colors of the Palestinian flag? Not to speak of the dogs we sent wrapped with explosives to blow up ammunition dumps at Sidon. Can you believe it? The Popular Front shot them dead. I saw the picture in that rag of yours, Joe. Canine kamikazes! Where are we going, my friend, where are we going? Don't say it – to the dogs. Well, at least somebody loves you."

Kadishzon was undergoing a painful divorce, with fire and brimstone and lawyers scratching at the soft pelts of three riven kids. He was like a stag whose antlers were being auctioned. Spotting a blonde head on shapely brown shoulders in the throng, he disengaged, waving at me as he elbowed off. Anat was deeply charming the Chicagoan millionaire. Send a few cents my way, honeybunch. Love, it's true, it makes the world go round. Which a drop of bland kiddush wine cannot. I know Anat hates all this razzle-dazzle as much as I do, but it is her cross and she bears it nobly. *No bliss oblige.* Empathizing, I sidled along the walls towards the exit. But there was someone there, standing awkwardly in a light khaki raincoat, beside an old *peshkvil* denouncing "ABORTIONS – THE NEW HOLO-CAUST."

"Good afternoon, Mr. Dekel."

A blurring of parameters. A slight shifting of the earth. One cannot forget the global village. In my own back yard, on my hallowed soil, Agent Kool, American G-Man, standing as if the floor was tilted under his feet, holding his hands in his pockets and surveying the crowd as if someone had stolen J. Edgar Hoover's death mask.

"Do you have a moment?"

I have eternity. Do we not have God's signed affidavit?

"One hell of a view," said Agent Kool. We are standing on the roof terrace of the Arts Center, overlooking the iconic landscape of the Old City walls, the tower of David and Mount Zion rising across the narrow ravine of the valley.

"Is this your first visit to Israel?" It doesn't hurt me, I suppose, to start out as a complete idiot and work my way up from there.

"I've been here twice," he replies, "once in 1978. Then in 'eighty-two, during the Lebanon War. There was a problem."

"There certainly was."

We are poised like Butch Cassidy and the Sundance Kid, wondering whether to leap out over the chasm. Below us, the posse paws, prattles.

"I was a Military Policeman in Vietnam," he finally volunteered. "Trying to keep the boys from getting killed in whorehouses rather than on the battlefield. They seconded me to the Investigative Branch. There I worked with a Jewish Sergeant named Jaybaum. We were investigating narcotics, which meant sitting in hotel rooms trying not to do the job, otherwise we would end up dead. So he taught me Hebrew. He had spent his early childhood in Israel, but his parents took him out because they didn't want him to land up in the army. We used to laugh a lot about that. It was damn hot and sickening. He used to say he had only one conclusion from the entire Vietnam morass: Happiness is a dry fart. But I was a quick learner of Hebrew. I was curious. I kept it up, when I got back home, found I could buy the Israeli newspapers and read them. It became a sort of hobby. Then, in 'seventy-four, they impeached Nixon and I joined the Federal Bureau. I was a clerk for three years, then somebody called me in and said: Hey, Kool, we hear you speak Hebrew, but you're not family. What's the story? I told them about Jaybaum. They ran a check on him and found he had died in a road accident the year before. They thought that was tidy. There was a job going in a new department. Hebrew an asset, but no Jews. It was a delicate situation. I was sent out here to tour the country, get acquainted, meet a few people. My superiors liked my style. I didn't bend either way. I judge a man by his character, not his religion. I do my job, and I don't get carried away. I do what the Bureau wants me to do."

"A good cop."

"You said it." He turned his head, and looked out towards Jericho. It was, again, one of those razor-sharp days. You could make out the brown hills of Moab, far but near, in the Hashemite Kingdom of Jordan.

"I was brought up in a small town community in Virginia," he said, "down-the-line Baptists. That's Jerry Fallwell country. What the Bible says, and so forth. Have you read Mark Twain? He was brought up on all those Old Testament stories, Galilee, the Jordan River. He thought the Jordan River was fifty miles wide and longer than the Mississippi. What a bitter disappointment when he traveled to the Holy Land and found it was just a stream. All those powerful tales. Where Jesus walked. Jerusalem. That's not a place to me. That's a way of life, a hope, a dream. There is a green hill far away, without a city wall, where the dear Lord was crucified, who died to save us all. There was no other good enough to pay the price of sin, He only could unlock the gate of heaven and let us in."

At least he had advanced from Lewis Carroll. Or was it a regression? As if to counterpoint his words, bells began ringing somewhere. This sort of convenient coincidence is grist to the Jerusalem mill. It never fails. The cornier the better.

"This could be the city of peace, like its name," he said, "the place which really teaches us how to reconcile and live with so many different viewpoints. A real model. But in the law enforcement business we have to deal with practical issues, not with the way we'd like things to be. I understand you went to meet this guy, Didi Schaeffer, and you found out he wasn't the same guy you met in New York."

"If you know, you know," I said. I, too, could be circumspect, even if I had nothing to be circumspect about, having no secrets that the whole world didn't know. My life, as I've noted before, is an open book, which only I can't read. "I hear you let the man who kidnapped me out on bail," I said, to show I had my sources too.

"Yes, we decided not to contest the application," he said. "We want the big fish. The one that swallows up Jonah."

"The Boojum," I said.

"Exactly."

Dust to dust. Nonsense to nonsense. We are traveling in circles. Down below, the hellish sounds of accordions. A "folk-dancing" troupe, which I had seen sneaking in from the blind rear dressed in crisp Zouave-like costumes, is about to break out in its rash.

"Is this the 'Colonel'?" I asked, "the Jew-hater who also hates keeping appointments with his own employees?"

"The Colonel is just a mechanic," he said, "a hired hand. He's small potatoes."

I would not wish to confront the family-sized spuds then. "So what can I do for the Union?" I asked, spreading my hands. "And when do I get my green card?"

"I wouldn't dream of suggesting anything underhand," he said hurriedly, "that would be dangerous and stupid. I admit, I've been giving you partial information. I couldn't be sure how far you were involved. The post-Pollard affair turned up some strange by-products. We have a very serious problem here, that's been developing for some time." The thump of folkish feet came from below. We walked away down the terrace to the path winding through bushes and flowers towards Yigal Tomarkin's war monument made up of bits of old tanks. I have never been clear whether this was for war or against it. An Arab youth walking his goat ambled up the paved pathway. We both watched suspiciously until he had passed. An *intifada* by goat turds? Anything here can be a weapon.

"Your friend, your editor Nahum Lauterman," he said, "I know you've spoken with him, and I also know he has talked to some contacts in the Security Services. But I can tell you with confidence that he has been warned not to proceed with his inquiries. The Joe Dekel Affair is under wraps. Information is being strictly embargoed. There will be no SHABAK leaks on this one. No bus hijack whistle blowing."

He was alluding to the most prominent scandal that had afflicted our hidden Guardians recently. When four amateur terrorists hijacked a bus, near Ashkelon, with flick-knives, the bus was stormed by crack army and SHABAK (Internal Security) troops, and all four hijackers were killed. But when a subsequent press report showed two of them had been led away alive and battered to death in captivity, the Service reacted with a ferocious cover-up. (It was not my rag that got the scoop, I am sorry to say, but a rival, God bless their eyes.) The Chief of the Service ordered his men to lie to several parliamentary committees of inquiry, but some of his deputies revealed the deception. Both the Chief and the whistle blowers had to leave the Service. Now, as we all know, it is squeaky clean and watertight, apart from the other revelations about torture in interrogation, the faking of evidence, et cetera, but how can you make an omelette without breaking legs?

So this man is well informed. I am happy for him. They say knowledge is power. Nice to hear there is a Joe Dekel Affair already, and that the cleansed Internal Security Service is taking such a kind interest in me. Are these my fifteen minutes of being famous coming up? Or merely the bell that tolls, I need not ask for whom? Agent Kool was playing out his rope skilfully and I can feel when I'm being reeled in. First he had whispered "Pollard," and started shaking my kishkas. Now he was climbing up the Richter scale.

"So what do you want me to do?" I said. "I have no battalions. My tank divisions have been retired with terminal rust and I have a wife with three mouths to feed. Are you suggesting emigration?" Sanctuary! Sanctuary! Was this nevertheless a recruiting drive? The dreadful Rabbi Kahane who had one turn in our Parliament had allegedly started life as an FBI informer, but for the left this was unusual. What does it entail? I racked my brains but could not remember anything about Efrem Zimbalist, Jr. except his leaping through closed windows. Would I get a hat, a coat and a gun? Or is it still called a gat? I seemed to have built up a core of serious enemies while barely lifting a finger. The hills stretched out before me towards Jericho, an old, barren, indifferent ground. What was Joe Dekel in these folds of dry earth? Just another bag of bones to crumble. Perhaps, if I went to America and became rich I could have myself cryogenically frozen, and wake up in the twenty-fifth century to find Yitzhak Shamir was still Prime Minister, Shimon Peres still whining on the sidelines, the *intifada* still going strong and my paycheck for June 'eighty-eight still not come through. Then again, perhaps not.

"I think you're a target," he said quietly. "I think your intelligence services want to see if you'll draw fire from a certain quarter. I have to confess that was my strategy, too, but I think some form of mutual trust might be better. I can't see how you can be any help being dead. At any rate, not to me."

"Thank you very much."

"You can believe it or not," he said, wanly.

I remember that phrase, from Ripley's tall tales: Did you know that in northern Oregon Chief Ogaboga of the Picayune Sioux grew his hair seven thousand feet long and had a penis on the side of his nose? That in the Hofamogo Falls of the Upper Amazon the water flows upwards? Believe It Or Not. I used to buy those paperbacks, second-hand, at Gertwagen's.

"Am I supposed to take it that you've flown over the oceans and eaten execrable airline food and been assaulted by a fiftieth rerun of *Smokey and the Bandit* just to protect Joe Dekel?" Even Ripley would have balked at that.

"I have some other matters on my agenda," he admitted. "Obviously as a citizen of the State of Israel, you could place your trust in your own intelligence services. After all, it's their *raison d'être* to protect and preserve you."

Yeah, in formaldehyde. "OK," I said. "Mutual trust. That's wonderful. So how about some proper information? So far I've got hints, nods, winks, elbows in the ribs and punches in the nose, recitations of Lewis Carroll and Sunday school hymns. Do you have anything more substantial?"

"I might," he said. "Can you meet me tomorrow morning at eleven o'clock in the lobby of the King David Hotel?"

More exotic locations. Paul Newman and Eva Marie Saint, in *Exodus*, plighted their troth there, over crème-bavarois.

"How will I know you?" I asked.

"I'll be the one with my face," he said, solemnly, revealing that he had read old Dodgson quite thoroughly. "Keep your pecker up."

The Talmud advises otherwise. He loped off, with his John Cleese Silly Walk. I stayed, holding the indifferent city. The Arab boy and his goat lolloped back, crossing my path with little pellets. I moved my foot. The goat shied away from me, down the hill, crossing the road, against the heavy traffic, the small boy in its wake, trucks and buses hooting, honking. Both rushed away, towards the new cafés and galleries standing guard over the houses of the Arab village plunging down the hill. By a trick of the traffic swirl and dust, they seemed to vanish into the Rasputin Piano Bar.

Once again I cursed Nahum Lauterman. One minute a friend is clapping you on the back, offering you his suntan oil on the beach, canvassing your opinion about the nubility of the passing fifteen-year-old maidens, the next his fangs are in your thigh. I once met a black South African in London who said that the true test of a friend was his response when a poisonous snake bit you on the penis. This was in the days before homosexuality was either a threat or a temptation to our pioneering generation. Today we wallow in the interstices of uncertainty, personal, public, social.

I phoned his office. He was out. I phoned his home. A cackling feminine voice in an unconvincingly broad Sephardi accent answered: "Nahum not at home . . . me charlady, know nothing . . ."

"I'm coming right over, Nahum," I told the bastard. "Don't move until I see the white of your eyes."

A thankfully undramatic taxi ride to Tel Aviv, Anat having her lingering obligations with the massed patrons of Jerusalem Arts. Afternoon receptions, evening soirées, never an undull moment. For myself, a rapid thrust through the urban sprawl in a local cab to Nahum's house in the outlying suburbs, a cool cavern of escape for Ali Baba after the day's tussle with the forty thieves. Five large rooms on two storys, fitted cupboards, piano, king-size freezer, very nice if you can get it. I remember him scrabbling with his Aliza and the two tots in a two-room hole in Talbieh. Now he lunches with cabinet ministers and film stars, and kisses the backsides of spooks. He opened the door to me shamefacedly, offering orange juice, 7-Up or booze, apologizing for the mess. Both the wife and the charlady were away teaching at seminars. The Filipino maid was on holiday. The elder boy was on Reserve Duty in the south. The daughter was at a Peace Now budget meeting.

"God rot your soul, Nahum," I said, "you've been holding out on me." I gave him Agent Kool's revelations without revealing my sources. Let him shuffle in the dark a bit. But he was very defensive, jiggling the ice in his orange juice as if it would turn it into something better.

"Well, did I promise enlightenment?" he appealed, when I had finished. "You're chasing a story that can't be told, yet. Do I have to beg you to trust me? We're both old haggard whores here, Joe. We've been fucked so often we just turn over and think about something pleasant."

"If I'm a walking target I want to know for whom and why," I said. "I'm not prepared to continue walking around with a sandwich board saying 'Shoot Me, I'm Joe Dekel' written in phosphorous on either side. I want at least to read the charge before the execution."

"In Iran," he said, "they bill the executees' families for the bullets. We're just amateurs in comparison. Believe me, Joe, mouths are taped up out there. This is a very delicate issue, a real tightrope."

"So you know the gist of it," I said. "I know you, Nahum. Your tricks and ruses, all that eyelash-fluttering and cooing. People tell you things in confidence. But when it means my life or death, you tell me. Or I'll reveal the expenses scam at the Hotel Grand, Barcelona."

"What a threat," he said, "in a country where the most right-wing minister in the cabinet takes a bribe from an Arab businessman for the importation of shrimps. OK, Joe. I owe it to you. But it's not an encouraging story."

And I thought it would be an inspirational epiphany. The Good News. Evangelicus Dekel. He leaned back, in a Japanese chair, which was supposed to straighten the spine but looked as if it would cause permanent dislocation, closing his eyes, gathering his thoughts in a familiar Lautermanish manner of separating the wheat from the chaff. I sloshed a Teachers in my glass.

"Lebanon," he said, finally, "August 'eighty-two. One month before the massacre at Sabra and Shatilla. You remember that fucked time. We were deadlocked around Beirut, bombing like crazy. Philip Habib was busy negotiating the withdrawal of the PLO from the city. Sharon was trying to torpedo the negotiation. The air force, navy, artillery and tanks were blitzing West Beirut as if it was Berlin. Remember Begin's quote about Hitler's bunker? We are hunting Arafat from house to house with missiles. The madness was in full swing. The only thing more horrendous than the bombing was the ceasefire, in which the bombing intensified. Meanwhile, yours truly, who was then, as you know, far from the august pinnacle he is now impaled upon, was reporting on the consolidation of forces in South Lebanon. I went to Nabatieh, where a bizarre 'conference' of pro-IDF forces was being convened by the military governor. Nabatieh, you remember, had been the linchpin of the PLO's little empire – Fatahland – before the invasion was launched. The Christian Phalange, led by Bashir Gemayel, wanted to add it to its fief. The Druze, who had been neutral in the war, objected. We gave it as a present to Sa'ad Haddad, our Pinocchio who was never going to lose his strings. Haddad was a Greek-Orthodox Christian, the majority population were Shiite Moslems, there were obvious problems to resolve. I got to Nabatieh and walked from my jeep to the Municipality, where the meeting was being held. Sa'ad Haddad and the IDF commander were going up the steps to the entrance. On either side, Haddad's militiamen stood to attention. As their commander passed, they gave him the Fascist salute. You may have seen it on the TV report at the time, later on that little shot was cut. Was it the only known time an Israeli officer was given that accolade? But this was just the beginning.

"Inside the building, some really bizarre bodies had gathered. Haddad's men, a delegation from the Phalange, a group of ultra-Fascists from the 'Phoenician Party,' who wanted to abolish Arabic in Lebanon as well as the Arabs. Rich notables from all over the south, delegates from the Shiite Amal, who had let our forces through unopposed, though, as you know, we would not be pals for long. I remember a group of Islamic fanatics, they might have been the same people who later made up the Hizballah, but they hated the secular PLO more than the Jews. As well as all these people who hated each other but were brought together by our gun barrels, there were a number of foreign guests. Some were familiar, the usual group of American Jewish notables bussed up from Israel to see the good work of our gallant boys in the war zone. An Irish journalist, whom we had bought for a good price, and some other eager hacks. But there was another group, which looked extremely out of place, as if they had dropped in from Mars. They were mostly young, fresh-faced Americans, uniformly dressed in black suits and ties. Crisp, starched white shirts, in a temperature that was pushing 100 degrees. They were sober and polite and wore those strange, beatific smiles that I remember from Baptist Midwest churches. The local commander, a Major Uri, one of those bright missionaries of ours who shone so briefly in Lebanon and then faded into a frazzle, introduced them to me as a delegation from the Arizona Church of Christ The Living.

"You remember that whole nonsense: Menachem Begin convinced himself the Christians of Lebanon, like the Jews, were an oasis of civilization in a sea of barbarian Moslems. Ariel Sharon's Master Plan – the Christian Lebanon, under his friend, Bashir Gemayel. When you see the world in simple terms it's so easy to drench it with blood. We had decided Sa'ad Haddad would be the Christian Savior of South Lebanon, a useful counterpart to the ambitious Gemayel. But it would be an expensive business, and we were spending over our ears on the war. So somebody found him some willing sponsors, Baptist fundamentalists from Ohmygoshland, who knew that war in the Middle East is a vital part of God's plan. The Revelation, the Antichrist, the War of Gog and Magog, Armageddon, the Second Coming. The Jews' return to the Holy Land prefigures the End of Days, the Tribulation, and then, the Rapture! The Righteous go up to Heaven to meet Christ. Hallelujah! Of course, in this plan the Jews have to be converted, or destroyed, before the Savior's transcendence, but that's a minor matter to those for whom ideology and *realpolitik* have merged in infinite flexibility.

"The Conference was everything it was supposed to be. The Notables made speeches that had been written for them by our intelligence officers. Amal swore undying brotherhood. Haddad said a new day of Justice and Peace had dawned. The PLO, pawn of Satan, had been routed. International Terrorism had been defeated. From now on, peace-loving people throughout the world could sleep securely, knowing there would be no more plane hijackings, bomb outrages, or the slaughter of innocents. All the Israeli officers present applauded. My brain felt stretched like bubble gum, and I had to leave the hall.

"In the afternoon, Major Uri took us on a helicopter flight around the area. There were five members of the American Jewish group and four of the Baptist Christians. One of them, I noticed, was different from the others, a small, heavy-set, gray-haired old man with a limp. He sat beside another older man, with one of those perpetually young faces crowned by close-cropped silver hair. The two others, young clones, had the unmistakable look of bodyguards. The Jews, who were from this Committee or that League, were uncomfortable in this group's presence. Except one, a rather small, wiry, heavy-lidded gentleman with a small beard, who went on a little private walk with the Christians when we reached the Beaufort Castle. We were put down dramatically on its proud Crusader summit, overlooking the hills in all directions. The Beaufort, drenched with the blood of our soldiers which our great rulers shed so freely . . . Under the Israeli flag, the three older gentlemen were having quite a bit of a powwow. Major Uri was proudly relating to the Jewish group the heroic tale of the Castle's capture. I walked offaways with an Intelligence Officer I knew, and pumped him for information. It was an interesting story. The silvery Christian was the Reverend William Risegood, pastor of the Church of the Living Christ. The heavy-set old man was a guest he had brought along, one E. Dermott King, a bona fide Texas oil magnate. They were proposing to set up a Christian evangelical TV and radio station in South Lebanon, among other charitable works which implied funding Sa'ad Haddad's Freedom Fighters. The Jewish gentleman in animated conversation with them was one Murray Waiskopf, from New York.

"While we were climbing down the ramparts towards a PLO arms dump, an argument exploded among the American Jews. Two brethren, with skullcaps, were shouting at Mr. Waiskopf. They were extremely angry. They rounded on Major Uri, who was completely nonplussed. One of them said: 'I'm not riding back with those people.' 'Gentlemen, gentlemen,' said my poor compatriot, out of his depth, 'we're all on the same side.' The more senior brother, a respectable man of authority, said: 'I am not on the same side as anti-Semites.' Maybe the heat had got to him, he lost his cool a bit. He said: 'You have the right to make your own alliances, it's your policy, but you can't expect us to swallow shit. That man has funded Klan activities. That priest has said on public television that God doesn't hear a Jew's prayers. You live in this part of the world, you have to deal with a lot of strange people. We support you down the line. But you don't have to import here people we have spent fifty years opposing in the United States.'

"It was bizarre. Like the schismatic air of Lebanon was pouring into every niche. When we got back to Nabatieh the two groups huddled, while Major Uri had to rush off because one of his Shiite guests had been assassinated in the back of the building. The town was chaotic, armored cars were everywhere. The American Jews were driven off in a van. We were soon overtaken by even grosser events – the PLO withdrawal, the Multinational Force, the blowing up of Bashir Gemayel and our entrance into West Beirut and the Sabra and Shatilla massacre. Horror piled on horror. That small incident at the Beaufort paled into insignificance. We all heard how the fundamentalist Christians made further inroads into Lebanon, set up their TV station, shored up Haddad, came to Jerusalem with him to kiss Begin, had a mass rally in Jerusalem. We opened the doors and they poured in, Risegood, Fallwell, Swaggart, the whole team. But then Lebanon peaked, soured, went off the boil, Begin went gaga and resigned, Shamir, the Kahan Report on the massacre, the elections, the National Unity government. Our wars with the Shiites and our withdrawal. So Lebanon is history. It's not our hot potato any more. We just die there in small doses, occasionally. We have come back to our roots, the battle for Palestine. The Peasants' War, as Benvenisti calls it."

A sad and grotesque tale, indeed, but what has it got to do with Joe Dekel? Apart from being the sea we all swim in, the polluted ocean our ship of fools has drowned in.

"*Quo vadis?*" I asked him. He rose and tottered to the fridge to get himself a 7-Up, and replenish my Teachers.

"What can I tell you, Joe. The old story, life and death move on. Yesterday's excess becomes today's norm becomes tomorrow's nostalgia. How do we pick the wheat from the chaff? You know as I do the continuing rumors of Christian Fundamentalist meddling: the denied links with the Jewish Settler's underground, the ecumenical cabal of extremists. Lebanon provided the soil for all sorts of mad alliances that chop and change with the weather. What are we supposed to believe, when the Christian Phalange, whom we armed to chase the Palestinians out of

Lebanon, then sold those arms to the Palestinians to bring them back to counterweight the Shiite Amal? When the Hizballah, our fiercest enemies, are financed by the Iranians who claim a *jihad* for Jerusalem but whom we arm against Iraq? In the nightmare maze, what's real and unreal? And who is really spying for whom? In the international market for information, how do you distinguish the facts from the noise? So you can't blame me for forgetting all about Mr. Waiskopf and the Reverend Risegood on a bad day at Nabatieh. But my memory nevertheless keeps things on file. When you said the name I did a little retrieval. And when my contacts in the Services ran like rabbits when I mentioned the names Waiskopf and Pollard in one breath I went on orange alert. I phoned a lady in San Francisco, who has written three books on the U.S. Fundamentalists, from which we had published extracts. She gave me an interesting tidbit: Murray Waiskopf attended the Church of the Living Christ's Convention in Phoenix last year. It was their biggest fling yet, a thousand delegates turned up, sang hymns and pledged ten million dollars. The Convention denounced George Bush for abandoning Reaganism and the Fight against the Evil Empire. President Gorbachev, the man with the Mark of the Beast on his head, was officially designated the Antichrist. The *intifada*, according to the Reverend Risegood, is the beginning of the three-and-a-half years of tribulation, in which the Jews will be savagely persecuted, leading to the Second Coming of Christ. That gives us May 1991 as the date of the Battle of Armageddon. The Faithful were all called upon to Prepare. Exactly how, we do not quite know, but the schedule is there."

He sighed, like a Jewish grandfather who has once again to contemplate the fact that his offspring have turned out proper schvantses.

"What can I do? I'm just a newspaper editor. I can hack away at received opinions. I can encourage those who share our views to speak out and keep going. I can annoy the government the way a wasp annoys an elephant. I can force the Security Services to sacrifice some scapegoat when they're caught pissing in the drinking water. But the juggernaut rolls on. The strategic alliances, the armaments deals, the corruption, the underhand and in fact open betrayals of everything we're supposed to stand for. You think you've scraped the bottom of the barrel when you find more in concealed compartments. So what's going on, in this shadowy matrix of Risegood, Waiskopf, the FBI, and our spies? What part does your friend in Amiel play? I don't have to tell you, if there is a connection, it can be like a binary bomb. Put 'em together you have some bang. The mosques, Joe, that's the whole story. The bottom line, with both sets of fanatics, is that both want to get rid of the mosques. The Third Jewish Temple will rise on the ruins. But to the Christians, of course, that's just Stage One. Stage Two is the destruction of that temple and the coming of the Kingdom of Christ. On our own account we've now had how many, three different groups caught trying or planning to blow the mosques up? So what if it provokes a *jihad*? Makes any dialogue between us and any Moslem Arab impossible? That's literally dynamite, my friend. Now add to that the murky outline of our alleged spies in Yankeeland, connect the dots, and you have one hell of an ominous picture: A possible link, inside the Security Services, within Mossad, SHABAK, LAKAM, God knows who, to the Fundamentalist cabal, and to their incendiary nightmares . . .? No, it doesn't bear thinking about. As if we don't have enough enemies, enough Saddam Husseins and Khomeinis. We have to manufacture them home grown. Line up for your wings at the pearly gates. Book your advance tickets now."

"Is that your only advice, esteemed Opinion Leader?"

"Love thy neighbor as thyself."

Easy for him to propose. He had lifted up a curtain to give me a glimpse of the Day of Judgement, and then gobbled a 7-Up. From Sodom to soda pop. Coming to Lauterman to get a load taken off my back, he had piled on four more tons. Sackfuls and sackfuls of exposition and not a rest stop in sight. What can I tell my poor wife, who labors around the clock to make this a better place to live? A land fit for Yuppies. And meanwhile one thousand hymn-swilling Christians in Phoenix are praying for our incineration. Go tell it on the mountain. Or even in the Café Cassit. I remember some wag who paraded round Tel Aviv with the latest (1980) Rhodesian T-shirt: "ARMAGEDDON OUTA HERE." Would even as dedicated a zealot as Murray Waiskopf play with this sort of fire? And why was Joe Dekel hauled into this? What has my embattled book got to do with Mount Sinai? And if the Didi Schaeffer who came up to me in New York wasn't Didi Schaeffer, who was he? A plethora of unanswered questions.

I mentioned none of it to Anat that night, when I got back from Tel Aviv, finding her already in bed with a new translation of a Latin American doorstopper entitled *On Heroes and Tombs*. Indeed. "How were the Arts?" I asked her perfunctorily. "How was Nahum?" she riposted ditto. "The living dead," I answered. "Same here." I shut myself in my study, opened up my Caligari's cabinet of weapons, cleaned the Luger and the Karl Gustav, which seemed to have developed spots of dirt. Then I switched on the PC and played Jumbo Jet, in real time, trying to get from Heathrow Airport to Frankfurt. After two hours the stupid machine informed me I was twelve hundred miles into the Atlantic Ocean and had five minutes of fuel left. Then it turned off my controls and announced "Oh dear, you have crashed with 269 passengers on board. Please report tomorrow morning at ten o'clock to the Committee of Inquiry."

I joined my sleeping wife, calmly unconscious. I tried to toss and turn quietly. Anat and I know there are times we have to leave each other to stew until something is ready. In this cacophony of a city, we cannot always achieve synchronicity. Sometimes we are living in different centuries, sometimes on different planets. Keeping a small head. Living hour by hour. Blood's stickier than water. Our close to two decades of sparring have produced no knockouts or submissions yet, though there have been enough falls . . .

I dreamed: I was on that Jumbo Jet, heading for Frankfurt via Iceland. The pilot had gone for a cup of tea at the airport and the plane had taken off without him. Apart from me, none of the passengers felt threatened. They were all plugged into the earphones, listening to the music channels, or the film, which was Pasolini's *The Gospel According to Saint Matthew*. The soundtrack was the timeless black spiritual: *Sometaams ah feel laak a motherless child . . . a long wa-ay from home . . .* Judas had sold the Nazarene and was about to hang himself. I made my way into the cockpit. Agent Kool waved to me from the controls. The dead bodies of Murray Waiskopf, Didi Schaeffer and Shimon Peres, our Finance Minister, were sprawled over the other seats. The altimeter's needle was whizzing round and round down from 40,000 feet towards zero.

"Shadrach, Meshach, and Abednego!" caroled Kool, rolling his eyes to match the needle. "'*And behold! I see four men loose, in the midst of the fire, and the form of the fourth is as the Son of God!*'" He spoke in the original text, and I wondered how and when he had managed to learn Aramaic. Was that, too, a dividend of Saigon? I looked back into the passengers' cabins. They were all melting, like the dolls in *The Wax Museum*, while the stewardesses were handing out the Duty Free. Lauterman clapped me on the shoulder. "*Put this on!*" He handed me a parachute. We jumped, baling out over the ocean. He winked at me. "*Give my regards to Anat!*" he called, and drifted away, waving cheerfully, towards the icy coast of Greenland.

I woke up. The sun was up too, but Anat had left, leaving a note: "In the office till late. No milk." I phoned her, and after the usual shouting down corridors, had three seconds to inform her I was meeting "the American" at the King David and if I wasn't back by Passover, she could have the joys of my family *seder* feast without me. Think about it, all those cold hard-boiled eggs. She told me not to do anything idiotic. Like what? Challenge the Mossad to a duel? But she did offer to get the milk on her way home. A veritable Camp David treaty.

She had taken Alexander, so I called a taxi and rushed over to the King David. He was not there, so I settled down behind an ornamental potted plant, with a Tequila Jaffa Sunrise I ordered from the skivvy and a copy of the *Jerusalem Post* someone had left behind, starting with "JOINT BID TO GET HUSSEIN TO TALK." A good image. Sing, ya pesky Hashemite dwarf! Ya'll never git me alive . . . Down the page, I read the Chief of Staff, Dan Shomron, told reporters that the Palestinians were turning to murder and "real terror" in order to keep the *intifada*, which was fading, alive for the world's press. He saw the light at the end of the tunnel. And this is the man who was played by Charles Bronson in the film *Raid on Entebbe*. How are the mighty declined.

Twenty minutes passed, and I had progressed to page eight: "YES, ISRAELI SOLDIERS DO LOOK LIKE 'SCHLUMPERS,' EX-ARMY CHIEF AGREES," when I decided to cut my losses and went up to the reception, asking if anyone had left a message for Mr. Dekel. I was passed an envelope with a note which said: "Profound apologies. Something came up. Can you meet me at the Damascus Gate, 12:00 p.m. sharp. Definitely to your advantage."

Disaster. This was going to be another of those days. The stupid Yank had evidently not registered that there is a war in the city. He has not translated the headlines and the ABC News into concrete reality. Only two weeks before, a Jewish Jerusalemite had been stabbed by a berserker at that very gate, and three weeks before that someone had shot and killed two Arab residents at the Jaffa Gate, just around the corner. In the old days we could sit kicking our legs against the parapets, ogling the crowd in and out, the tourists, the myriad sects of the city, the *shabab*, the taxi drivers. No more. The bastard had set a trap for me.

I should have listened to Anat, or at least to my own brain. But I am incorrigible. Whisking off my hattie I proceeded, out of the hotel, catching the number 18 bus, which left me at Mamilla, from which I walked down. A blustery day, this, with clouds doing their usual scud past the sun before she notices. On my right, the majestic walls of Suleiman the Great. On my left, Notre Dame de France (no Quasimodos need apply), the truck park, the ex-watermelon stalls. The shops lining Hanevi'im and the Nablus Road are shut by the ubiquitous commercial strike. There are, amazingly, taxis by the Gate, and people walking in and out, a thinner flow than previously, and even a school of tourists being shepherded through the closed Old City. "Where are all the caaffee shops, Seymour?" Out to lunch, me old dear.

The Damascus Gate. Very picturesque. But no gangling Yankee G-man. I am definitely not going to sit here dangling my toots, waiting for the *shabab* to close in. Go away, sir. You are not wanted. This is our land. The Border Police patrol closing in, smelling trouble and skulls to crack on my behalf. No thank you. But I stood there, indecisively, seeing my watch tick past 12:04, an Arab taxi driver, keys jangling, stepped up to me and, before I could tell him I didn't want to go anywhere, even though I did, back home to bed, said to me in English: "Are you Joe Dekel? I have a message from Oral Kool."

It sounded like a toothpaste ad on American TV, but I said: "I am Joe Dekel."

The man handed me a note. This was my day for written bulletins. It said, in the same handwriting as the other note: "The man who gives you this note is Nabil, a friend. You can trust him. He'll bring you to me. Please excuse the mumbo jumbo. We need to talk in a safe place."

I looked at the man. He looked at me. His hand gestured to a taxi, door open. A more unwise course could not be imagined. People are murdered this way. A throat cut, a body found several weeks later in thick thornbushes. Bleeding heart or not, one doesn't need to be starry-eyed about the dire realities.

I stepped back and shook my head. The man looked about, then took from his pocket a handgun, which he pressed into my hand before I could move, butt in my palm.

"The gun is loaded," he said. "Check it if you wish. There are four live rounds. That is an insurance policy. We are on the level. If we trust Oral Kool, so should you. He is not a double-crosser."

I have never been known to have a better judgement, but perhaps I should have acquired one somewhere along the way. I got into the car beside the driver, leant down and checked his claims. The bullets appeared kosher. I pointed the gun at his head. He looked worried. I put it aside and asked: "Where are we going? I need to know where."

"Not far," he said. "Ramallah. A quiet safe house. It's guaranteed."

"By whom?"

"By the people you met in New York. Let's go, people are looking at us."

Someone might have glimpsed my impulsive gunplay, God help us. "Let's go," I said. "How many times can a man live?"

"Only once," he said, "that's for sure."

We screeched like banshees up the Nablus Road. Past

117

Nahalat Shimon, the American Colony, Sheikh Jarrakh, the police headquarters. Old neighborhoods that don't seem to change. The olive trees behind moss-grown stone fences. The brown, brown earth. Stone houses with old women leaning from balconies. Groups of small kids. In any other context the picture of innocence. Today, they mature young, and scrutinize the passing car earnestly. My driver waves as he goes past.

"It is amazing," he said, shaking his head. "In our society it used to be sacred that children listened to their elders. Today, if the elders don't listen to their children, ho!" He tossed his head as if out the window. "Wait a minute. A roadblock. You keep the gun."

Oh, thank you. A dark brown jeep across the road. A Border Policeman staggering towards us, giving us the old eye. Identification cards. Driving licenses. I know I am done for now. The armed policeman curls his lip at me. "I have urgent business in Afula," I said. "This is the quickest route. I had to take a Special. My car's in the garage. Any problems?"

"Why is everybody in a hurry?" He looks at me. I give him my best businesslike look. "Gravelworks," I say. "Eldan Contractors, Strauss Road." He curls his lip even further to my driver, and writes down his name in his notebook.

"If anything happens to him," he means me, "we know who you are."

"I will look after him one hundred per cent," says my driver, in candid innocence.

"Keep to the main road," says the policeman. The jeep backs, we are, amazingly, waved through.

"That was good," the driver said to me, as we passed by. "Very quick thinking. I like it. I am Nabil Abd el-Khalil." He put his left hand past the steering wheel to grasp mine. We shook. "Those bastards," he said. "I thought they had us there." He shook his head admiringly. "Gravelworks, that's fantastic. You are an artist. Good gosh." He kept shaking his head and chuckling to himself as we accelerated up towards Shuafat.

There were three more roadblocks. Two waved us through, the other was a long queue of vehicles at the outskirts of Ramallah. This one was pure army. Tired reserve soldiers, definitely the *Jerusalem Post*'s "schlumpers," all sagging uniform and pouches, especially under the eyes. "You're traveling with him?" They look from me to Nabil. "He doesn't give a fuck for politics." I toss my hand, "He's taking me to Karnei Ze'ev, I have a cousin there. It's better than taking my own car and getting stones through the windshield." "You should buy the new window guards." He's telling me what I already know. "Anyway, I have to search him." They poke about in the car and on Nabil's person. I have the gun in my shoulder bag. "I don't care what you do," the tired soldier says, "it's all shit. We're wasting our time." "I know," I sympathize, "I had to serve in Gaza last month. Oil on troubled waters." "The politicians," he says, "put a stick up their ass and turn it, slowly. Then they'll know what it's like."

Into the town. The wide main road, patrolled on either side by army jeeps, prowling. The old men on stools, beside shuttered shop fronts. Some younger people, lounging. All the colored Arabic signs and logos over the opaque, closed center. We turned swiftly aside, up the avenue leading west, alongside gracious large homes nestling behind unspoiled gardens. The stone fences everywhere were either aerosoled with slogans or bore the signs of only partly successful wiping, forced by the patrols in their eternal war to check out what the population is doing and stop them doing it. One, in English, says: "LET MY PEOPLE STAY – NO DEPORTATIONS." A language perhaps the soldiers can't fathom. Scant hope, at any rate, that foreign news crews might penetrate the wall of sagging pouches today.

The whole thing looks like a kind of enforced Sabbath, a Rip

Van Winkleland where the law has decreed that everyone must sleep, or else. Nabil said: "It's a quiet day. Last week there were demonstrations. The army chased the people into the hospital compound and threw their tear gas inside. Four people were shot in the main square. Look, there's something they missed – " A ragged Palestinian flag, with the forbidden green, red, white and black, was fluttering across a telephone wire.

"When they have banned a flag and a song," said Nabil, "then they have lost. But we have not yet won."

The clouds had stopped their game of tag with the sun, and the day was another pre-spring beauty. The brown hills, the blue sky, the contoured fineness of the low houses fitting into the landscape. No high-rise monstrosities here, with or without planning permission, but wait and see. Once we have our bitter quarrel settled, they too can have the benefits of statehood . . . An efficient prison service of their own, a bureaucracy, long queues at the passport office. Everyone should have a right to be driven crazy by their own people.

We drew up in an alley twisted away from the main street, in which three other cars were parked. One was a rented Europcar with a King David Hotel sticker. I could guess this. The house was a gracious two-story dwelling belonging to someone who would have difficulty claiming membership of the starving masses. On the other hand, rose bushes and flowerbeds seemed to have been churned up by some recent disturbance, and there was a pile of spent shells in a corner.

A man was waiting by the door. Gray trousers, short-sleeved shirt, mustache. "Welcome. Everybody is in the back room."

I walked through a spacious hall whose walls were hung with decorative tapestries and objects. Brass plates, a coffee pot, an old saddlehorn. Framed photographs of persons foreign to me. A traditionally robed young black-eyed lady with a headscarf nodded me through a salon lined with cushions to an austere white room with French windows opening out on to a back garden which dropped down a slope westwards towards the rolling west Judaean hills. There were six people already in the room, seated on black carved chairs. Oral Kool, in a rumpled gray jacket, half rose to wave to me. An elder man with distinguished gray hair in the George Habash mold, grasping worry beads, nodded majestically. An immense old fat man wheezed beside him. Two Moslem clerics with matching brown beards eyed me impassively. The sixth person, like the first, was familiar, but wholly unexpected.

"Good to see ya, Joe." Slumped in a comfortable traditional robe, her gray hairs spread against the high back of the chair, brown eyes with a butter-wouldn't-melt look, gazing at me behind a swirl of cigarette smoke. Dorothy Morgenthal looking perfectly at home. Which she wasn't. At least, what right had she to be?

An absolute conspiracy. Without a shred of an excuse. I saw the headlines: "AMERICAN HAUSFRAU IS SPY FOR HIZBALLAH. AMAZING TRANSFORMATION OF BABUSHKA." That Bruce Lee stuff at Nederlander Schatz's apartment ought to have alerted me. I should have known. I should have known what?

"Sorry for the surprise, Joe," she said. "I'm as flummoxed as you are. I came off the plane late last night. I would have called you but it was three a.m. Then these guys collected me punkt at seven." She drooped a suspicious eye at Oral Kool, who offered me a tray of baklava. "Home cooking," he said, "you wouldn't believe it." A young man came in with a tray of coffee.

No one bothered with introductions. Oral Kool kicked off with the earnest air of a football coach at the start of the season.

"I have to say first of all that I have no authority to speak for the United States government. I am purely engaged in a criminal inquiry for the Federal Bureau of Investigation. I have no jurisdiction or authority here of any kind whatsoever, but I have Embassy agreement to discuss the matter which is of course of grave concern."

"And Mossad. You liaise with the Mossad," said the fat man in a gravelly voice.

"Not on the details of the inquiry," said Kool. "I wouldn't be here if that were the case."

"If it was not the case you would be on a plane flying back to Washington in half an hour," said the fat man. "Who are you trying to kid?"

"I was vouched for by your own people," said Kool. "You have had direct word from Tunis."

"We deal, you deal, they deal," said the fat man, "everybody makes deals for us. OK, we are playing this game. Let's agree, Mossad is in confusion. They have a leader who doesn't want to talk to anyone, but who needs to keep a door, because Washington says so, to the reactionary Arab states. Hussein, the Saudis, even the butcher Saddam in Baghdad. Not to speak of Cairo. Also, they have deals with Assad, to keep the lid on Lebanon. They kill each other, but they talk in the shadows. Only to us they won't talk. Your Ambassador in Tunis sends bulletins to the Israelis about his discussions with our delegation and they have orders to throw them in the rubbish. Meanwhile, they keep shooting our children, every day. You are playing with us. If you are serious, then tell the Israelis to come to the table and get the negotiations going."

The distinguished man with the worry beads spoke up softly. "Oral Kool is a policeman. We are trying to be as accommodating as we can. So we will speak to any representative, to policemen, postmen, dogcatchers. This co-operation is in our interest. It is classified as goodwill. We know we speak even to SHABAK when it comes to the security of the mosques on the Haram al-Sherif. This is not just an issue which affects the Palestinians. The whole Moslem world is involved."

"But if it is SHABAK themselves who are working with the conspirators . . ." The fat man wheezed and shook his head.

"We do not know that for sure," said the Elder. "All we know is, the enemy is fragmenting. There is no consensus in Israel, either in the public or among the Security personnel. This is an opportunity, but also a danger. We cannot tell what dark forces are gathering for what can only be called the 'final solution' to the Palestinian problem. Today they are extremists, tomorrow it's government policy. Transfer, genocide, destruction of all Palestinian culture and society, physical annihilation. We have to work against this with our Jewish and Israeli friends, and with the United States."

123

"Ask the United States about Nicaragua," scoffed the fat man, "and Guatemala, what deals they did with Shimon Peres. Selling Uzis to kill off the Indian population. And what about Bolivia and El Salvador?"

"Emotionalism will get us nowhere." The gray-haired man turned apologetically to Dorothy Morgenthal, saying sadly: "We are too used to flowery rhetoric at political meetings and other marginalities. We have to fight our addiction to a purist failure. We are now, how do you say it, players. We will not be puppets of the United States or anyone, but we must not go and sulk in the corner. Our people have put up with our failure too long. Now they are demanding results." He looked back at his rival. Two old militants in competition. The Moslem clerics were silent, stroking their beards. I wished I had a beard to stroke, but I didn't think they would take kindly to my caressing theirs. Nevertheless, I was dragged in.

"Our friend Joe Dekel, here," said Oral Kool, "whose political commentaries you may be familiar with, has spoken recently with one of the settlers, in Amiel, who we are pretty sure is involved in the new Jewish Underground. What was your impression, Joe?"

"He's very big," I said. "He doesn't like Arabs. His friend's baby was killed by a petrol bomb. He obviously knew more than he would tell me. He tried to break my neck." As a briefing, from a potential FBI agent, I was aware this was defective, but it was all I could offer. They didn't like the mention of the baby. Had I been brought up here to give this drivel? I remembered I still had the gun in my tote bag. Perhaps I should just aim it at my head.

"All right," said Kool, "I'm aware that you're in the dark. For the benefit of newcomers and to recapitulate, I'll go over the story, as we know it." He proceeded to relate to the gathering more or less the gist of what Nahum Lauterman had already told me in between the gulps of 7-Up, skipping Lebanon, but going directly to the strange alliance between the Church of Christ the Living, the Jewish settlers in the West Bank and the Golan Heights, and maverick American Jews. He added to my store of knowledge that Didi Schaeffer (the real, not the fake) had been present with Murray Waiskopf at the Church Convention at Phoenix, Arizona, last year.

"This year's Convention," said Kool, "is set as a grand spectacular in Zion National Park, in Utah. A symbolic choice for their location. It's due in mid-April, six weeks from now. We have reason to believe an attempt on the mosques will be made to coincide with that meeting. As the Reverend Risegood speaks of the Coming, he will be able to report on its first Divine Phase. The destruction of either the Dome of the Rock or al-Aqsa. This has to be stopped at all costs."

It would certainly put a crimp in our style. As Lauterman had said, no question then of dialogue or reconciliation. Just war to the end. Moslem against Jew. No politics, just primal vengeance. As we sit in our bunkers, we'll dream nostalgically of the days when we could have struck a deal with Yassir Arafat, or even the Rejectionist Front. Doctor Strangelove, please copy. Doesn't Pakistan have The Bomb? Not to speak of ourselves.

But the participants at this meeting seemed to have more interest in fixing spheres of responsibility than the actual nitty-gritty of Doomsday. I was reminded of Monty Python's *Life of Brian*, in which the revolutionaries sit passing resolutions while poor Brian is taken off to be crucified. The film ends as the victims tied to their crosses sing: "Always look on the bright side of life." I now knew exactly how they felt. I kept trying to catch Dorothy Morgenthal's eye and getting coded eyelid drooping which I think meant Wait till later. The Moslem clerics were eyeing me suspiciously as if I was flirting with this sixty-year-old grannie for reasons of perverse Jewish obscurity. They didn't know what I was doing here. I didn't know what I was doing here. But Agent Kool prattled on: " . . . Naturally, the Israeli

Security Services have been told what we know, or what we suspect, about the U.S. side of the equation. We would assume the Prime Minister would have no hesitation in rooting out this sort of project. But we also know there are internal party constraints on his ability to crack down on settler excesses. The U.S. government wants to give him space to maneuver in the little box he's created. Which is, I presume, why I have been authorized to speak with you people independently. You have to appreciate the parameters. It's the old question in unstable situations: Who's really minding the store?"

Something had obviously stuck in the fat man's throat and he was coughing and trying to bring it up. The distinguished man clicked his worry beads. So much static electricity must have been generated by the clerics' beard-stroking it could have powered the municipal grid. I was glad at least that Kool was not quoting the Snark at these people. We must thank God for small mercies. But then the mustached minion who had showed us in came and whispered in the older man's ear. He put his hand up: "I am sorry, gentlemen. I have just been informed there is an army and SHABAK force on the way to this house. There has been a leak. We will continue this discussion later."

The four Arab participants got up hurriedly, and, with a volley of dirty looks at us strangers, but with an air of routine, filed out through the French windows. The mustached minion motioned to us, and the woman I had seen as I came in entered with three large jalabiyas. We put them on, and wound kafiyas round our heads. Dorothy looked the spitting image of Golda Meir on her famous jaunt to meet King Abdullah of Transjordan in 1947. Agent Kool looked like a Miami Beach poolside attendant with an eccentric uniform. I had no time, thank God, to see what I looked like. We were bundled out down the hill, Mustache leading us like a stubborn shepherd with recalcitrant sheep. I remember thinking we were as conspicuous in this garb in this hi-life suburb as we would be in Dizengoff Square. But at least we were not instantly identifiable from the air, a wise precaution, as two minutes later a helicopter clattered over the hill. Following our attendant's lead, we raised our heads and waved at it. It swooped away, towards the house.

From behind a stone fence two teenagers with serious looks emerged and had a brief pow-wow with Mustache. He turned to us: "We should not all be together. The two of you go with the boys." He led Agent Kool left down the hillside while Dorothy and I were ushered to the right, down a weedy gravel trail. Teenager One said to me in Hebrew: "The helicopter will come back when they find you're not at the house. So if we can, please run a little."

We ran a little, Dorothy amazingly fleet of foot among the stones and brambles. What can you expect of Madame Tai Chi? "This reminds me of a kibbutz *tiyul* we did in 1946," she gasped to me at a pause. "We were tricking the British soldiers and carrying pistols from Safad to Gush Halav. But on that occasion there was a lot of singing." Mercifully, she did not demonstrate. We arrived at a wider dirt track and an old tractor. We climbed on board and Teenager Two gunned the engine. We lit out across the fields like Sylvester Stallone in pursuit of the Soviet Fifth Army, Teenager One scanning the sky for any sign of the chopper, till we came to a stop at a fence of barbed wire, with bedraggled signs proclaiming: "NO ENTRY. MILITARY AREA." There seemed nothing beyond it but sugarbeet. It must have been singularly potent. We disembarked, ran alongside the wire, then through a gap in it, to a grove of olive trees, part of which had been uprooted. The whine of the chopper now sounded. We ran from tree to tree like rabbits. A strange thought: Here I am, on the run from the army that is supposed to be protecting me from the people I'm running with. So, life is full of ironies.

Suddenly we were at a stone fence with a house behind it. Chickens, a goat, an alarmed child. We ran through backyards, the teenagers leading. Washing lines, old saucepans, baking ovens, impassive robed women letting us by. I remembered a cliché from Lauterman on a good summer's day: "Nevertheless, this is still one of the best countries in the world to hang your laundry out to dry." Small mercies. We ducked under a small entrance into a house. Two teenage girls, three or four small children, an old grandmother under a quilt, an old man, with a massive white handlebar mustache, sitting on a stool. The usual elegiac niceties of traditional hospitality were not observed. Teenager One spoke to the old man, in clipped tones, with the air of a Sergeant Major. The old man nodded, unfazed at this rudeness. The teenage girls brought armfuls of cushions.

The Hebrew-speaking boy turned to me and said: "You will stay here through the night. There will be no problem. Tell me if you want someone to be informed." I gave him Anat's name and number. Dorothy brushed away the offer. "My hotel doesn't even know I exist yet. At any rate, that's what the sheets looked like."

The old man perked up at the sound of English. He had evidently not bothered to learn the new masters' language. "I remember," he said to Dorothy, "in 1937, in our National Rebellion of that time, we had a Jew staying with us. A very brave man. Are you a Communist?"

"Not really," said Dorothy, "but my first husband was a Schachmanite. They were really something else."

"I have been in the Party for fifty years," said the old man. "But my sons are with the Fatah. They have some ethnic delusions, but we are all in the same boat. You will explain Schachmanites for me."

Oh God, I thought. How do they find me? I took the cushions and settled down for the duration.

Night in the village, and an eerie silence, broken only by the eternal screek of the crickets, a hacking cough over the next house, a crying baby, the far clap-clap of some sort of release of ammunition, whether in training or live action, unclear.

Yes, the fluttering of the newly-raised Palestinian flag, on the electric cable leading to the mosque, the only building wired up to the grid. Indoors, kerosene lamps lend a time-warped, other-worldly glow to the restlessness of the sleeping. Small bodies turning over softly, the lap lap lap of the old grannie's lips, the periodic snuffling snores of the fifty-year Party member. I poke my head out the window. Three lithe shapes in T-shirts and jeans, with pillowslip hoods over their heads, are busy pasting up a notice on the wall at the junction of the village's two streets. In the morning the locals will amble by and get an eyeful of the umpteenth Popular Committee's communiqué for the running of the *intifada*. No one is supposed to know who the anonymous flyposters are, but I think I recognize the loping stride of our guide, the Hebrew-speaking Teenager One.

Dorothy is sleeping soundlessly on her pile of cushions. Not at all my image of a *femme fatale*. Where is the lush-haired blonde/brunette, svelte, plastic-mackintoshed broad, with cigarette holder and gat – You don't have to call me, honey, just vistle . . . You know how to vistle, don't you? Instead I get this old leatherneck New York lady with her nunchaku sticks and iron stomach that can digest Yassir Arafat's breakfast slops. Have I deserved this? I probably have. Poking my head where it's not wanted. It's a habit I must kick. I put my lips together and blow, lightly, but making no sound.

Eventually, after an afternoon of *intifada* horror tales, I managed to corner her, outside in the yard, with only the chickens for company and Teenager Two looking out in the street for surprises. She apologized again for the surprise. I asked her point-blank whether she had been in on this plot from the start. Had she set up my "chance" meeting with the fake Didi Schaeffer, and why me, for God's sake?

"Of course not, Joseph," she said. "Who do you think I am? Fu Manchu? Ned Schatz phoned me, from the Virgin Islands. The Waiskopf affair is making big waves. The FBI have been uncovering some unsavory connections and hints of even worse to come. A major flap in the upper echelons of the Community. The Anti-Slander League has been hauled over the coals by people even they can't ignore. There's always been opposition to their open pandering to all sorts of Reaganite beasties. Mixing the meat and the milk. The kosher with the treife. It's un-Jewish. There are counterforces. Ned asked me to meet a certain Rabbi at the very pinnacle of the establishment. I go and see the man. He tells me the FBI are touting this amazing story. The Reverend Risegood, Waiskopf and the West Bank settlers. The mosques plot, which you just heard. The rumors of the Israeli spy, which we talked about. All heap bad medicine. Big Chief no like-um. Relations with paleface much endangered by hot-headed braves. The FBI are sending their investigator to Israel to talk to Palestinians. Tribe wants to send goodwill messenger to say Chief not involved in war dance. I have the ear of the Apache Enemy, so I get the job. I phone Tunis. I get the Chairman's endorsement. I book air ticket. *Voila*." She paused. "Imagine, me who has a file thick as your arm from Civil Rights to Vietnam, working with the FBI." She shook her head mournfully.

This clears my mind about as much as mud churned up by all the chariots of war. "Squaw talks in riddles," I said. "Mad Dog Who Bays At The Moon still in dark."

She abandoned analogies. "It's a new ball game in the Com-

130

munity, Joe, despite the outward show of unity. Since Pollard, they mistrust Israeli intelligence, and by extension, the Israeli government. The FBI has received assurances of Jewish co-operation from the highest level. Israel is one thing, but American Jews have to live in America. Provoking *jihad* is not their game, and the West Bank is not their Mecca. Not all of Palestine can be made into New Jersey."

This explains some things. Why SHABAK might allow Agent Kool to stomp over their turf, for a while. He who pays the piper calls the tune. When Washington wants something, it has its way. That, at least, I've learned by watching the weather-cock. If something isn't being done the way Washington says it wants, it means it doesn't really want it. So much for *realpolitik*. But what have I got to do with all this? Me, the eternal innocent, Hiawatha seeks isolated teepee.

"I really don't know, Joe. This man came up to you, baited you with the story about your book being blacklisted, and led you to a dead Murray Waiskopf. But you were supposed to turn up the day after, weren't you? Was that body supposed to be there? And why use the name of Didi Schaeffer, unless it was to lead you to the real Didi? There's still a lot of murk there."

You're telling me. The break-in at the hundred-year-old Jew's. My kidnapping from Morningside Park. The "Colonel," who is a "mechanic," for whom? For the Reverend Risegood, or for someone else?

I was getting no further towards enlightenment. Every step of the way drew me deeper into the morass. I gazed out the window again. The hooded flyposters had gone, probably to paste up more copies of the leaflet on different walls, of different villages. Here, at least, was something straightforward: A people fighting, with time-honored methods, for some sort of minimum dignity, to be treated as more than dogs. Civil disobedience, protests, riots, solidarity in the face of brute force, all of these seem simple enough to me, though they are not to the mad rulers of my country, who seem to think they can turn the clock back to a halcyon mythic period of benign master and willing slave. Not to speak of those who wish to return to primeval taboo totems . . .

The tales told that afternoon were dreadful enough, gushing out from the men and women of the family sheltering us from our own, with Dorothy scribbling it all down as fast as she could in a big dog-eared notebook. She never got to explain about Schachmanism to the old man, as the testament of assaults, abuse and degradation overflowed: The display of spent "plastic" bullets and other projectiles fired by the army into the village. The plastic coating merely thinly covering a black lethal metal ball. Live shell cases, pebbles fired from the famous "*hatsatsit*" or gravel gun, even marbles, which at least the children could play with. These were particularly prized items. Not to speak of the familiar tales of dumdum bullets which fragmented in the body. Women shot while leaning over washing lines, passers-by caught in the crossfire of soldiers shooting stone-throwing kids, the five-month baby blinded in one eye. The families scattered by demolition of houses of alleged petrol bombers. All the familiar daily dosage our own press couldn't fail to record. Lauterman, I have to say, was adamant he would report every incident, however obscure. The beating and breaking of bones with clubs and iron bars. The arrests of children eight years old. The harshness of the regime at "Ansar Three," the concentration camp of Ketsiyot in the Negev desert, which our paper had dubbed "the Graduate School of the *Intifada*," as the longer inmates were incarcerated there, the more points they gained with their people.

"Everything they do to weaken us strengthens us," said the old man. "They leave us nothing to lose. Once, before the *intifada*, there was a benefit, if you co-operated, you could live a sort of life. Today they offer us nothing but the big stick. Everything we do, we need a permit which they make it almost impossible to receive. You have to show you have paid all your taxes, to the last penny. But nobody has enough money. The merchants have been ruined, so they have no reason to go against the poorer people. Even the rich are not rich any more. You cannot live in luxury in a slum. Every Palestinian is an enemy for the government, so they cannot any more divide and rule. They have crushed us so hard we have become one element. They have made us an absolute unity. What we could only dream of in speeches and pamphlets is now an everyday reality. The *intifada* cannot end because it is a way of life. In fact, we are medically healthier. Everybody has to grow their own vegetables and things for their own house, because there is so little to buy. It is a healthy diet, from nature. One year ago, they tried to stop us growing our own vegetables, can you imagine, the army coming to pull up the tomatoes? But they have given up on that. They would have needed to have two soldiers for every Palestinian."

I remember it. My paper ran an item: "DEFENSE MINISTER'S WAR AGAINST THE CUCUMBERS." Perhaps if the Diaspora Jews do emigrate in large enough numbers, we could put them to work plucking up the Palestinians' allotments, as well as sweeping the streets and collecting the garbage. A sorry plight to contemplate.

"In the old days," the old man continued, "we used to fight among ourselves, to have feuds. There was also crime. But now the young men of the Committees take care of that, since we have no more policemen. If you are caught with hashish you will lose your life. If two neighbors fight the young men will come and order them to make up, or they will both be beaten. It may seem harsh to you, but we all accept it. We are building our own state, our own morality, under the nose of the Israelis. To stop it, you have to arrest us all. Or 'Transfer,' which means Genocide, because we will resist to the end."

Our century repeats itself with staggering irony. Or can the cycle be broken? Slumped down, on the pile of cushions, an ex-Intelligence Corps NCO (long ago, in Moishe-Ganef days), beside a gray-haired New Yorker who was brought up on the blue and white Jewish National Fund collection tin (One Acre After Another We Will Redeem Our Homeland), and an entire tribe of Moslem Arabs reprising our own battle for dignity. The total reversal of roles is the invisible chain that binds us together. And outside, the curfew rolls, and the hooded youngsters roam the streets, pasting up tomorrow's rebel rules.

Sleep comes, without the necessity of a dream, because one's waking life is it. Nevertheless, a rude awakening, out of whatever dark swirl, by a dig in the ribs and a harsh whisper in Hebrew: "Wake up, Dekel. We have visitors."

"Tell them to wait in the lobby."

A forlorn hope, as I join Dorothy and Teenager One at the window. Down the path at the junction I had watched earlier, a tarpaulin-backed jeep was idling. Two other vehicles could be glimpsed behind it. One was a light Mercedes, the SHABAK's favored mode of transport. The other was a civilian van. The figures in the cars could not be made out.

"Do you notice something strange?" Teenager One whispered to me.

He was right. Like Sherlock Holmes, and the dog that didn't bark in the night. There was no telltale crackle of static on radio that denoted contact with headquarters. The intruders were maintaining radio silence. They were a self-defining force. As we watched, figures did emerge from the vehicle. Some were uniformed, some were not, but all were equipped with weapons and combat gear. They fanned out, silently, among the houses.

"We move," Teenager One whispered. I could not fault the logic of this proposal. We moved, ushered out through a courtyard, over a series of fences and past other back yards, till the figure of Teenager Two waved us back. A brief exchange in Arabic.

"They came from both sides of the village," Teenager One

said to me. "This way." We stumbled towards a series of terraces leading to three houses up the incline of a hill.

There was a sudden burst of gunfire. A short clatter from a sub-machine gun. Then a loud bellow, through a megaphone, in Hebrew: "COME ON OUT, JOE DEKEL. WE KNOW YOU'RE HIDING HERE. WE'LL BREAK EVERY BONE IN THIS VILLAGE BUT WE'LL FIND YOU. YOU AND THE AMERICAN WHORE."

I knew that voice. I had heard it blaring at an Arab worker hefting crates at Amiel, the New Pioneering Valhalla. The true blue-and-white Didi Schaeffer, calling Yankee Go Home. What an irony. As if he hadn't misspent his own youth in Brooklyn. Another burst of fire. The whine of ricochets. Then a sudden explosion, and a ball of fire rising from where we had first seen the raiders.

"Shit! What was that?" I grabbed Teenager One. He shook me off, laughing: "Somebody has petrolled the jeep."

All hell breaks loose. Firing in all directions. Screams and yells from inside the houses. Flares shot up from the surrounding hills and hovered like light bulbs over the village. The picturesque Biblical landscape, the low stone houses with solar heaters, the gardens of trees, the allotments, the hindquarters of a startled scuttling goat, men in pajamas transfixed at the doors of their abodes. A loud cry in accented Hebrew: "Don't shoot! Don't shoot!" It might as well have been in Urdu.

Teenager One cried out in Arabic. Grabbing his colleague by the hand, they began leaping, stone to stone, down the hill towards the main square, where two other fires were now raging, after unmistakable grenade explosions. Dorothy's face was white as chalk. I could not see mine.

"Jesus Christ!" she cried out. "Jesus Christ!"

But he was not present either. We sat, in the midst of thorn bushes, watching the event unfold like some macabre light show. The flares kept going on, illuminating the running shapes of the village men and women, carrying children in their arms, the bulky figures of the armed men, firing, it appeared, at random. Then they were the leaping forms of the younger men, and the older children, throwing stones and objects at the invaders.

Then, out of the hill behind us, a helicopter rose. A searchlight's beam shot out, raking the scene of battle. A vastly enhanced loud-speaker boomed across the hills and valleys: "THIS IS THE COMMANDER OF THIS SECTOR. I'M CALLING ON THE OPERATING UNIT IN THE VILLAGE: CEASE FIRE IMMEDIATELY! I REPEAT: CEASE FIRE IMMEDIATELY! THIS IS AN UNAUTHORIZED ACTION!"

The helicopter hovered over the village, almost touching the rooftops, sending washing lines flying, raising a cloud of dust. The searchlight punched a cycle of blinding white into the midst of the battlefield. The loudspeaker blared out again: "I REPEAT: THIS IS AN UNAUTHORIZED ACTION! CEASE FIRE IMMEDIATELY! ALL ACTIVE UNITS REGROUP SOUTHEAST OF THE VILLAGE PERIMETER AND AWAIT FURTHER ORDERS! THIS IS THE COMMANDING OFFICER OF RAMALLAH SECTOR SPEAKING. YOU WILL CEASE FIRE AT ONCE! REGROUP AND AWAIT FURTHER ORDERS!"

A tongue of flame licked out from the ground. Someone had been gross enough to bring along a flame-thrower. Was it with me in mind? Or had it fallen into the "wrong" hands? (What might be the "right" hands for a flame-thrower?) At any rate, the helicopter was wreathed with a crown of fire for about three seconds. Then it exploded, crashing down on to the houses below.

There followed an eerie silence. The broken machine burned fiercely, sending a plume of black smoke into the gray-lit sky. The flares died. The shooting had stopped. Everyone seemed stupefied. I grabbed Dorothy and yanked her up from the thorns. "We have to go, we can't stay here." We dragged each other up the hill, past the houses, ripping through weeds and brambles, finding ourselves suddenly on a paved road, facing a line of jeeps and armored cars crackling with radio static.

We staggered up to the front jeep. Soldiers were standing on the curbside goggling in disbelief at the scene below. A man with a major's pips gazed at us from the jeep's front seat through thick spectacles. Dorothy confronted him defiantly.

"My name is Dorothy Morgenthal," she rasped. "I want to speak directly to your commanding officer. This is . . ." Her mouth moved, lost for words.

"I am my commanding officer," said the major, taking the radio mike from his companion. He spoke into it: "I have Miss Dorothy Morgenthal. Repeat, Miss Dorothy Morgenthal." He turned to me: "Are you Joseph Dekel?"

At least he didn't say he'd seen my picture. Or read my book, come to that. I nodded, lost for words too, if not for dreadful thoughts. He turned back to his radio.

"I have Joseph Dekel and Dorothy Morgenthal, over."

"What is their condition?" a crackling voice came over the set, as if speaking from Timbuktu. "What is their condition, over."

"They are ambulatory," said the Major. "They do not seem injured, over."

"Hold them in your vehicle," said the crackling voice. "Send the ambulances down to the chopper, with cover, to fire only if fired on. Yochai's forces will be with you in five minutes. When he arrives, bring your absentees back to base." There was a pause. Then a sharp intake of breath. "What a fucking stinking fuckup. Over and out."

I understand nothing. I can see nothing, but khaki uniforms, steel helmets, the scuffed material of old seats worn by sweaty bodies. I can smell nothing but engine grease and gun oil. Hear nothing but the maddening crackle of radios waiting for somebody to say anything. Dorothy Morgenthal in shell-shock beside me. All the unanswered questions again, rolled into one: Was all this blood and destruction carried out for my benefit? On my behalf? On my account? Or have I become some metaphoric figure of hate, a sort of scapegoat on whose hide the sins of my generation are visited?

Come out, Joe Dekel, we know you're there! But I'm not sure I know I'm here at all. A part of me is still curled up at home, watching *Dempsey and Makepeace* on Channel One, hefting an iced tea as my weapon. I watch, I peep through the hole of my television at the follies of the world. I read, I weep at the blunders and senselessness of the daily press's agonies. I even read my own columns with disbelief. This cannot really be happening. The bloodthirsty Rabbis, the petrol bombers, the generals who chase teenagers in helicopters, the apostles of revenge who set bombs in tape cassettes to destroy passenger aircraft . . . We all seem part of some medieval passion play which has spilled off the stage, out of the dark imagination of some guilt-wracked painter on to the pages of life.

The army base, a strange amalgam of transience and permanence, like an inhabited ghost town. The low barrack huts, the neat shrubbery along well-laid paths, the freshly painted fences, as if the whole enterprise is ready to be sold at a moment's notice. The flag-lowered drowsiness of night replaced now by the harsh white of massive lights, glaring on the hubbub of armed soldiers cramming on to their vehicles, the thunder of gunned engines, more static, barked orders and rushing boots.

Dorothy and I were shoehorned into a small room in a hut and locked in for an indeterminate time. There were two plain mattressed beds and a flush toilet, with one towel and a shredded old newspaper. We sat on the beds, looking at each other. Then she fell asleep. My own eyelids drooped. I saw a column of tanks, trucks and armored cars, heading for the sun. As they got closer, their steel flanks began to melt, the tank cannons drooped and sheared off, chassis buckled and men plummeted in an eerie silence into cloud-swirling deeps. A tinny voice in my ear repeated over and over: *"You have run out of fuel. Please report tomorrow morning at ten to the Committee of Inquiry."* A key was unlocked in my head. It was the door of our cell being opened. We were ushered forth, groggy, out of the barrack hut, down a neatly signposted path to a larger, stone house which obviously had been the commandant's in Jordanian days. This might even have been one of the camps I remember bursting into, in those foul-glorious Six Days of 1967, to marvel at the abandoned Hashemite officers' quarters, with the double shower and bidet. The height of decadence. Now the camp commander's office was a spartan affair of desk, hard-backed chairs, white walls minimalistically hung with framed photographs of the nation's leaders: The Prime Minister with his gray walrus mustache, the dour wrinkles of the Minister of Defense, the State President with the curled lip. A true coalition of national unity. Crammed beneath this austere trio was a group which was rather less united: The commander, a bulky youth with gray hair, a gaunt colonel from Military Intelligence, Agent Kool, tight-lipped beside a nondescript black-suited-and-tied clone with a briefcase, obviously "from the Embassy." Two civilians with the telltale undereye bags and bloodhound gloom of SHABAK, and, with the rumpled look of a man dragged out of the marital bed and helicoptered over from Tel Aviv's Sde Dov airfield, mine own editor, Nahum Lauterman.

He pulled me down at his side, Dorothy on the other. All the Israeli army personnel and spies stood up as another civilian entered the room. He was small, just a little larger than our Prime Minister, bulky and bald, with shaggy gray eyebrows, looking, in contrast with all the other sad sacks in the room, as if he had just cycled the Tour de France, and won, after a perfect eight hours' sleep. Sweeping into a waiting chair behind the desk, he waved everyone back into theirs. Lauterman nudged me in the ribs and whispered "*Numero uno.*" So we were being honored by the rarest sighting of all, the country's top internal spook. How wonders never cease.

"OK," he opened, in English, in a headmaster's voice, as all us mere mortals shuffled our feet. "So our best friends don't speak to us. Commitments? Let's not be little children. They read the newspapers and decide we've gone crazy. The Mad State. So who should we blame? Society? Our mothers and fathers?" He looked around us as if we should all be ashamed of ourselves. I was born ashamed. The others merely slumped further. The lecture continued: "They're used to dealing with El Salvador. Hey, Orlando, keep those death squads quiet this week, damn you, we have a crucial vote in Congress! When you think you're dealing with amateurs, you send amateurs. Tell me, should I laugh or should I cry?"

Agent Kool pursed his lips but said nothing. The Man From the Embassy, moving his own lips as if he were a ventriloquist dummy operated by extremely remote control, said: "We are now co-operating fully with your own investigation. All the relevant documents are being forwarded."

"Wow, I'm so glad to hear that." The Chief Spook leaned forward on the desk and pointed his eyebrows directly at Dorothy Morgenthal, Nahum Lauterman and me. "It's a mystery," he said. "We tried turning the whole nation into an army and what did we get? Slackness, insubordination, incompetence. Vanity, vanity. Do you want my job? You can have it. Here, you can get to work right away." He thrust out his own briefcase towards us, then grabbed it back as if we might take it. He pointed us out to the Embassy Man as if the latter had not noticed us and told him: "You see these people? If this was El Salvador, they'd all be dust and ashes by now. Even *Señor* the Editor. But this is Israel. It's spelt I-S-R-A-E-L, not P-A-N-A-M-A. We try to keep a grip on our geography."

"We are well aware of that," said the Embassy Man, as if he had just glimpsed at an atlas. He wanted to say more, but held back, glancing nervously at Dorothy Morgenthal. But the Chief Spook had turned to speak to Lauterman in Hebrew:

"I'm convening the Editors' Committee for ten a.m. We're expecting your co-operation, Nahum. This is the story: What happened tonight was an internal foul-up. The chopper crashed by accident. The families of the five village dead will be offered compensation. We have arrested eight settlers, who we know have been involved in other attacks on villages. They will be charged accordingly. The rest is up to the courts. There will probably be the usual political interference. What do I care? I'm only a civil servant. As far as the United States' investigation is concerned, we are asking for a local and foreign blackout. The mosques are under our jurisdiction and we will protect them by any means necessary. If we have internal problems, we'll solve them. Everyone knows how explosive all this is. I'm asking for your help in this, Nahum. At the end of the day, we're all family, and like all families, we fight among ourselves. But this is an issue of National Security, the real thing, not party politics."

Without waiting for an answer he turned to me, ticking off the recalcitrant truants one by one, giving me a pained look that made it evident my chances of a good term report were zero. "Ah, Mr. Joseph Dekel . . ." Definitely one who has seen my picture. Profile and *en face*, the works. The spider looking at the flea. As long as he's already had his nightcap. "Yes, Dekel. For you, it seems, life is imitating your art. I glanced at your book, but I can't abide thrillers. They always make me feel I'm missing out on something. Why isn't my life like George Smiley's? Not to speak of James Bond. But anyway. I understand you have a beautiful and intelligent wife, and you're thinking of starting a family. I think that's excellent news. Make us a good Peace Now protestor for the next generation. Believe me, we will need them. Just go home and pick up the threads. You want to go hob-nob with Arafat and Co. abroad? Don't let me stop you. It's your funeral. The state wants to prosecute you? I'll give them your file. It's just like three thousand others. Believe me, you're so far down on the list you won't believe it." I am quite prepared to.

He dismissed my existence, and turned to Dorothy Morgenthal, switching back to English: "And as for you madam . . ." He sighed, drooping his head towards the desk. "I have looked you up, you have some track record. In 1948 you ran guns for us. You organized major fund-raising drives in 'fifty-one and 'fifty-six. In the sixties you marched with Martin Luther King and joined the Freedom Riders in Mississippi. You went to jail for the blacks. Now you think Arafat is the same as them, a poor schwartze with a noble cause. Should I argue with you? Life is too short. But you're an American Citizen. You have an inalienable right to shoot your mouth off. You can shout, you can scream, you can publish my name in the *New York Times*, if they let you, or in *The Nation*, if they won't. So you met Yassir Arafat. I'm not allowed to. When you next meet him, give him this message from me: I'm going to do my job. End of message. This country might tear itself apart but I'll still be out here doing my job. That's what they pay me for. Whatever my opinions are, I carry out what my elected Prime Minister orders. That's the bottom line. There will be no special deals on the one hand, and no putschists, either, on my territory. Others can speak for themselves."

142

Having exhausted his personal touch, he snapped his brief-case open, and beckoned to a flunkey. "See that our curfew breakers get home safely. We have to get down to business here." Civilian and military stooges motioned Dorothy and me out of our chairs and towards the door. Lauterman and Kool remained seated, gazing at us with sheep's eyes. Oh, these lambs in lambs' clothing. The Big Chief shuffled secret papers, but we were out of class. Escorted firmly down the bulb-lit corridors out to a waiting Mercedes car. The driver, a mute Neanderthal, drove us back to Jerusalem. Neither of us seemed to have anything to say to each other that we could enunciate in this floating coffin ambience. We looked out of the opaque windows, on opposite sides of the car, seeing nothing, gazing into the passing darkness.

Move over Woodward and Bernstein. The unfree press lays another egg. The humiliating obligation of powerlessness. Shut up. Close your eyes. Go to sleep. I arrived home, after Dorothy had been dropped off at her hotel, chauffeur-driven back to my womb. Anat was waiting up, having been warned and soothed by a telephone call from Lauterman.

"Honey, you won't believe what went on tonight."

"What?" she asked, pouring a tea.

"I haven't a clue." I had to answer.

Even Flight Simulation is too dangerous. Let alone massaging one's Lugers. Sleep, dreaming of melted tanks again. A molten hailstorm, scalding the populace, scattering them to uncertain cover in open trenches, blitzed bunkers. No profound puzzle here. In the morning, the events of the night had not made, even in sanitized form, the daily press. It was all just the same sad litany of blighted Peace Processes and spent bullets. The *sicarii* have made an arson attack on a left-wing Member of Knesset's house. Two million dollars' worth of heroin bagged at airport. Swing to right expected in Municipal poll. The Prime Minister will offer elections for an Autonomy in the Occupied Areas. Tourist bookings for Passover are down.

Anat decided to take the day off, away from Jerusalem in miniature, and we called on Dorothy Morgenthal. Whisking her away, from the echoes of the night's horrors, to a guided tour of Our City. Not the City of tourist brochures and frenzied *pesh-kvilim* but the quiet corners of our own balm: The Hut, The Gallery, the Yemeni Falafel, the Artists' House Cafe (nobody there I knew, the younger generation now, all born since I retired), then off in Alexander to the hills and pines of the

Jerusalem Forest. The landscape looking west, not east, the burning colonies left behind. The brisk mountain breeze on our faces. Nevertheless, here and there, the charred areas, scars left by the previous summer of revenge, when scorching dry weather aided the *intifada* youths' arson attacks against the trees. Why should the Jews picnic when our lives are destroyed? Why indeed? We sat and unwrapped the sandwiches Anat had prepared at home. But Dorothy's mind was still absorbed by the night.

"Those people who were killed. I can't understand. How can this just be business as usual? I feel responsible. If the two of us hadn't been there, they would still be alive."

Every step we take in this country is a walk in a minefield, blindfolded. The heart freezes, but pumps on its routine supply to keep the body ambulating. Dorothy lacks the defenses we each wear as a second skin, the invisible armor of protective inertia, the habitual turning of a blind eye to the misfortunes of others, the preservative coating of coward's restraint. If we take our finger out of the dike, the oceans of pain, of anguish and anger, torments and troubles will overwhelm us. And by opposing, end them?

"It's one thing to read about it in the papers, see the snippets on television. It's different to see it happening in front of your eyes."

But one even gets used to that. Dorothy realizes this. "I just feel totally out of my depth here. I've always had this distance – I just can't make the mental leap. In America I can deal with the mad twists of power. The language of money against the individual. Maybe it just seems simple. But here, where I'm told it's the simplest choice of liquidation or survival, I'm lost. There are too many subterranean currents, too many lethal passions I can't take on. Militant Islam, Christianity, Judaism . . . Wars of a God I don't believe exists. Begging your pardon, Joseph." I am not offended, I don't believe in that God either. "The pitting of uprooted refugees against uprooted natives. It doesn't make sense, except at the basic level of my tribe against yours. And I can't accept that at all."

Well, tribes are such strange animals, with our filthy habits, fetishes, totems. Bizarre dances at the full moon, taboos, menstrual secrets. If we don't cherish what keeps us together we might have to navigate by our personal preferences, our private ratio or emotio, we'd have to make our own decisions. That will not do at all. Better to open a book, or a newspaper, or switch on a TV set, which tells me who to hate and who to love.

"I have a friend in New York," said Dorothy, "a reform Rabbi, who wants to deal with the situation in the Territories here as we did in the South in the sixties. He wants to flood the West Bank and Gaza with progressive Jews, who will join the Palestinians in vast numbers, in solidarity against the oppressor."

"The West Bank and Gaza are flooded enough with American Jews," said Anat, "what we need are less, not more."

"We're always blinded by past triumphs," said Dorothy. "Like generals, we're always ready for the previous war. Marching side by side with Martin Luther King and the young men from the SCLC. Jesse Jackson and Andy Young. But we forgot, we had the Supreme Court on our side. The state was actually drawn in to support us. Paratroopers took the black kids to school. And still it took years to get anywhere, to achieve those taken for granted demands . . . All the blood and fire expended just to get a basic dignity for human beings. Maybe one day they'll sit back and marvel at what happened here as well – so many wasted, blighted lives to reach the obvious – a decent life for both peoples."

We fell silent, looking at the trees bending softly in the wind. A last cloud of the winter appeared to be determined to have its say before the long dry spell. It began tossing drops of water in our sandwiches and faces. We waddled back to the car. On the way home I bought the evening newspaper. The night's events finally unfolded in the grisly warp of a distorted mirror: "FIVE KILLED IN VILLAGE INCIDENT." The settler movement denies any involvement. The army is investigating. The army is always investigating. Every shooting, every breaking of bones or spilling of blood is a surprise requiring an inquiry. Every incident is an exception, but not one that proves any rule. Interestingly, the chopper "accident" is headlined as a separate item. Two dead, two badly burned. The Editor's Committee had evidently met, with predictable results. When we're sheep, we're sheep properly. No dodging forth out of line. Our bleating, too, is world renowned. Well, who am I to complain?

Dorothy returned to her hotel, determined not to fall victim to our malaise of disconnection. A wodge of Peacework to be achieved while she was here. Contacts to be made, bleeding hearts to be patched up, information to be gathered. The next day was Friday, my cue to disappear for my weekend of atavisms. After which, the Municipal Elections were due. Should I cast my ballot, and for whom? There is little choice in this city. It is sane reactionaries against The Madness.

I spend the weekend speaking to my God, who, as usual, does not answer. Given the state of the world, that's not surprising. He is probably in sackcloth and ashes somewhere, on some far hill, or some dark shebeen. He too appears schizoid. Or is it His schizoid nature we reflect? Job dared to raise an unspoken reproach against the Lord, who answered him with a veritable blast of unanswerable domination: I made you, so put up or shut up. Man's bluff of presumption was called. Or was it just the arrogance of the tyrant, a mark of cruel uncompassion? I am not suggesting a reproach here, God forbid. Just a query. No need to respond directly . . .

Anat continues to read *On Heroes and Tombs*. The chapter headings are somewhat evocative: "The Dragon and the Princess," "Invisible Faces," "Report on the Blind," "An Unknown

God." I have enough on my plate. Saturday night, we phone Dorothy, but a message reveals she is pow-wowing in Tel Aviv. The besieged forces of Peace, counting the ashes.

The new week. I vote in the Municipal Elections. I cast my vote for Old Sandpaper, our incumbent Mayor, building-planning traumas and all. Anything to keep the religious-right coalition from turning the city into a Beirut/Belfast. It's bad enough as it is. Next day we watch the TV analysis. Old Sandpaper, thank God, hangs on. Elsewhere the right continues its consolidation at the expense of the Labor Alignment. In the Arab sector (within "green line" Israel), a poll shock as Moslem lists show sharp gains against the left-wing lists, mainly the fatigued Communist Party. So now all the saints are marching.

But not all is lost! Prime Minister Shamir definitely promises to unveil his "autonomy" elections plan. Palestinians will be allowed to collect their own garbage and sweep their own streets under our benign rule. The Premier is due to visit Washington and has to come up with something, however unreal. Thus we arrive at our near apotheosis: Fantasy as state policy. They have caught up with me after all.

Dorothy returns to the capital, with sackfuls of documents attesting to the slings and arrows of the *intifada*. Rather than taking the usual precaution of committing the stuff unmarked to the mail she wants to take the whole lot out in her suitcase past the beady eyes of Airport Security. She knows, I suppose, they won't detain an American. I used to be on their list, in the old days. A bored SHABAK officer used to invite me into a little office, whenever I or Anat and I made our sporadic breaks for air abroad, and sweat through my meager belongings, hoping perhaps to find Trotsky's lost manifesto in my underwear. I used to take lists of film symposia participants, or TV press handouts, to satisfy the security officer's thirst for written material, but he always waved me on wearily. Eventually they cut me out of the roster of the nation's fifth columnists. I seethed with rage for three years. But Dorothy can probably take sheafs of letters out from or for Yassir Arafat, such is the power of our Sponsor's passport.

She had not much further information about the U.S. side of our imbroglio. Nederlander Schatz was incommunicado in the Virgin Islands. The powerful brethren in New York had been appeased. Assurances of Mossad and other official co-operation had been accepted. Agent Kool had been recalled, without even waving me goodbye. Dorothy waved me goodbye, as she climbed into the service taxi taking her to Ben-Gurion Airport. "I'm not much use over here," she said. "All I can get is a blood pressure count that nudges me towards the grave. I don't intend to forget those people in Ramallah. I'll do what I can, which is precious little, don't I know it? We shout and yell, but the bullets still fly."

Indeed they do. Two more Palestinians shot as she was winging her way across the seas to Manhattan. It's mere routine. Unrest, containment. The dead vocabulary of hardened hearts. Leaving me in my limbo, with Anat. Dangling over our abyss of uncertainty, veiled threats, unresolved mysteries, gags and enforced silences, *coitus politicus interruptus*.

Who needs blacklists and official Silencers when we have our own fears? This would not do at all. I braved the service taxi to Tel Aviv again, plugging my ears to evade the ethnic patter, and bearded Nahum Lauterman once more in his office overlooking the mudge and muck of the commercial quarter and the opaque windows of the alleged Information Retrieval Center across the street. He pretended to be busy, ploughing through a pile of expenses slips queried by the income tax man. "My God, Joe," he said, "dinner for six at the Gay Hussar, London! Where on earth did that come from?"

"I want answers, Nahum," I said. "I don't care if the head of SHABAK, God, and all the Ayatollahs say Keep Off. The Public Has The Right To Know."

"You know very well what the public here Wants To Know," he said me. "Fuck all. They just want to lie back and be raped and imagine it's them doing the raping. It's a lost case, my friend."

"You know me," I said, "I'm a lost case too. I have absolute Faith," I recited, "in the Coming of the Messiah. And even if he tends to be tardy . . ."

"You'll be at the bus stop every day. It's an endearing trait of yours, Joe. Loyalty to outmoded principles. Justice, Truth, Fair Play, and the beer should always be cold. We are entering the nineties, Joe. The world can't deliver. The whales are dead. The trees are wilting. People are dying in London of poisoned yogurt. Can you believe that? It just came over the wires. Madmen are putting glass in baby food. Tap water makes your hair fall out. So tell me, why should you be spared?"

"Don't sell me any more damaged goods," I said. "Open the door or I'll break it down."

He sat, holding at arm's length a receipt which seemed to be covered by a large smudge of mud or blood, or perhaps just a spilled Turkish coffee.

"What on earth do you think this is? It might be a car rental form, on the other hand it might be my chit for the Cairo Citadel Baths . . ."

"Your time is up, Nahum," I said. "I want no more evasions, just some straight talking for a change. Item: Who did I meet in New York and why was I singled out for the contact? Item: Who killed Murray Waiskopf and why, and why was I made involved? Item: What's the state of play with the real Didi Schaeffer, the man who told me I was a corpse, and did his best to make good that statement? Item: How does the boss of SHABAK, whom you obviously breakfast with daily, know my wife and I are considering conception? How many more intimate titbits have you provided? Does he know where I hide the porno tapes?"

"Just gossip, Joe," he said, still eyeing his stockpile, "you know this is an incestuous country. You so often find yourself in bed with people you never even wanted to say Hi to in the street. The country's too small. There are no secrets. In America, on the other hand . . ."

He stopped, brow furrowed by another hieroglyphic message from an immediately profligate past. "What? Oh my God . . ." Then, leaning back, apologetically. "Come on, Joe, you know I don't discuss your private life with anyone. The man is a fan of your columns. He's read your book, despite his disclaimer. I hear he's read every trashy spy novel in print. Apparently he used to read your TV column. He said it saved him watching anything. He is not my buddy, if that's what you think he is. He's a tool of people I despise. But I'm supposed to be the big cheese of the Fourth Estate, *nein*, Yozef? I hob-nob over the chopped liver cubes. You know that I attack his handiwork daily, that I try not to let him get away with murder. But what do you want, on this matter we are dependent on him. Are you going to mount a twenty-four-hour watch on the mosques? Or on the mad groups who have vowed to blow them up and scourge the infidels from the Holy of Holies? If there are dangerous elements in his own constituency, only he can root them out. It's not a matter of affection or even trust, Joe, it's a strategic common interest."

"And the Christians? The Church of Christ the Living? The Reverend Risegood and your Lebanon plotters?"

"You're the one who prays, Joe. Pray for me. Pray for all of us. Put me down for twelve Ave Marias. I'll tell you this piece of gossip: Your Agent Kool is off the case. He has been withdrawn by the Bureau. Somebody twisted somebody's arm, out in Yankee-land. Maybe you'd better make that twenty Ave Marias."

"And all that stuff about the Church Convention? Agent Kool's warnings in Ramallah?"

"You're asking me? It's in the stewpot, Joseph. Somebody high up will put on pressure. It's not in our mortal hands, old friend. Maybe Ron himself will phone from California, demanding the postponement of The Rapture. God's schedule is infinitely flexible. As a Believer you know that, Joe."

"*Allahu akbar.*"

"Precisely. You know how it is. We stagger on from crisis to crisis. This is not Western Europe, where emergencies might crop up, but social inertia rules. Everything can be blown off course here by a puff of the wind. We seem to be the true Orwellian country: War is Peace, Love is Hate, Ignorance is Strength. We just rattle about, like dice in a box. Let's just be thankful we're still alive. And apropos, Joe, if we're talking Orwell, don't get too paranoid if you notice some people watching your house or your wife. I believe the Chief has you under protective surveillance. So don't use filthy words in the bath. Tell Anat. I have put in a severe word on your behalf. If anything happens to you, I go to town on the story. If anything happens to me, it goes to press anyway. If not here, then in Deutschland, or France, or even England, God help us. We are the Free Press, guarantors of Liberty! Doesn't that warm the cockles of your heart?"

"No." I was following the train of thought of his references to the Englishman's dystopia. The vision of the future offered by O'Brien, torturer of Winston Smith: A boot treading on a human face, for ever. Our boot, someone else's face . . . Nothing comforting in that reflection, however much we can report "the facts" . . . We used to think you only needed to tell the truth, and the truth would set men free. Now we know that truth is in the eye of the beholder, that our truth is another's lie, and vice versa. Should we weaken, then, and surrender, to the loudest voice, the noisiest bully, the greatest coercive force?

Do I love Big Brother? Hell, no.

I took the service taxi back to Jerusalem, leaving Lauterman with the detritus of his petty tax scams. Taking the bus from the city center to one stop before my normal one and walking round to check out his claims about the Big Chief's seeing eyes. He was right. There was a man parked in a Ford Fiesta thirty yards up on the other side of the street, reading a paperback novel. Was it mine? I couldn't see from that distance. He had that laid-back look of the professional snoop, the kind that melts in the crowd. Or was he The Enemy, staking out the house for other sinister forces? I couldn't tell, least of all for lack of knowledge of who my Enemy was or was not . . .

Welcome back, full-blown paranoia. Now at least I am in full harmony with my environment. An ecological fit. I walked jauntily to the house, looking at my watch. Five-fifteen, Anat should be returning in half an hour or so from the office, barring storms in artistic teacups. I sprang up the three stairs to the door and took my keys out. I stuck my key in the lock and turned it. The door blew up in my face. I felt a massive blow on my side and a clap of thunder inside my head. Then a sort of odd, cold, tranquil silence.

Then the sirens. *Waah-waah! Waah-waah! Waah-waah!*

3

AYE, HAVE A DREAM

I 'VE ALWAYS WONDERED about those TV pictures of victims, lying torn and bleeding on the ground. I've always wondered who was in those ambulances, screaming to the hospital from the scene of the disaster. Now I know it's me.

Soneh Amcho. Hater of your people. Everything is very black. There is movement, a sort of rocking, an engine whine, the dull turning of rotors. The feeling of being raised up, up, towards a sun which has been put out. No light, no heat. Nada. Just a ringing in my ears, resolving itself into a haggard cry from somewhere:

"The Name, Dekel! The Name!"

Jahweh. The true monicker, the Forbidden. He shall be my rock, my salvation, my refuge in time of sorrow . . .

"The Name! The Name!"

"Bugs Bunny."

A shaking hand seems to let go. The cold increases. Snow. Ice. February in Manhattan. The slippery streets of New York, with all their burglar alarms triggered . . .

A man approaches me with no face. He is swathed completely in bandages like Claude Rains in *The Invisible Man.* Coal-black glasses hide his eyes. He hands me a white manila envelope. I open it. It is my death warrant, an ornate and rubber-stamped document, in Biblical Hebrew, signed by the two Chief Rabbis, the Sephardi and the Ashkenazi, just to make sure. I am to report the following morning, to a warehouse on the Lower East Side. The figure vanishes, its bandages unraveling down the steps to the 116th Street subway. I take the number 3 train south. The alarms continue to ring. The passengers, weaving in a kind of fog, all appear nevertheless to be familiar. School

157

friends in the shabby khaki of their Reserves service, toting rifles, flame-throwers, mortars. The train jars to a halt in the tunnel. The rattle of the compartment doors. The police, dressed in shabby raincoats and fedoras, are trampling through the cars, checking identity documents. Their faces through the smudged compartment door window: Agent Kool and Detective Flynn. But the only document I have is the deed I've been handed. I get up and squeeze by the immobile soldiers, down to the rear of the train. Opening the back door I proceed down the tunnel, along the ghostly lit tracks. The alarm bells fade into water dripping from crumbling masonry above. Plop plop plop. I feel it in my bloodstream, an oily, diseased scum.

"How many fingers, Joe?"

Fifty-seven. There is a scrabbling in the dank wall ahead of me. I move gingerly down a slope from the tracks, by an abandoned, rusted mining cart piled with what appear to be black glittering rocks. Behind the cart there is a knocking on the rock-face, and a slab falls out, revealing the gaunt, spider-webbed features of Nederlander Schatz. The Hundred-Year-Old Jew, determined to reach at least One Hundred and One. He gestures to me with a withered claw. I walk up to hear his stentorian wheezing. "I told Theodor Herzl it wouldn't work. The immigrant ships. They sank with all hands. No one reached the promised land. The people who are there now – all impostors. Tell the world – the real Jews – still in bondage – " His voice fades into a drooling gibber. I replace the slab and move on. A chink of light ahead, a small circle of stars, above, coming from the pinpoints in a manhole. I climb, rung after rung, up a rusty ladder, pushing the manhole cover aside.

I am in the East Village, somewhere around Houston or Great Jones Street. The entire street is the backs of buildings, with immense faded painted signs: "THE AMERICAN SOCIETY OF BUDDHIST STUDIES." "ORIENTAL SEASONS LIMITED." "ANTI-SLANDER BOOKS INC."

"ATOMIC WASHING MACHINES." The alarm bells again. At the end of the road a jeep and an armored car stand waiting, amid the crackle of radio static. Two men are standing in front of the jeep's hood, dressed casually in short pants and white shirts. One is short and slim, the other tall and bulky. I recognize the two Didi Schaeffers. Four figures sit in the jeep behind them, faces hidden by black cloth hoods, with small holes for eyes. I know one of them is "The Colonel." They want my document. I back away, down the potholed road. The usual writhing white steam exudes from the subway vents, one of the white wisps beckoning to me. "Over here, Dekel!" It is Nederlander Schatz, released from his mortal coil and *en route* to the Next World. "Come with me! I have secured places! Discount rates!" But I am paralyzed. The earth beneath begins to move, the asphalt melts and breaks up. Something is thrusting its way to the surface. Bells ringing everywhere. The hooded figures from the jeep advance, with burning crosses. Both Didi Schaeffers lie dead on the ground. The hooded men's feet tramp over their bodies. A celestial choir sings:

There is a green hill far away without a city wall
Where the dear Joe was crucified who died to save us all . . .

"Tell us your name, Joe! Just your name!"
The wailing ghost of Ned Schatz.
If you will it, it is no fairy-tale . . . A bulky shape from the depths. The pointed ears, the squat head, the cloven hooves, the forked tail, the glittering gold bracelets, necklaces, earrings. The hooded figures fall down and worship the molten calf. Large pendant earrings of dollar signs hang from the creature's ears. I wince at the cliché. The voice of Agent Kool resonates in my ear:

But oh, beamish nephew, beware of the day,
If your Snark be a Boojum! for then,

THE SILENCER

You will softly and suddenly vanish away
And never be met with again!

The golden calf breaks the asphalt and ascends, coming to a stop beneath the "ATOMIC WASHING MACHINES." Newsmen pop flashbulbs from every angle. A vast hubbub of voices. Police hold the throng back, throwing up barriers. The sirens: *Waah-waah! Waah-waah! Waah-waah!*

I try to call out, but no voice emerges. My throat is dry, my larynx has been cut. I feel a bubbling sensation in my windpipe. I try to cry out again. Nothing. Again. A dry croak. A firm hand closes on my shoulder. A voice: "It's all right, sir. It's all right. Everything is under control."

A room. That at least I can count on. I can feel the closeness of its walls. A hospital bed I know, from the other side of hell, that coarse linen that always has Property of the Ministry of Something printed on it. But other than that, ignorance. The alarm bells are still ringing. Thoughts of the fictional tales of fake rooms, arranged to entrap their inmate. The jailed spy who is apparently sprung from prison to a safe house, where he hides, behind close curtains, with the subtle sound of traffic, until he telephones his contact, blowing his cover, and finds himself back in jail, the curtains having hid a special cell with taped sounds. Or the science fiction tale of the set of an entire town, specially constructed in the nuclear ruins of the earth, shifted about just to fool the protagonist that the aliens haven't taken over.

Or Orwell's Room 101. The worst thing in the world.

Rats.

"How many fingers, Joe?"

Ninety-nine.

A boot, grinding on a human face, for ever.

Nevertheless, an abrasive cheerful male voice: "Dekel? My name is Avi Tsemach. Remember? We spent time in Reserves

160

together, in the Jordan Valley, in 1972. I was just a medic then, but you were already a live wire. Telling jokes, entertaining everyone. The life and soul of the party. So tell me now, buddy, how do you feel?"

With difficulty. "My wife, my wife all right?" Was that ugly slur my voice?

"She is A-OK. No signs of damage. She was not on the premises when the device exploded."

"Eyes. M'eyes?"

"A narrow escape, habibi. That's one solid door you have in your apartment. Luckily the device was not that powerful. You should see the normal injuries in this kind of action. You got off lightly, habibi. A good zap in the face, a broken nose, lacerated jaw, a good whack around the eyes, but no fragments. The covering is just a precaution. Your left arm broke, so we set it. Ribs bruised. Left leg scraped a little. Your ears will be ringing for a while. Am I right? Not to worry. You have survived, virgo intacto. Can you believe it? God protects his own, doesn't he? In a while I'll remove the eye bandage and return you to the seeing world. Back to the Man with the X-Ray Eyes! Remember they showed us that film, at the Jordan Valley outpost, when we were stuck there over Passover? Ray Milland, as Doctor Xavier. He invents these special eyedrops which make him see through the skin of people, bones, objects. But as time goes on he can't avoid seeing, he sees deep into the secrets of the universe. In the end he has to pluck out his own eyes. That was one hell of a movie, eh? There was a colonel in the Medical Corps Research and Development who tried to do something similar. Today he's in the National Institute for the Blind. But you'll be A-OK, Dekel."

"Where am I?" Babble babble babble.

"A secure medical facility. You are under State Protection, Dekel. Grade A. Like Suleiman Rooshdie. Did you read his book? I can't wait for the Hebrew translation. Getting on the wrong side of the Ayatollah. It's an unwise career move."

"Why my here? Where wife? Want make phone call. Want m'lawyer. Call Na'm Lau'erman, edi'or, H—. Demand bress gonference." I sound like a lobotomized rhinoceros.

"You're getting excitable, honey. There's no problem. It's the drugs that are talking. Painkillers, they have harmless side effects. You'll experience hallucinations. Enjoy them while they last. If you need something, there's a bell right here. I'm going to shoot you full of something real snazzy now, but don't worry, we won't charge you extra. Did you know that Heroin was a Bayer Company brand name? But this stuff is not addictive, don't worry. Pleasant dreams."

He shoved a needle in my arm. It was a relief to feel some sensation beyond the ringing. Then my brain became unstuck again, soaring in the realms of speculation . . .

I know, I should have listened to Anat. The small still voice of my rationale. "Whatever you do, don't be an idiot, Joe." That impossible eleventh commandment. Take a step outside your womb and you're doomed. Finally co-opted. State Enfolds Dekel In Hairy Embrace. The Prisoner. Come back Patrick McGoohan, all is forgiven. *I am not a human being, I am a real number!* Whatever happens, I will not edit the *Village Journal*. But no one bothers to ask me why I've resigned. Just that repeated question in my dreams: "The Name, Joe Dekel, the Name!" Whose Name? Hermes Trismegistus? Jesus the Nazarene? Ole Man River?

I don't know what they've shot me full of. Scopolamine, the Truth Drug. Ve haff vayz of makink you talk, Englischer schweinhund! Hollywood sweat, down papier mâché walls. The gleaming world of the imagination. A pot-pourri of scattered images, Manhattan again. The West Bank. Jerusalem, the never-never land of holy dreams. Tick-tock, tick-tock. A time bomb is shackled to my ankle. How are the flighty fallen . . .

A different room. Or so it seems. The walls are closer, but invisible. The ringing is a little less insistent. A pool of light falls across a table. I seem sunk in a soft leather chair. A smaller circle of light illuminates the interrogator's face, like a Melies moon, with rubbery, moving orifices. I think that one's a mouth, those are eyes.

"Murray Waiskopf, Joe. The man you went to see prematurely."

Oh yes, I know *his* name.

"Why did you go there on the night before the day you were due to?"

Curiosity killed the cat. Miaow.

"What did he tell you before he died?"

Soneh Amcho. Just one last insult.

"Who killed him, Joe? Of course you know."

Dorothy Morgenthal, with her nunchaku sticks. Of course, everything would fit. Wheels within wheels. They had an argument about the Jewish Destiny. He tried to rape her. She clipped him on the kop. Well, that's how Raymond Chandler would write it.

"He slipped and fell on barasoap." The rhino mumble again.

"Very funny, Joe. Always the humorist. We try to help you and you play dead. Your country keeps you alive and you shit on it. The little boy who wants to kill his father. You want to sleep with your mother? It can be arranged. We can make wishes come true."

"Want my wife. Want my lawyer."

"They are both dead. The world has come to an end. You didn't want to co-operate and your worst fears have come true instead of your best wishes. The conspirators blew up the mosques. Nothing is left but dust and ashes. The Arabs attacked Jerusalem with a nuclear bomb, in retaliation. So we wiped out Mecca. The Americans and the Russians followed suit, in panic. Nothing is left but us, in this bunker, with ten years' supply of K-rations. Loof meat, baked beans, powdered milk, peach segments. From now unto everlasting. Holy Holy Holy is the Lord Blessed-He-Be, the Earth is filled with His Glory."

"Still want my lawyer."

Dark again, the cold returns. A parade of Rabbis floats by my bed. I recognized a number of Hassidic Sages of old: Rabbi Menachem, who when told about a foolish man who went up the Mount of Olives and blew the ram's horn for Redemption, threw open the windows of his house, looked at the world, and said: This is no Redemption. Then came Rabbi Zusya, who explained God's commandment to Abraham thus: Get thee out of thy country means get out of the darkness you have inflicted on yourself. Get out of thy birthplace, that means the darkness inflicted on you by your mother. And out of thy father's house, the darkness inflicted by your father. Only then can you find the land that I will show thee.

These Rabbis had the gift of the gab. They needed it, they had no battalions, no Chariot Tanks, no Lion Cub planes. Now we have the hardware, the software has deteriorated into rhinoceros drivel.

Did Dorothy Morgenthal kill Murray Waiskopf? Would Hillel kill Shamai? Does the left hand strangle the right hand? The right hand seems to have few compunctions. Till when will our aggressions turn solely outward?

Again the room of light pools. The Melies moon and me. This time there is more sensation in arms, legs, torso, face. The bandages have been removed, sometime, without my noticing. This room is no hallucination. But my head still feels as if twenty tons are pressing from each side. The ears, tolling again. The Melies moon has a document in the pool of table light. A hairy arm passes it to my free right hand.

"Is this the document you were expecting Murray Waiskopf to pass on to you? What were you supposed to do in return?"

Printed letters swim in front of my face. I try to focus, through the tonnage, filtering them through sluggish synapses: ANTI-SLANDER LEAGUE: MEDIA WATCH MEMORANDUM. SUBJECT: JOSEPH DEKEL.

As part of the ASL's monitoring of prejudice in the media, we shall from time to time address ourselves to matters beyond the press, television or radio. Our memoranda will also deal with books, plays or films that can lead to preoccupation due to their lack of balance in presenting issues of our concern.

The present case is a minor novel by an Israeli journalist strongly identified with left-wing causes, which has been offered for publication

in the United States. The book presents a shallow and distorted
view of Israeli actions and attitudes vis-a-vis the "Palestinian"
problem. It has enjoyed a moderate success in Israel, but falls into
the category of those works best left to internal debate and discussion,
free of the implications which would arise in terms of Arab and
PLO propaganda outside its native land . . .

I flicked pages. There was a photocopy review, from the
Jerusalem Post, and a long list of organizations that took me back
at least into the previous century: The Israeli New Left,
Ha'Olam Ha'zeh – New Force, Israel Socialist Organization –
Matspen, Ad Hoc Committee For Peace In Lebanon. A stream
of coffee shops floats across my brain.

"What on earth does this mean?"

The moon snatched the paper back. "Little brothers are
watching you, Dekel. Even paranoids have enemies. It's nothing
much, just routine. I'll let you have it in return for one small
favor."

"Aah?"

"The truth, Joe, no more lies. No more holding back, evasions, memory lapses. Why are so many people after you?"

"True love?"

The moon face smiled. Someone came round the other side
of me, from the blind rear, and clipped me on my already
overloaded head. The bells stopped ringing. I fell out of my nice
soft chair on to a cold hard floor. The moon stood over me,
silhouetted now against the light. A veritable eclipse.

"We treat you nice, you just continue spitting in the well from
which you drink. You're broken in three pieces, Dekel. We
stitched you up together. We can easily undo that work."

"Told you all the truth I know."

"It's your attitude, man. You don't respect authority. You don't
respect your own history. You don't respect your own birthright.
What do you respect, Dekel? Apart from our enemies?"

"Al'ays respect a well-made British TV series."

Somebody kicked me in the face. I blacked out, literally. Then the dreams returned, in waves. The grinding roar, of massive boilers. A sense of floating through a red zone of intimidation and fear. Rabbis, Priests, Ayatollahs, spinning coins before my eyes. Anat, desperately searching for me on the keyboard of my PC. Agent Kool, leaping from tree to tree. Ned Schatz and Dorothy Morgenthal, forcing Yassir Arafat's head down into a plateful of tshoolent and gefilte fish. The prattling mug of the self-proclaimed Avi Tsemach, who had seen Dr. Xavier with me in the Jordan Valley in some forgotten Reserve binge, in the Palaeozoic Age: "Don't worry, Joe, we can control the pain. You'll have strange dreams, but don't let them get you down. At the end of the road, we are returning you to reality." Thank you for nothing, schvantz face.

Sleep on, my little cutey, sleep.

Yes, mama, yes, dada. Mmmmmmmm . . . The night flight. The Prophet Mohammad, I'm told, flew in the dead of night from Mecca to Jerusalem, on his fabulous steed, the *buraq*. He stopped off, apparently, at the Wailing Wall, where the faithful stick their little notes requesting this and that, and currently the battleground between the Rabbinical authorities and a group of American religious women who want to pray there without formal sanction, a heinous sin indeed. Onward! Onward! Into the Valley of Death, now groaning with fully laden fruit trees, apples, oranges, grapes as large as potatoes, luscious berries of every kind. Signs abound throughout the Garden: "INSECTI-CIDES! DO NOT EAT! MINISTRY OF HEALTH AND PUBLIC SAFETY." Everywhere, we are protected. But still I can't love Big Brother. I beat my wings, flying up again towards the sun. But it screws its face up at me, and becomes the familiar Melies moon, the interrogator. The Name, Joe Dekel! The Name! I wrap my wings around me and curl up, back, as far as possible, into the womb. The Rapture! Suckled by amniotic fluids. The only secure promised land. An eternity appears to pass, of floating within the boiler roar. Then a shutting off, a quiet. A shaking, a swaddling in sheets. Is this it, the burial in the arid soil? My throat is parched. My eyes, ears, limbs ache. Is the influence wearing off? Pain. Internal kicks, bumps, shoves, contractions, yelling and screaming through the fleshy orifice . . . the slug emerging from the chrysalis . . . ?

"Wake up, Dekel, wake up! Reveille!"

A gross bass voice I seem to recognize. I struggle with my eyelids, winning a heroic victory. A room again, if slightly different. The walls are further away, the bed is just a normal one, no hospital smell or contraptions. Two windows, closed, shuttered with Venetian blinds. An air-conditioner roars. My sweat has dried on me. Tinnitus again.

A very large man sits on a small chair by the bed. He is skullcapped, clad in a prayer shawl, with the phylacteries wound round his arm and forehead. He holds out to me a familiar book, with a familiar feel, of other days, of better balms.

"It's Sunday morning, Joe. *Shakhris*. Let's pray together."

That harsh voice and grating breath of a big man who has no problem letting the environment know he's around. No mistaking his identity.

My compatriot enemy, Didi Schaeffer.

Be not afraid of sudden terror,
Nor of the storm that strikes the wicked.
Form your plot – it shall fail.
Lay your plan, it shall not prevail.
For God is with us.
Even to old age I will be the same.
In your gray hairs I will sustain you.
It is I who made you and I who will bear you,
I who will sustain and save you.

We speak the same words, but we mean complete opposites. I am talking about him, his plans for mutiny, his dreams of eternal domination over the "strangers" in our midst, his dreams of holy destruction and rebuilding on the ruins of war. He is talking about me, the dire conspiracies of the "leftist Mafia," the media traitors, the stabbers in the back of the renascent Jewish Nation.

He offered me his prayer shawl and phylacteries, as he only had one set with him, but I declined, doing my piece *à nature*. For twenty minutes we mumbled together, in this room in the middle of nowhere, lit by a dim bedside lamp. Talking to God. I, as usual, pursuing my monologue. My protagonist, with the zealous air of those who have a direct two-way line. If this is the norm I should complain to the celestial Telecom Company. I have not been connected. Didi Schaeffer, on the other hand, behaves as though God hands him down set orders, every briefing, like an efficient brigade colonel.

"Sit down, Joe Dekel, let's talk."

Is there a mirror in this room? Goddamnit! I can feel my stiff leg under the pajamas I appear to be wearing. My left arm is encased in plaster, on which no one has yet scrawled any messages. There is a thick dressing over my nose. My jaw feels as if I've gone twelve rounds with whoever is the current Muhammad Ali. My eyes still feel sore, as if my eyelids are concrete. But these aches and pains are cause for celebration. I am no longer floating on whatever tide of chemical guck my ex-Reserves colleague shot into my veins. I have come down to earth, and now I feel chained to it as if by a metal ball.

"Thirsty, Joe?" He opened a fridge which was humming away under the air-conditioning and extracted an orange-juice bottle, whose cap he flipped open with his teeth.

"I thought you were under arrest," I said, "for attacking that Arab village, not to speak of the Israel Defense Forces, with a flame-thrower. Killing innocent civilians. Not to speak of blowing me up."

"I didn't blow you up, Joe," he said, choosing a Pepsi Cola for himself, giving its cap the same treatment. "We don't kill Jews. The Sicariim think we should kill a few, just for discouragement, but we don't hold with that at all. We think we should kill our enemies, because they are our enemies. Our own people can be redeemed. You were not going to be harmed in the village. The Arabs petrol bombed our jeep." He looked at me very seriously and thoughtfully, as if figuring out whether I was, nevertheless, Yassir Arafat in disguise, with plastic surgery. "It was a stun grenade that got you, in your house. Your injuries came from the door hitting you. They probably clapped that cast on you for decoration, to make you feel it was a closer call." He shook his head and sighed. "You are right, I was arrested, but I escaped. People help us, in the services. Aren't you always complaining about that in your leftist columns? You, and all the other hacks: Silvie Keshet, Boaz Evron, Ziva Yariv, Amos Kenan, all the Arab-lovers. Preferential treatment for the Jewish terrorists. Arabs and Jews should be equal. But the good Jews in the police and the prison service know different. They know we are fighting for their future and for their children. They know what a PLO state would mean. In World War II, the British and Americans fought the Germans with their own methods. Mass bombing, massacres of civilians in cities. Dresden, Hamburg, Berlin. Now they scream and yell if we hit an Arab petrol bomber with a plastic bullet. The hypocrisy of the goyim, that's not new. Of our own kind, that's more galling. But we have to carry that burden. It's part of the task, Dekel. I am carrying you on my back."

"Let me off. This is my stop."

I have completely lost track of the situation. My leg, my arm, my face hurts. My ears tolling an alien mass. I need another shot of Avi Tsemach's potions, to take me back to my floating dreams. I try to muster my thoughts, stringing them together like chipped beads on a frayed string. If this is a secure medical facility I want to speak to someone in charge. It can't be the norm in such institutions for the person you are supposed to be being protected from to walk in and *daven shakhris* with you.

"You threatened my life, in Amiel."

"I didn't. I told you you were a dead man. Because you seemed to know about the spy."

"What spy?"

"Our spy, Dekel, don't play dumb. The one we have behind Pollard. The one your friend in the FBI is chasing with his *Alice in Wonderland* knives and forks."

"Forks and soap." I corrected him, "Forks and soap."

"I don't have a sense of humor, Dekel, all these jokes just pass me by. Don't tell me you don't know, Dekel. Don't play the wide-eyed virgin. Why is everybody so interested in you? You think it's about your stupid boycotted book? Believe me, nobody cares. I used to stop a dozen of those before breakfast. Murray did them on the assembly line. He sat by the phone and called all his old friends in the business. Why do you need this headache? he'd ask them. You publish anti-Israel material and

171

feel you're a great liberal these days. But deep in your heart you know it's wrong. Am I threatening to kill your wife and children? No, I'm just expressing my sorrow. You, who have contributed, fought, struggled with us over the years, for a just cause. And they know, the United States has enough anti-Semites waiting to pick up the pieces of our disunity. American Jews are not complicated people, like some fucked-up Israeli self-haters who love everyone except their own people. So you get frozen out. My heart bleeds. But who cares? Books, plays, films, 'art.' It's Hellenistic masturbation. Nothing good comes of fucking up the mind in the name of 'intellectual freedom.' But all that's small beer. Now Murray got a little too deep in things he should have left alone. It was his nature, to be a busybody, to pry and snoop and find things out. So somebody got to him and killed him, and there you were, on the scene. Naturally, some people thought he'd passed on the little gem to you, why, I can't really say. People are naturally suspicious, in the *Spy vee Spy* world. The Name, Joe, the Name of the mole our people have deep in the Administration. The spy who would put Pollard in the shade, and really fuck up our U.S. ties. You get my drift?"

This was not something I could really take on in my present parlous state. "Are you telling me the Israeli secret service killed Murray Waiskopf because he knew the name of their American spy?"

"I'm not saying it was them," said Didi Schaeffer, "though who can tell? They're after me too. But somebody killed Murray to stop him passing the Name on. He must have had some reason, mustn't he? A loyal friend like that. But there you were, catching his final words. What were they, Dekel?"

Soneh Amcho. "He said he didn't like my face." He looked at me, pursing his lips shrewdly, as if wondering whether to feel my neck again. "Come to think of it," I asked, a little late in the day, "how did you get in this building? Special favor again?" I began moving on the bed, edging my way across it to a door I had noticed on the other side of the room. Come to think of it too, as my mind cleared more and more along with the increasing pain from my limbs, I had only his word it was Sunday, Monday morning or any other morning. It might have been Tuesday, three a.m. for all I knew. I might have prayed without need. Still, it's all bonus points, totting up, in the final count. God doesn't speak, but boy, does He listen. And who else is listening here? The Name, Joe Dekel, the Name. The double act, a stale old trick, if one can accept Didi Schaeffer in the role of soft man. The mind boggles. But I have no Name to give them. Will anyone accept an honest lack of knowledge in this day and age?

"The door is open, Dekel. But where will you go?"

"Home." I edged off the bed. He didn't rise to stop me, just twiddled his thick fingers in his straggly beard.

"You'll find that a problem," he said quietly, with a trace of sadness in his voice.

"Home, to my wife, and unconceived child . . . Or did you kill her? Was that bastard lying to me?"

"Your wife and unconceived child are well. I'm not your real enemy."

"Ah? So who is?" I thought I'd better keep him chatting in his chair as I tottered, holding on to the wall, towards that receding door.

"Yourself," he said.

Touché, shmendrick. We'll have a return bout in the fall. Or was this still spring? I couldn't tell whether I'd been under Avi Tsemach's sweet dream-makers for six months or six hours. The door, mercifully, drew nearer. He watched me as if I was a cockroach crawling towards a baited trap. I crawled on. We cockroaches are stubborn, if short-sighted. The door was within reach. It was a solid affair, padded along the edges to shut out the light. I turned its handle. It opened.

Blinded by the brightness. A blast of hot air hit my face, virtually scorching my pajamas. I put my hand over my eyes.

The contrast was overwhelming. From icy air-conditioned dim-
ness to this. Midday in the Negev desert. Or Sinai, or God
knows where. Perhaps I'd been jetted to the Kalahari, to hide
among the Bushmen. I staggered, stumbled and fell on gravel
earth, tearing the skin of my uncast arm. The plaster scratched
along the rock. I crouched, on my one hand and knees. The heat
was like the inside of a furnace. I felt my skin was melting off.
Perhaps, like a snake, I'd emerge in something more comfortable, or at least a smidgen less painful. I tottered back on my
feet. Squinting through my fingers, then removing them, trying
to make out the landscape. It was the desert all right, more the
harsh red rockland of the Negev gorges than the empty dunes of
Sinai, now back in Egypt where they belonged. I staggered along
the gravel trail, which suddenly plunged, almost taking me with
it, into a canyon of majestic red ridges, fingers of rock thrusting
up towards the sky. Vague memories stirred. Was I in Egypt
after all, in the harsh, stern vistas of the Mount Sinai range? The
twisting path leading to the uncanny Saint Katherine Monastery,
abode of mad monks living among the neatly piled skulls and bones
of their predecessors, stretching back hundreds of years?

Moses, Moses! I steadied myself. No burning bush. At least
that's a relief. I fingered my tortured skin, to make sure I was not
still traveling along Avi Tsemach's chemical trails. But there was
no need to pinch myself, I ached and burned at every pore. I
looked back. The building I had come from was a stone hut set
under a rock ridge. Its whitewashed walls burning in the sun, its
shuttered windows, its door now closed. It seemed like some
mad hermit's retreat so beloved of the Levant's millennia of
madmen, prophets and seers. I slipped and staggered on down
the path. It twisted back into another ridge. Coarse bushes grew
along the trail and in the niches of the rock. If I were a
geographer-botanist, like my old friend Gingi Arse-Face, I
could locate myself by vegetation alone. But Gingi Arse-Face
was long gone into exile in Los Angeles and my knowledge of

flora and foliage was defunct. I moved on, between cacti. A strange sound seemed to be twirling in the wind, beyond my chiming ears. Except there was no wind, no trace of atmospheric movement, just the hammer and anvil of the wilderness.

Nevertheless, the sound increased, from a low wailing murmur, swelling to a chorus of song. I finally knew I had cracked at last, my brain boiled away and bubbled into steam. Angels were singing, somewhere around the curve of the ridge, high voices wafting on the heatwaves. I stopped, tripping around a rocky corner, coming out upon a blinding space, with the burning sun in my eyes. The voices were now louder and clearer, belting out words I could now make out, in English, whether I wished to believe what I was hearing or not:

> On wings of living light . . .
> At earliest dawn of day . . .
> Came down the angel bright . . .
> And rolled the stone away . . .

There seemed little hope for my sanity. I shielded my eyes and looked ahead. A fair-sized amphitheater stretched ahead of me, built of what appeared white stone. It was filled with people, men and women, the men in white shirts and black pants, the women plainly and chastely dressed for so sweltering an occasion, in somber and drab colors. An immense, plain black cross, made of material like the monolith from *2001*, towered above and behind the throng. The chorus issuing from a thousand throats:

> The strife is o'er, the battle done,
> Now is the victor's triumph won,
> Now be the song of praise begun – *Alleluia! Alleluia!*
> The powers of death have done their worst,
> But Christ their legions hath dispersed,

Let shouts of holy joy outburst – *Alleluiah! Alleluiah!*
The three sad days have quietly sped,
He rises glorious from the dead,
And glory to our risen head – *Alleluiah! Alleluiah!*

Something told me I was not in Kansas any more. The crowd
fell silent, as I staggered forward, the only disheveled figure in
that multitude of neatness, set in the middle of absolutely nowhere. A number of black-suited-and-tied young men with dark
glasses moved towards me from both sides of the amphitheatre,
but a tall, gangling figure mounted on a podium in the center of
the semicircle leaned forward and waved his hand. He was a
silvery-gray-haired, distinguished-looking figure, with the air of
a Real Estate Agent of the Year about him, his voice booming in
the craggy waste:

"Whoso delivereth himself unto Christ, that man shall be
Delivered. For the Lord hath said: I have seen the affliction of
my People, which are in Egypt, and I have heard their groaning,
and am come down to Deliver them. But they refused Moses,
and made up the Golden Calf, and offered sacrifice unto the
idol. Oh, ye stiff-necked and uncircumcized in hearts and ears,
ye do always resist the Holy Ghost. As your fathers did, so do ye.
Which of the Prophets have not your fathers persecuted? But
when Stephen, the Beloved Disciple of Christ spoke these
things unto the People, they cut to the heart, and they gnashed
on him with their teeth. But he said to them: Behold, I see the
heavens opened, and the Son of man standing on the right hand
of God! Do you see him, brothers and sisters?"

"*Alleluiah!*"

"Do you see the sinner come to repent?"

"*Alleluiah!*"

"Do you see the man who was blind, and now he can see?"

"Praise the Lord!"

"Come forward then, friend, and be Saved!"

176

This was not my idea at all. But I could hardly turn round and reverse up the winding gravel path, back to Didi Schaeffer's equally stern catechism. I was caught between the angels and the deep red desert. The gray-haired Real Estate Agent thrust his arms towards the sky.

"Let us all pray, for this poor sinner's Rebirth in Christ, Our Lord!" Leading the entire congregation in resumed ardor:

He brake the age bound chains of hell,
The bars from heaven's high portals fell,
Let hymns of praise His triumphs tell – *Alleluiah! Alleluiah!*

I now noticed that the black-clad clones advancing on me again were not unfamiliar. One face I definitely recognized, though without its crowning head bandage – the plug mug of the would-be assassin Dorothy Morgenthal had floored with her oriental weapon in Nederlander Schatz's apartment. The Man Who Had Not Brought the Ampules, now rectifying his mistake by brandishing towards me a rather mean-looking hypodermic needle, which he seemed intent on using.

"Hello, Jewboy," he said dryly. "Man, are you in the wrong place today."

Out of the mouths of babes and scoundrels. The congregation behind him sang:

From death's dread sting, thy servants free,
That we may live, and sing to thee . . .

Spong! the needle goes into my free arm, right through the pajama sleeve. The Bandaged Man's sweat is right up against my own.

"Fuck your ass, boy!"
"*Alleluiah! Alleluiah!*"
Somebody switched the sun off.

177

"Is he awake?"

"Should be."

"Are you awake, Mr. Dekel?"

To wake, perchance to dream . . . This room was not the previous closed hole. Large and airy, one wall seemed to consist of smoked glass looking out on to the clear sky. On another, above the camp bed I was laid out on, a portrait of my lost city, Jerusalem. It was one of those nineteenth-century Roberts lithographs, those majestic pastel-colored paintings which exaggerated all the facets of the city, so that one looked at lofty turrets and grandiose battlements across an awesome gorge, with a small group of robed and turbanned pilgrims prostrating themselves at the view.

The silver-haired man was seated on a simple armchair between myself, the lithograph and the big window. Didi Schaeffer sat beside him.

"Do you want a drink, Mr. Dekel?"

The Man With the Ampule handed me an orange juice. Oh, these alcohol-free zones. I sat up. The silver man waved a finger and Ampule Man headed for the door.

"My name is William Risegood," said the silver man. "You know Mr. Schaeffer. I have had your new cuts and bruises dressed while you slept. I am advised you are in reasonable shape."

That's because you're outside my body, not in it. I rose, my legs, amazingly, obeying my brain, and tottered over to the window. The vista of the craggy canyon stretched below me, magnificent red rock sculptures, gigantic slabs of layered rocks presiding over chasms whose ends I could not see. Bursts of

178

vegetation and beds of wild flowers breaking out in the oddest places. A genuinely primeval if picturesque air, as if Walt Disney dinosaurs might be expected to cross the frame at any moment.

"Zion National Park," said Risegood. "Aptly named, by the Mormon pioneers who found this place after their long wanderings. I find their beliefs, as I suppose you do, odd. But they had inspiration. That divine emotion, so often scorned. I have no doubt the spirit of God entered into them, and drove them towards their promised land. Expulsion and wandering, Mr. Dekel, that is at the center of our Judaic-Christian religions, the loss of Eden and the wages of sin. The Mormon founder, Joseph Smith, committed the sin of pride, in adding to the true scriptures, and his people wandered and suffered like the Hebrews out of Egypt. But your people have come home. That is a new dispensation no God-fearing person can ignore. God works in mysterious ways is an old cliché, but clichés are so often simply Truth. Only the Godless are afraid of simplicity. Don't you think so, Mr. Dekel?"

"Utah?" I said. "I'm in the United States?" I was being particularly slow, and certainly unfit for the cracker barrel.

"God's own country," he nodded. "Not, of course, to devalue your own. In many ways I envy you, Mr. Dekel. You have lived in Jerusalem all your life, I understand. You have the holiness of the City at your disposal every minute of the day. You are a religious man, I'm told. You pray every day, do you not: And to Jerusalem, thy City, return in mercy, and dwell therein as thou hast spoken. Rebuild it soon in our days as an everlasting building, and set up speedily within the Throne of David. Rebuild it soon, in our days, are those not the words, Mr. Dekel? *Be'karov be'yamenu.* Not in the unknown, far future. Not in the infinite never-never time. If you pray for it, surely you must desire it? Mr. Schaeffer and I agree on that. To think otherwise is to be illogical. And true religion is never that. Irrational, yes, but not illogical. But I am told you believe otherwise. You think

179

the infidels who have built their temples on the Holy Place should have their 'rights,' to retain their mosques, retarding the Lord's work. How is that?"

"The Lord's work is the Lord's work. He comes in mercy, not with sticks of dynamite."

"And the Lord's wrath, Dekel? And the hot breath of his nostrils? Before whom let all the inhabitants of the earth bow and fall? The God who smote Korah, and Babylon, and Pharaoh? He has the balance in the palm of His Hand. Good and Evil, Holiness and Sin. You cannot have the one without the other."

"Sin is a human construct. We define it ourselves. The scriptures are not a How To guidebook. Sowing death and destruction and war in Israel is not the worship of God in my book."

"Liberalism, a secular infestation. We allow it to paralyze us while our opponents laugh and follow their own iron path. Can you see a Moslem hesitating to unsheath the sword? I have been in Lebanon, Mr. Dekel. Where neither Christian nor Jew can afford the luxury of those sentiments. Wearing those blindfolds will not prevent war in the Land of Israel. All we can do is plan to ensure that when it comes, it comes on favorable terms to us, not to them. We're already in the midst of the Days of Tribulation, Dekel. Blinding yourself will not change that. God and Satan have already girded themselves for the Last Battle. The war in the Levant, the hostage taking, the so-called '*intifada*,' they are all clear signs. If we are Believers, we should read the Angel's writing on the wall."

"Put me down as a conscientious objector." I could not take this. My body and soul had absorbed enough punishment. Blown up at my front door, or stun grenaded, torn from my wife, editor and lawyer, shot full of guck by Young Dr. Xavier, interrogated by the Melies moon, and then apparently flown, if I could believe what I'd just been told, under the influence of their induced nightmares, half across the world, to be lambasted by a massed choir of Christian Fundamentalist lunatics, their crazy Reverend, and the hypodermic Ampule Man. Not to speak of the encounters with Didi Schaeffer. To whom I uselessly addressed myself: "You're mad to co-operate with these people. They want to rebuild your Temple only to destroy it with you inside. Then they'll fly off to heaven, leaving you charcoaled."

"They have their Faith, I have mine," he said. "Time will tell who's right. Who should I trust? Peres? Shamir? Rabin? Dr. Yeshayahu Leibovitz? You?"

What could I tell him? If I accused him of trusting "strangers," he could throw that right back in my face. Aha, the anti-racist, universal-brotherhood Dekel reveals his true face, just like ours! If you mix God with politics, you take the consequences. At the end of the day, we each make our choices. God whispers so many different things in our ears. So do I, too, hear Voices?

"What do you plan to do with me, then?" I had fallen back on the bed, as my legs had decided to call it a day.

"I don't know. What do you suggest?" he said, calmly, looking at me with an expression of pain. "Am I a murderer, some kind of mafioso, who has opponents tortured and killed? God is terrible enough in His wrath to those who have abandoned His path. There comes a culling of humankind. Does this sound chilling, even monstrous? But God unleashed the Flood, and spared only Noah and his family, of all the multitudes of Man. Or does God change, in accordance with the latest modern social theories? I am simply a servant, doing God's will as revealed to me by His Scriptures. Your Scriptures, too, are they not? Do you not pray yourself: Let all the inhabitants of the world perceive and know that unto thee every knee must bow, every tongue must swear . . . Let them all accept the yoke of thy kingdom, and do thou reign over them speedily, for ever and ever. And the Lord shall be king over all the earth, the Lord be One, his Name One."

The literal mind. It will bury all of us. Go fish for spiritual metaphor. I am too tired, too wracked with chemical withdrawal. He said: "You see, I have no mandate for hesitation. Let the sinners be consumed out of the earth, and let the wicked be no more; Psalm 104. You are an obstacle, Mr. Dekel. It appears by chance you might have come across a piece of information which people are prepared to kill for. But you keep claiming you haven't got that item. Personally, I'm inclined to agree. But people I have to work with are not convinced. Until the Lord's kingdom is established, I have to work with worldly substitutes. It's a give and take situation. So I'm afraid I shall have to give you over to people who are not, alas, men of God. I believe you just missed meeting my colleague at Ossining due to the intervention of the authorities. But in Zion National Park, no one can hear you scream."

I'll be damned, the bastard had a sense of humor after all. The Ampule Man and his friend marched back in the room, followed by a short, stumpy individual dressed in neatly pressed camouflage fatigues and a green beret, with beautifully shiny brown boots.

"Mr. Dekel, let me introduce Colonel Jonas O'Donnell."

The Colonel smiled at me, revealing two cherubic dimples. But I had only a snatched glimpse of them on his chubby cheeks before his companions moved forward and threw a hood over my head. I struggled, as far as was physically possible in the circumstances.

"The Colonel," the Reverend Risegood's voice continued smoothly, "interrogated prisoners in Vietnam, Honduras and El Salvador. He is a somewhat rough-cut diamond, I'm afraid."

"Schaeffer!" I said, desperation overtaking dignity, calling to him in Hebrew: "Are you just going to let this happen?"

"So perish all thine enemies, Israel," he replied ditto. So

much for ethnic brotherhood. I suppose it's all of a piece: Let the *goyim* do the dirty work.

"If I give you the name," I called out in English to The Colonel, "will you not torture and kill me?"

"What's the name?"

"Armando Callahan," I said, rapidly, "Third Assistant Secretary to the Commander of the Joint Chiefs of Staff, Washington, DC."

"What a funny man," he said amiably. "OK boys. Let's take this consignment to the yard."

Hustled out of the room, without any chance for a parting shot. The burning heat of the day wrapped my hood. My feet dragged on paving, then gravel. Wind hit my face. The churning rotors of a helicopter. Hauled, tripping, scrapped, into its maw. The Colonel shouted in my ear: "In Vietnam and Salvador we threw prisoners out of the choppers into the jungle and the sea. Where do you want to be thrown out, Dekel?"

Let me out at the corner of Ramban Street, kind sir.

The chopper took off into the sky.

183

A Song of Degrees:

I lift up mine eyes unto the hills, from whence cometh my help:
My help cometh from the Lord, who has made heaven and earth.
He will not suffer thy foot to be moved: he that keepeth thee will not
slumber . . .
The sun shall not smite thee by day, nor the moon by night;
The Lord shall preserve thee from all evil: he shall preserve thy
soul . . .

In my ill-fated book, I had myself kidnapped to Lebanon, and held there as part of a complex web of intrigue between rival secret service agents, who had both been army colleagues of mine in the long-past days of National Service. Even I found it difficult to make out that plot, much as I found it difficult to unravel the twists and turns of "reality." This one defied even more any semblance of order or reasonable causation.

Icarus. I flew up, up towards the sun, but it could hardly become any warmer. My wings had been left in the hold to be jettisoned as a chunk of ice over the ocean. I held tight to the metal bar of my seat, anticipating the Colonel's resumption of his old habits, but I seemed to have been left alone in my shell.

Does one's entire life flash before one's eyes? Hardly flashing, but languidly drooping. The vibrations of other flights, in other times, over landscapes of battle. The Sinai, route of ancestral wandering, dunes burnt and defiled by pulverized convoys of Egyptian tanks and trucks, June 1967 – the stench of the dead clogging the nostrils . . . or helicoptering over the West Bank, a year later, in search of elusive Fatah guerrillas in the brown

184

folds; the Biblical hills hiding Biblical penalties . . . we might have all have been blindfolded then, for all we could see, physically and morally, of the decline to come . . . snatching defeat from the jaws of victory, again and again . . . never penetrating below the surface of our wishful thoughts, our tight-assed desires . . . the entire nation blindfolded, waiting to be dropped in the sea . . . And my own life? Lurching from dream to dream, hauling my cocoon after me, long after the scheduled shedding of skin and butterfly rebirth . . . Anat's face, receding from me . . . a familiarity breeding, not indifference, but the inertia of ingrained habits . . . where's the romance, where's the anger? Now nothing but fear remains . . . Everyman's fear of physical violation, and an added, "genetic" flavor: the Jew in the hands of Torquemada, ethnic terror and holocaust funk, the sheep in the abattoir . . .

Make a joke, Dekel. Parachutists' jokes . . . we go up, we come down, we go up, we come down – boring! You'll have to do better than that . . . At the moment the entire idea is to remain suspended, as long as possible . . .

The Colonel's hand grasps my right shoulder. I tense, holding on to the seat bar with all the strength of my free hand. But his other hand simply whips the hood off my head, searing into my blanked-out eyes the harsh contours of the small chopper's interior, the pilot's overalled back, the winking controls, the open rectangle of the door right ahead of me, the jagged majesty of red ochre Grand Canyonesque terrain, a mile or two below. We are hugging the tops of massive knolls, cropped and sandpapered by time. No sign of the Ampule Man or his sidekick, who must have stayed behind with their vicar on earth. I braced every nerve end for the inevitable crisis, but the Colonel, beside me, smiled, like a squat cherub who had seen it all, and, letting go of my shoulder, leaned out of his seat and tossed my hood out of the open door, watching it whip away in the wind. He leaned back and shouted in my ear.

"Banzai, Joe Dekel! You're safe now! All your worries are over! Everything is under control!"

When I hear those words I reach for my final confession. I held on to my seat. But he continued grinning amiably at me, pointing out through the door towards the grandiose landscape, miraculously transformed into a tour guide, like those retired captains in the Israel Defense Forces who had all been in the first armored truck to crash the Old City of Jerusalem's Lion Gate in the Six-Day War and went on to make a good living from it.

"One hell of a view, ain't it, Joe?" My new friend, metaphorically jingling his bell. Shouting out landmarks, as the mesas, peaks and chasms ground by, shimmering on my battered retinas with strange hues and timbres, like the stargate sequence of Kubrick's *2001*. "Beartrap Canyon down there, Joe, ain't that something? And that peak is Langston Mountain. Up ahead is Job's Head, and Firepit Knoll. God's palette, I always think of it. These are God's natural art galleries. No wonder those boys back there have spectacular dreams of the Holy Land, when their expectations are formed by this, eh, Joe? Check it out: Zion Canyon, the Three Patriarchs, Angels Landing, the Virgin, the Sentinel, the Twin Brothers, the East Temple, the Altar of Sacrifice, the Streaked Wall . . ."

Miracles and wonders. I nodded, just to keep him in good humor. As the chopper banked, chattered on above the tableaux, he left me slumped on the seat and stood, one hand lightly holding on to the side of the open doorway, the tip of his boot literally over the side, in the posture of a veteran skydiver, for whom anything closer than 20,000 feet down is virtually ground level. Then he walked back and sat by me again. My hand tightening again on the bar.

"You don't have to worry Joe," he yelled, "the stories you've heard about me are exaggerated. I'm your rescuer, not your assassin. We're heading for a meeting with an old friend of yours."

AYE, HAVE A DREAM

Aye, old master Todt, in the Bergman movie, black cape, traveling chess set and all. I'm past being amazed any more. If Walt Disney walked through the door, with a bag of cashew nuts, I would simply grab a handful. The kindly face of the transformed Jew-hater twinkled at me like a Melies sun. My life has become a papier mâché backdrop. The tiny helicopter droned on. But, astonishingly, nevertheless, fatigue overtook both my pains and my terrors and I dropped off, into a limbo of semiconsciousness, suspended in a blob of wet putty, gibbering faces from outside gawking and gawping in at me as if I were a baboon in a cage. Time itself suspended, until, abruptly, the vise-like grip of the Colonel's hand on my shoulder: "Wake up, sailor! Dry land! We get off here. Journey's end, OK, Joe?"

My eyes opened again on the bright desert light, then focussed on an unexpected view: The flat asphalt of a runway, radar dishes revolving above long barrack huts, flat-roofed two- and three-story buildings. The clear contours of a military base. An ambulance was rushing up the asphalt towards the chopper's doorway. Two blue short-sleeved uniformed men reaching to carry me down under the slowing rotors. Another uniformed man swung open its doors. A stretcher was pulled forth and I was placed on it. Colonel O'Donnell helped lift me into the back of the ambulance and then climbed in beside me. The doors were slammed shut, the siren wailing familiarly above me: *Waah-waah! Waah-waah! Waah-waah!*

This is where I came in. Bathed in a red light, like some early, cheap, science fiction movie, The Man Definitely Without the X-Ray Eyes. A uniformed paramedic held my head. O'Donnell, eyes twinkling in the monochrome.

"Cheer up, Joe. What did I tell ya? You're safe now. See, I've brought you to your buddy."

"Hello, Joe. How are you feeling?"

Again, that inane question. I managed to turn my head half an inch, a movement that made me feel it was coming directly off

187

my body. The lanky, curled-up man still wearing his old tatty raincoat. But that earnest face, that innocent look. My true nemesis, the voice that answers me from the hills. Not the Lord, after all, but my own personal, undetachable G-man: Agent Oral Kool.

"Sorry, Joe. We lost control there for a while. But normal business is resuming. We're going to look after you from now on."

Who the hell is we? But I've finally lost my voice completely. Not even the dull old croak.

"Your wife will be flying over, Joe, on the first available flight. I notified her as soon as we were radioed O'Donnell had you in hand."

"I told you, Joe, I don't really hate Jews," said the Colonel, adding, inevitably, "why, some of my best friends are Jews."

"Colonel O'Donnell is a CIA operative, Joe," said Kool. "He has been working for the government in the Church of Christ the Living. He has been keeping the Reverend Risegood under surveillance for some time."

"I did drop people into the sea from helicopters," the Colonel explained, "but that was a long time ago. We use new methods now."

A kinder, gentler America. I, too, watched TV in the days when I was still in one piece, body and soul, not a shattered wreck heading for the knackers. Drill? Spanner? Scalpel? Take him away, gentlemen, this man is beyond all help.

"I've spoken to your Chief of Security too," Kool volunteered, as if to soothe my savage brow. "Several further arrests have been made among your Mr. Schaeffer's colleagues. Serious inquiries are underway inside the Israeli security services. Certain heads are expected to roll."

Everyone is being so eloquent, but my powers of articulation have been quashed. The smooth voices, blending with the ambulance siren. *Waah-waah! Waah-waah!* My innermost self, keening, my id shrieking. Pain overwhelms all. Except fatigue, which wins the battle again. Down, down, I plunge, into the canyon. The ancient words of Job are written on the walls of the bottomless pit:

Why died I not from the womb? Why did I not give up the ghost when I came out of the belly? Why did the knees prevent me? Or why the breasts that I should suck? . . . Then had I been at rest . . .

Does Faith survive, in absurdity?
Where else can Faith survive?

Phoenix, Arizona. Out of the ashes, Sun City, the long, straight boulevards, the sprawling suburbs, the mountain horizons. Parks, universities and gardens. Over it all, the deep blue sky of spring.

Recuperation. That's the name of the game. Lying in a proper hospital bed and watching the green sway of a tree outside. No papier mâché backdrop to fool me, but the genuine serene article. A large American black nurse named Charlene lifts me with one arm to smoothe the ruffled sheets, then drops me back again.

My wife arrives. A tense moment. How does she react to my folly? Charlene leaves us, for a half-hour of unspoken empathy/ recrimination, hands held, fingers discoursing. I know, I almost got myself killed. I am a dunce, a clod, a schlemiel. I endangered our unconceived child. The panic of separation. The dread of hostage limbo, the endless pangs of uncertainty. Not to speak of the recurring tinnitus, the stubborn legacy of the grenade . . .

At least they had chopped off my plaster. As Didi Schaeffer had reckoned, it was a ruse to slow me down and panic me, there was nothing wrong with my arm, except bruises and the pins and needles of enforced rigor. I had no reason to be an invalid. They moved me to a private room in an annex with an extra bed for my wife so we could restore full, if contraceptive, contact. Hesitation still remains . . .

Believe it or not, the days of Passover. My heritage catching up with me. Throughout my country and among my scattered brethren, people are eating cold hard-boiled eggs, bitter herbs and unleavened bread, reading the traditional passages from the Passover Haggadah: Slaves were we to Pharaoh in Egypt, and

190

the Lord Our God took us out of there with a strong hand and an outstretched arm . . . And the Egyptians ill-treated us, humiliated us and imposed a hard bondage on us . . . does this not ring a bell?

Anat brought with her the gunpowder smell of home news, the latest tales of Semitic woe: Palestinian Arabs still being shot daily, in demonstrations and protests. Four were killed in a village near Bethlehem, where Border Police had opened fire indiscriminately and had to be held back by regular army units. As the army medics tended to the Arab wounded, the Border Policemen shouted insults at them, culminating in their worst epithet: "leftists!" The police units, apparently, had been entering the village daily, calling out through their loudspeakers: "Bring out your wives so we can fuck 'em." The villagers finally responded to this provocation with predictable results. My country, my people. As strange a mélange as ever. On the other hand, the world news: At Hillsborough football stadium in England, over ninety fans were crushed to death accidentally in an overcrowded ground. We take about six months to kill that number, so perhaps not all is lost. In China, students have taken to the streets of Peking to demand democracy. In Afghanistan, war continues. As in doomed Beirut, of course.

We ebb and flow, between advance and retreat, between creation and destruction. At least we are not requiring the Palestinians to build Pithom and Ramses, merely the settlement of Amiel. Whose affliction, whose labor and whose oppression does the Lord God hear now? But of course, if He's a mere tribal deity, why should He give a fuck for anyone else? The Lord will give strength to His people, the Lord will bless His people with peace . . .

Anat and I perform the Passover show *à deux*, with wine and ingredients borrowed by Agent Oral Kool from the bemused and curious Phoenix Jewish community. Of course officially I do not exist. Colonel O'Donnell, having completed his in-flight

191

interrogation, had dumped me over some remote God-forsaken part of Zion, from several thousand feet, so retaining his reputation as an inveterate Jew-hater and cold-blooded assassin. America is full of these odd stragglers of *semper non fidelis* and botched glory. Oliver Norths of the world unite, you have nothing to lose but your stains. Officially, back in the homeland, I am on a long convalescence from the bomb outrage which has allegedly been attributed to the *sicariim*. Nahum Lauterman wrote a stinging editorial: How long are our guardians of Law and Order going to drag their feet on this menace? The increasing threat of right-wing terrorism, with its open challenge to the state. Privately he sent a message with Anat: I'll play it any way you want, Joe. Do you want me to blow these bastards out of the ballpark? Or will we let them show they mean business? Putting the decision to expose the lax Security Services in my hands. Oh boy. More vacancies for heroes. Big deal! But what can I do? Wracked by so many scandals, what would the impact of this one be on SHABAK? What was in fact happening in that shut-off world, as Didi Schaeffer put it, of *Spy vee Spy*? What impact could disclosure have, and what in fact could I disclose?

Agent Kool drove Anat and myself, on a brief outing from our secure house among army wives and children and dogs in the Papago Army Camp, a mile or two down the road to the Phoenix Desert Botanical Gardens, to show us, among the rows of Joshua trees, saguaros, yuccas, ocotillos, familiar prickly pears and unfamiliar pereskias, a bizarre plant looking like nothing on earth, all twisted pipes and evil thorns.

"*Voila*," he said, like a proud father, "the Boojum Tree. A rare sample. Named after you-know-who. I tried to give you as many hints as I was able. Apologies for being obscure."

Cacti. They suck in and hold their water, and then defend it against all comers. No wonder we named ourselves after one of these floral sons of bitches, the Sabras of the Prickly Pear . . .

But we are certainly not out of the briar patch yet, my saga no nearer to resolution, as I trail loose ends around the world. Who killed who, why and how? Some of the missing jigsaw pieces can be vaguely glimpsed, through the fog, but so many gaping holes. So the Snark was a Boojum. I pursued Jewish zealots and found Christians, who were seeking their own displaced Zion, to be saved. The Reverend Risegood's majestic vision of Jerusalem had no place in it for ordinary people's purrs and squabbles, for real desires and needs . . .

"All right," I said to Oral Kool, under the Boojum Tree, "unobscure it all for me. Why not take it from the top and work down to the bottom. Here I am at square one: OK, I, Joe Dekel, hackus anonymous, innocently snoozing through the Palestinian-Jewish Peace Conference in New York University, when an undersized runt, with a press tag for, what was it, the *New Jersey Jewish Courier*, tells me he's my Silencer and invites me out into the street. It's February. Snow, ice and slush. My bones are dying inside me. The PLO and Dorothy Morgenthal are squabbling over Roger Rabbit in Grandma's Cafe. The boy sells me some damnfool line about my book being blacklisted and then vanishes into the IRT subway. Discuss and explain."

He sighed. Definitely infected by our Levantine mores. Scratching his head, gazing from the Boojum Tree to Anat and me and back. Looking out over the sprawling city of pioneers turned urban glut. Individualists in serried rows, stretching to the horizon.

"All right. God knows you've earned the Right to Know, Joe. As far as it can be pieced together. There still are a lot of unknowns."

"The Unknown is my daily bread."

"But will our trespasses be forgiven?" He seemed to lose himself, in a coil of his own thoughts, then straightened out and walked us slowly past the cacti.

"You have to begin," he said, "by looking at it from the other end: Nederlander Schatz, the hundred-year-old Jew. Here's a man who has worked all his life for the Zionist Cause. He loves Israel, but is unhappy about the direction that state is now going. This man, as he's had all his life, has his finger on the pulse. He's been worried for years about the political bias of his own creation, the Anti-Slander League. He feels it is too tied in with one side of the American political spectrum, what we may call the New Revivalist Right. He keeps an eye, particularly, on extreme mavericks, such as Murray Waiskopf, an old colleague. Waiskopf has become, Schatz considers, dangerously involved with Evangelical Fundamentalist Christians. There is a split, Schatz knows, between American Jewish leaders and the Israeli leadership over this alliance, which was cemented during the Lebanon crisis, in Israel's involvement with the Lebanese Christians. Waiskopf, Schatz discovers, has become a conduit between Israeli secret servicemen and the Reverend Risegood, whose visions of the future in the Holy Land are particularly alarming. Even more disturbing, Waiskopf has independent contacts with elements of the extremist right-wing Jewish settlers in the West Bank, Gaza and Golan Heights, notably those almost openly speaking about rebellion against the State of Israel in the event of what they consider a sell-out to the Arabs, a settlement of 'land for peace.' Schatz detects an ambivalence within the Israeli establishment about these heavily armed fanatics. He knows influential figures in the current Israeli cabinet encourage, fund and supply them. So far, unobscure, Joe?"

"Clear as mud."

"It gets a little clearer. As you know, the Israeli government is a schizoid compound, and the secret services can't fail to reflect that. Schatz smells disaster coming, deeper schisms, private armies, the Algerian OAS scenario with no De Gaulle at its end. Endemic confusion, putschist tendencies, provocative terrorism. The mosques on the Temple Mount are an obvious target. Schatz decides to put a firecracker under Murray Waiskopf by leaking the story of his dubious alliances."

"Using me."

"Exactly. He might try the American press, but there are tensions he considers dangerous. Anti-Jewish elements would exploit the story. The friendly press might bury it none the less. But, Schatz thinks, what better than to find an Israeli journalist who has not only a political and professional but also a personal motive to dig further into Waiskopf's deals. He searches his files and contacts for a connection. He has his friends trawl through Murray Waiskopf's Israeli blacklist dossiers, not a big problem for the wily old fox, with his fingers in so many pies. This produces a jackpot: A successfully suppressed manuscript of a thriller by an unknown Israeli journalist – you. Even more convenient, he sees your name in a list of participants at the current Peace Conference in the City. It was Nederlander Schatz, Joe, who elected you as the patsy."

"Where can I find him and kill him?"

"Join the queue. But he is armor-plated. He may have seen a hundred birthdays but he wants to see the hundred and first. It's amazing, how people cling on. But you have to understand, he was not being that ruthless, in his own eyes. He was not to know that, (a) Dorothy Morgenthal would lead you to him by a coincidental route, and (b) how things were going to turn out."

"And the fake Didi Schaeffer?"

"A great-great-grandson. His real name is Martin Schatz. The old man whisked him away with him to the Virgin Islands when the trick turned lethal. He's still out there, as far as I know, wooing Mafia molls on the beach. Charming them with smiles and soap."

"Go on." So I am a cog in a derailed wheel. What else is new? Tweak on Gepetto, somebody's nose must be growing.

"The plan was straightforward: Young Martin Schatz, using the name of Murray's ex-assistant, since departed to Israel and so hopefully unavailable to screw things up, set up a rendezvous in an office drop which Murray often used to store his files. The building on 29th Street. There he would hand you your own file, as bait, and documentation on Murray's alliances with the Reverend Risegood and the West Bank Jewish network. But there was a triple hitch. (a) Murray Waiskopf had been informed that old Schatz had got at his files, that you, Joseph Dekel, were to have his secrets leaked to you, and, by checking with the Super of the safe house, who had been tricked by Schatz into supplying a key, the time and place of the handover. That much we know from Flynn, at NYPD. (b) Murray shared another vital secret with his friends in the Church of Christ the Living – something Nederlander Schatz had no inkling of, which might have made him abort the whole exercise, had he known the tangle he was causing. Because Murray Waiskopf and Risegood had a gold nugget of information. They knew something that gave them power over the Israeli secret services who might otherwise wipe them off the map."

"Don't tell me. It's on the tip of my tongue."

"I sincerely hope not, for your sake. Because this is what your kidnappers and nemeses all think that Murray told you with his last breath: The identity of the deep cover Israeli spy in this country who stayed in place after Pollard was flushed. The spy who doesn't exist, the one who, if and when revealed, would really put a spanner in Israeli-U.S. relations. And that, of course, was where I came in. Hopping my assigned route from Pollard to the other spy, which, I can't tell you by what route, led us, to our surprise, to the Reverend Risegood, and from him to Murray Waiskopf, and to you."

Charmed, I'm sure, to be at the end of this daisy chain. But there was still item (c). "All right, G-man. Sock it to me. I'm punch-drunk. Give me the works. What do I care?"

"(c) You got impatient, and went to the address ahead of time. Turning up the night that Murray Waiskopf was setting a bug to catch Young Schatz, except that someone else was waiting for him. Flynn found the bug under the table. Waiskopf still had the receiver on him. His killer was not interested in that. The killer, his operators, had got the whole thing garbled: They'd got wind of an assignation between Didi Schaeffer, whom they knew as Murray's sidekick and connection to the West Bank network, and an Israeli leftist journalist attending a Peace Conference with the PLO. It's the devil, you see, having an alliance between people of opposing religious creeds. You know what I mean? Between the Snark and the Boojum. We can't tell what happened inside Risegood's head but we can guess at age-old prejudices: A man like Risegood would be brought up to believe all Jews were treacherous anyway. No great shock to think that Waiskopf had betrayed him and his main secret – the name of that spy, which kept the Israelis in line: his insurance against the kind of policy switch which made Israel dump the Christians in Lebanon."

This man was not making me feel very secure. But he was in his element, enjoying the exegesis, waving at the Boojums and Saguaros. Lethally sharp prickles at every turn.

"You see the pattern now? A tragedy of errors. Risegood's killer follows Waiskopf to the assignation place. He smashes his head in and leaves him to bleed to death in the night. Only you turned up, the bad penny. If you'd been five minutes earlier, you might have been killed too, I expect. In many ways you're a lucky son of a bitch, Joe Dekel. One might call you the true Almost Man."

My epitaph. Well, at least it was obviously not Dorothy Morgenthal who bopped Waiskopf with her little oriental thrill-sticks. A relief to find not all my nightmares are true. Only ninety-nine percent.

"So who's the killer?"

"We're not sure about that. Your bandaged man is the obvious suspect. But we lack that evidence. It'll be one of those forensic cases. Bits of hair, fluff, wool. But you can see the problem, Joe? Once you turned up at Waiskopf's last moments, that only strengthened Risegood's fears. Did he reveal that crucial name to you in his dying breath? Did you pass on the name to Schatz? When Dorothy Morgenthal took you to see the old man, all their suspicions were confirmed. They tried to kill you both, and when that failed, and Schatz skedaddled, they grabbed you. But we arranged for O'Donnell, with whom we were already working, to keep out of the way so you could be recovered. We let the kidnappers pull bail, to give them enough rope. You can piece together the rest. I kept tabs on you, as well as I could. They were still after you, but there was also Didi Schaeffer, who was on the spot too. He could soon prove he was in the clear, as he was in the West Bank at the time. They realized an impostor had used his name. Nevertheless, he had to prove his colors. Thus, the attack on the village, a misplaced act which put the wind up his secret service allies. The mosque plot could not be kept under wraps for long. SHABAK and Mossad could grill you any time. So a major operation was mounted to lift you out – stun grenade, a waiting fake ambulance. An unwise use of their internal network. Risegood was not keen, but his backer panicked: The Texan moneybags, E. Dermott King. The whiff of espionage involvement made him leery. Who wants to alienate the CIA? Even the Federal Bureau can worry men like that these days. He insisted that all the leaks should be plugged. You should be flattered, Joe. So much attention, and all to find out if you knew that Name, and who you'd passed it on to, for instance your editor friend? 'O what a tangled web we weave, when first we practice to deceive . . .' Not Lewis Carroll that. Shakespeare. So here we are, and you still say No, Joe. Under the Boojum Tree, Joseph, you swear you haven't seen the Snark. I know you well enough now to believe you, myself. After all, why should Murray Waiskopf tell you, a sworn enemy and traitor in his eyes, that final, crucial secret? Except that, when a man is dying, who knows? Eh? Whadaya say, Joe? Give us a break? So what were Murray Waiskopf's last words?"

Et tu, Brute? *Soneh Amcho*. Hater of your people. We keep coming back to that. The pits we dig for ourselves out of love, let alone from hate. I can't deliver to either my deliverers or my persecutors the Holy Grail, the Philosopher's Stone, the *summum bonum*, the *heiros gamos*, the *imago dei*. The Man With No Name, that's me. Only my own, that poor personal patrimony I drag around chained to my face. *Dekel*. Meaning a palm tree. I sway in the breeze while monkeys scurry in my fronds, searching for coconuts. My namesake, Joseph, had a technicolor dreamcoat, which I have never had. Dreaming as I do in plain mufti . . .

It is better to trust in the Lord than to put confidence in man . . . Anat and I drain the fourth cup of Passover. Our little two-headed ceremony is almost over, apart from the traditional old songs . . . Who knows One? I know One, One is Our God who is in the Heavens and on the Earth. Who knows Two? I know Two, Two are Joe and Anat who are stuck between the spheres . . . Who knows Three? I know Three, the Unholy Trinity of the Reverend Risegood, Didi Schaeffer and E. Dermott King . . . Who knows Four? I know Four, my four "benefactors," Agent Kool, Detective Flynn, Dorothy Morgenthal and the Hundred-Year-Old Jew . . .

Anat's response, in our hideaway, to the lethal web drawn by Kool: "Where will it end, Joe? We have to pull back, to find our sense of balance again . . . I refuse to become the cliché: The weeping widow standing over the grave. I want us to do what has to be done to remain alive. If it means leaving the country, let's leave."

Our fathers, after all, were refugees. Why should we be any

luckier? But if I am in someone's sights, it could be anywhere. Flights to Mars are not yet being booked. At the end of the day, we are all trapped. As the last verse of the last Passover song recounts:

> *And then came the Lord Blessed Be He,*
> *And slew the Angel of Death,*
> *Who had slain the butcher*
> *Who had slaughtered the ox*
> *That had drunk the water*
> *Which had quenched the fire*
> *That had burnt the stick*
> *That had eaten the dog*
> *That had bitten the cat*
> *Which had eaten the lamb*
> *Which father had bought*
> *For two sous.*
> *One lamb. One lamb.*

Being a lamb is no picnic.

I could be no further help to Agent Kool, who knew I could not stay dead for ever. He just asked for a little time so my rescuer, Colonel O'Donnell, could wrap up his affairs re Rise-good and safely return to his CIA fold. I Was a Dead Man For the FBI. So Anat and I flew out, from Phoenix to New York, on false names. Mr. and Mrs. Cohen. Originality run riot. Dorothy Morgenthal picked us up at the airport and drove us to her apartment on Broadway. Consumed with guilt: "I am really furious, Joe, about Ned Schatz using me. I thought, when he phoned me at the start of the Conference, he was just being his usual prying self. I didn't know what scam he was setting up. If I had known . . ." I could see the nunchaku sticks coming out of the closet. "I finally got through to Ned, in the Virgin Islands," she added. "He swears blind he would never have made his moves if he had known Murray Waiskopf's 'other secret.' 'I won't help the Israelis dig their own grave.' he said to me, 'I'd just hand them back the shovel.' Do I believe him? Probably, yes. I don't think he would have exposed that. Ned wouldn't overturn that applecart."

"Would you?"

"If I knew the name of an Israeli spying on the United States? The bottom line of dual loyalties, Joe. Eating Arafat's breakfast, yes. The espionage game, no. That way lies madness. Look at that poor bastard Pollard. Sold down the river by the people he lost his liberty for. A soured dream of Zion. And Waiskopf too, I feel so sorry for the poor bastard. What do they hope to gain, with all their conspiracies? Security? For whom? They'll tip us all in the pit. Sometimes I just despair . . ."

One lamb. One lamb. All we would like to do is graze. But Dorothy had found her second wind, after her trauma in the village near Ramallah, and was stubbornly trying to get her West Bank human rights findings published, as a book. She was working on the text, editing, organizing. No patience with my tale of blacklists. "Times are changing, Joe. It's a dying gasp. There are more and more cracks." Aye, I have fallen through them all . . .

What paths to escape, then, lie open? Anat entices me to her museums. The Modern Art. The Frick. The Guggenheim. The Metropolitan. Dragging me through the European Sculpture, the Egyptian, Greek and Roman crafts, the labyrinthine galleries of Old Masters, Spanish, Dutch, French. My favorite Vincent Van Gogh Cypresses, painted exactly one hundred years ago. People who tried to see through nature and get to the other side. I appreciate, I yearn, I sympathize, but how is this going to save my skin?

"It won't hurt you Joe, to get a little aesthetic pleasure into your life. It might just soothe, that tiny bit that makes the difference."

I don't know. The old saw, how can we sue our own government, for incompetence, malpractice, misfeasance, for making one's life a misery and reckless endangerment of life and limb? Finally, in desperation, having brought you to the brink of death, they offer you, like Mafia chiefs, their protection, a massive armed guard, burglar alarms, quintuple locks. One doesn't know whether to laugh hysterically or cry. Cezanne: The Card Players. Everything subsumed in their enclosed world. Maybe I can crawl into the painting, hide in the right-hand player's long blue cape. After all, there are four pipes on the wall, and only three pipeless players. The vacancy for Dekel has been signaled in. But I lack Anat's talent to find escape in beauty even at the ugliest points. My escape has always been into the chaos of television and computer games, the Babel of electronic mind rot.

The Rabbi of Apt once said to God: Lord, I know I have no merit and no virtue to set me among the righteous in paradise after my death, but if you are going to put me in hell among the wicked, please take note I can't get on with them. So please take all the evil-doers out of hell, so that you can put me there.

"There's not much point in staying here," says Anat. Despite Art. The aesthetic balm.

Blend in with Manhattan's eccentric millions. Put my hattie back on and no one will notice. Eat bagels and ogle Van Gogh until the forces of vengeance close in. Or should we fly out to the Virgin Islands to join the Hundred-Year-Old Jew and his loyal great-great-great grandson? One encounter was enough. Not for me, the sinewy palms of exile, the Mafia dollies' coconuts . . .

One lamb. One lamb. Better your own mudhole than another's. I am a sedentary, not a wandering Jew. At least if they bury me I need go no further. They got me. One more Yid, despite it all, goes home.

"Let's organize my resurrection," I suggested to Anat.

"I was hoping you'd say that."

My beloved, the lily among thorns. We gaze into each other's tired eyes. We've grown accustomed to each other's face. Over eighteen years, we've ignored the lines, the graying hairs, the bags under the eyelids filling with all the artefacts and flotsam of ebbing and flowing times, the aftermath of post Six-Day War hopes for change, the stagnating occupation and its slow fuse of rebellion and resistance, the Yom Kippur War, Lebanon, all the shocks and traumas and terrors that seeped into our blood cells and pores. And now, the personal attack, the hand on our jugular, as the public breaks into the private, blasting open the door of our violated hide-out.

"You'll be in as much danger as me, honey, when the bastards who think I'm dead find out."

"You amaze me, Joseph. So what else is new?"

Loose ends flapping, the sword still to our neck, we telephone the national airline's office. I book a ticket, in my own name. The hell with them. I still yam what I yam. Luckily, Anat had brought my passport with her from the Holy Land and Agent Kool, waving his magic wand, had returned it to me with an appropriate exit and entry stamp. How he had got the former I didn't want to ask. "Just take it and go in good health." He tendered his goodbyes at the Bagel Nosh. A hot chocolate and a schmeer. "Don't panic. We're still ahead of the game. O'Donnell is clear. Just take care, hey? And don't go after Jabberwocks."

Who, me? I will just tend my garden. And so the hater-lover returns to his womb: The gruff stewards, the execrable advertising videos in my home tongue, the recordings of last month's news, the unseeable movie, the non-stop homeland tunes, on courtesy earphones, the emergency drill, the vomit bag. The echoes of usual airport security questions: Did you pack your own bags? Did anyone give you a gift to take home? Is this all your own baggage?

Metaphysically, phenomenologically, these questions cannot

be answered. But I said: "Yes. No. Yes."

Holding hands, across the Atlantic, Europe, the Mediterranean. We landed. We stood in line with our passports. The sunken policeman in the booth flicked through our documents and asked me:

"What about the Army Exit permit?"

"It fell out and got lost."

He gave me a jaundiced stare and rifled through the list at his elbow of the damned and the banned. No Joe or Anat Dekel. Nobody wants to arrest us. The state waves us wearily into the promised land. We have Nothing to Declare. No one waiting for us in the crowd of eager citizens searching for their loved ones. Our fate gripped in our own hands. We took a service taxi to Jerusalem, the coastal plain, the Latrun Road, the barely visible rolling hills in the swish of passing traffic. And then, in the darkness, the magic lights rising, the massed dots of the new housing estates on the hills heralding the older Jerusalem, the tail end of the Jaffa Road disappearing in a welter of modern traffic junctions. The ascent to Zion, like an entry into any medium-sized town around the globe, but with that special frisson that, despite all obstacles, shivers the timbers, goose-pimples the skin . . .

And nevertheless, and despite it all . . . Is there that genetic factor of history? No, don't tell me about dreams, chimeras, shadow-boxes, castles-in-the-sky, promised lands. At least here I can afford the rent. Barely. And even if the grocery stores close early . . . So what? So I live here. Is this a cause for heroic postures, pride, shame, guilt, despair, the peacock's strut or penitent's slouch?

Our home. The taxi took us round the back streets directly to our door, which, as Anat had told me, had been mended. The mail, reassuringly, clogged the mailbox. We opened the door cautiously. It did not blow up. We stepped inside our familiar walls. Everything seemed in place. The PC and the TV and the video. Nothing was missing. The fridge was humming on empty. *Alles in Ordnung.* We dared to breathe our sighs of relief.

The phone rang. I went and picked it up.

"Welcome home, Joseph Dekel."

The inescapable. Those brash, blaring tones.

The familiar voice of Didi Schaeffer.

4

MOUNT, ZION

NAHUM LAUTERMAN ASCENDED to the Capital, risking his new Peugeot 405 in the dodgem course from Tel Aviv. Meeting us at our traditional watering hole, The Hut, over three Bloody Marys. A stone's throw from the hot bustle of main street, Jaffa Road, several stones' throw from the Old City's continuing defiance and rebellion. Yuppies like us sit and ramble away their complaints and frustrations. My friends – I still have a handful of those – have already ambled over to tell me they're glad I've survived. The antlerless sculptor Kadishzon, still festooned with divorce lawyers, kissed me on the head as if he were Snow White saying goodbye to the seven dwarves. Dina B—, who edits a youth magazine, shed a tear and held Anat's hand. The civil rights lawyer Adam shook my hand firmly. The troubled glint in the eye expressing the hope that the *sicariim* do not yet have their number. We might be in the Third World, but if our enemies target every bleeding heart we may still have our own pyramid of skulls. Joining the Palestinian Arabs in the cemetery. In Life And Death They Were Not Separated.

"I'm ready to do it," Lauterman said. Shaking his head at Anat and myself, "I'm ready to go for broke. Publish and be damned. Now you're back we can try and piece the jigsaw together. I've had enough of being used as a doormat. The time has come for a little self-determination, in practice, not just declarations. Freedom of the press."

"I've heard of it, Nahum."

"As our allies say, let's kick some ass."

It's an attractive proposition. One's own backside is sore enough. Not to speak of the rest of the body, and my ears, which

209

are still ringing with the concussion of the stun grenade, as well as my Enemy's diatribe. That blaring voice on the phone just as we entered our sanctuary: "In a good hour, Joseph, and with the help of the Lord."

"The Lord is helping some strange people nowadays."

"Both of us can say that with sincerity, Joseph. We are birds of a feather. You hate me saying that, don't you? But we are both driven by Faith. Two Jews who pray together are tied by a bond which no one in the outside world can understand. We are connected, by a thread, to a source of ultimate energy that controls the cosmos. But where does it lead us?"

"To jail," I said. I should have put down the phone, but I didn't. We are an argumentative people. "Do not pass Go. Presidential clemency is assured. How many people has God told you to kill this week?"

"No one, Joseph. Why do you persist in this calumny? Self-defense, every human being's right. You want to evict me to make way for Arafat. I don't pretend to understand your reasons. You say that I am stealing land we know is our own. You claim that you can make peace with Ishmael. How do you expect me to react?"

"As the sweet soul you are, Schaeffer. What is the purpose of this call?"

"To congratulate you on your miraculous escape from bondage, Joseph, and just to let you know we know where you are. To let you know we have friends in influential places who tell us when people come and go. To welcome you back to your homeland, your birthright. After all, you could have remained in Arizona, teaching Hebrew to sons of émigrés. But you are tied to your country, Joseph. I do not despair of you yet."

"I know you are a great patriot, Schaeffer. That's why you work with Christians whose credo is the final conversion of the Jews. People who'll help you build the Third Temple so that it can be destroyed. A few sticks of dynamite to blow up the mosques to provoke the Holy War, the war of Gog and Magog, which we are supposed to lose, so that they can have The Second Coming and The Rapture. That's brilliant thinking, habibi."

"I don't care about the Christians and their raptures." I should have known better than to tank him up. It's my big mouth every time. "I don't fear them because I know their Messiah is false. He isn't Coming Again because he never came the first time. I know my True Messiah is nigh. His birth pangs will be felt by us both. But the enemy of my enemy is my friend. You think wars can be avoided just because we don't like them? That they can be prevented by us playing dead? The Arabs will fight. Why don't you believe them? They're your friends, but you won't listen to them. You only hear what you want to hear."

"I certainly can't be hearing this then."

"You'll joke yourself into the grave, Dekel. We are all outsiders to your 'friends.' They won't give up, even if it takes them three hundred years. Was Mohammad a pacifist, like Uri Davis? Our only hope is to harden our hearts. Of course, it's difficult, after two thousand years of exile, of bowing and scraping to alien kings. Of being corrupted by so-called Christian values of turning the other cheek, when all they turned to us were Torquemada's hot irons. But that's what the State of Israel is all about, if it's about anything. Read your own secular idols, Ben-Gurion, Dayan, Golda Meir. All sincere socialistic atheists, like you. But I forgot, you're a God-fearing man."

"What do you fear, Schaeffer? Do you fear God?"

"I fear God and I do His bidding. The God of Justice and Revenge. The God who answers the question: Till when shall the wicked triumph? They break thy people in pieces and afflict thy heritage, they slay the widow and the stranger, and murder the fatherless. Six million Jews in the ovens. And the repeat performance planned for us here. Ye fools, when will ye be wise? He that planted the ear, shall he not hear? He that formed the eye, shall he not see? He that chastiseth the heathen, shall he not correct? The Lord knoweth the thoughts of man, they are vanity. Yes, the Lord had you in mind, Dekel. But the Lord will not cast off His people, nor will He forsake His inheritance. We both say these words every day, Dekel. But to you, they obviously mean nothing. A meaningless ritual, like a kibbutz Passover, with bread rolls exchanged under the table. You are not a Jew, Dekel, I wash my hands of you. Who forsakes his people, his blood is forfeit."

I could find no riposte to that. Sometimes no joke can be appropriate. Except the joke of human presumption, the sheer conceit of the species.

He rang off, and Anat looked at me as if I had allowed a corpse into the house. Hopefully not my own. Our re-entry to the womb had lasted all of five minutes, and we were immediately plunged back in the trench. The whiff of gunpowder still about our nostrils, the next day, as Anat and I watched Nahum Lauterman sip his Bloody Mary in The Hut.

"So what do you suggest, Nahum?"

"I think we have to act quickly," he said, "if only for your own protection. Here we have a wanted man who's six foot tall and built like Sylvester Stallone in a hair shirt that all the forces of the Law can't find. Didn't Mao Tse Tung say the gorilla is a fish who swims among the people? And look at the way you're being treated. No airport queries, no SHABAK at your door, yammering for a debriefing. The Chief just wants you to sink back into oblivion. Silence is golden. But silence isn't safety, in this case. No, I think you're more secure with noise. So I'm prepared to write up your story. But I shall have to be both cunning and cautious, or the censor will just leave me with a wad of blank pages. I'll have to think this out . . . The consequences . . . Of course, the PM will breathe fire at the publisher, strange financial traumas will occur, coincidentally, in the region of the owner's pocket. But I think I can convince my Gods. They've supported me through enough skirmishes to know I don't issue the General Call-up for nothing."

He called Adina, the waitress, and beseeched her for a second Bloody Mary. He was going to swell up and explode with tomato juice. He thought at us, his mouth moving. "We'll prepare a dummy, a fake edition of the weekend supplement for the censor and his pals. Meanwhile, we'll print the real one in secret, with your story. I'll do it in one issue, all the eggs in one basket. 'The Incredible Tale Of Our Own Correspondent, Joseph Dekel.' 'See the Spy Who Never Is.' 'Thrill to the Armageddon Connection.' 'Tremble as Maniacs of All Faiths Unite.' But I'll have to debrief you, Joe. I'll have to put you through the wringer. The works. With a story as explosive and bizarre as this, we have to be sure of our ground. Who should I use? Milek Stuckman? Too sleepy. Amnon E—? He's on your side. I'll use Padan, our ace skeptic and hatchet man. He'll go over every inch of your story. We'll check what we can, carefully, without alerting the hounds. The hell with all my friends in high places. I can't hide for ever, playing Upstairs Downstairs. I've given them enough rope and they've hung us both with it. Time we took our fate in our hands."

If anyone can get away with it, it's Lauterman. Woodward-Bernstein he is not, and our rag may be noble, but it's still enmeshed in the cat's cradle of our national economic labyrinth, debt, deficit, greased palms, unseen nudges and winks. A good editor (from the publisher and owner's point of view) is one who knows the difference between tweaking the lion's tail and hitting it in the face with a mallet. And Lauterman knows, as I do, how full my twisted tale is of holes, false leads, flaws, potentially wild errors and apparent contradictions. But I'll say this for my old friend: You can only push him so far. And he is right, both Anat and I would be better protected, in our current state, by exposure rather than silence.

Anat agrees: "Let's get it over with. Let's have our fifteen minutes of being famous. It'll probably merge anyway with the entire circus. Today's outrage, tomorrow's wrapped falafel."

Is she right? Has anything got a chance of standing out for more than a passing headline in our lurid Hieronymous Bosch parade? Spy revelations, terrorist attacks, hostages, death on the roads, peace initiatives, recession, political scandals, Rabbi wars; everything tumbles in the Levant dryer, a mass of dirty laundry endlessly revolving, as no one fixes the malfunctioning machine. We sit, fascinated, in life's washeteria, wondering: When will it ever come out, and why did I forget the detergent, and why does it swallow so many coins?

The Silence, versus Babel. Can there be a golden mean?

So the process began. Lauterman drove us southwest, to the coast, at Ashkelon, where he had a little beach house belonging to our Far Eastern correspondent who was travel-lagged in Thailand. A quiet hide-out overlooking the sea and the blissful absence of tourists, scared off by the general ambience of violence in our *intifadaed* Nation-State. The waves rolled in to the beach. Soldiers from an adjoining base pounded their daily morning run up and down the thick sand, stripped to the waist and sweating loudly. Anat had postponed her return to the Jerusalem Art scene, graciously given unlimited leave by Old Sandpaper, who told her: "Just keep that husband of yours on a leash. We have enough problems in this country."

Nahum's ace reporter, Padan, arrived at the seashore with his little bag of tricks, his cassette recorders, his bug-detecting devices, with which he swept the entire house and the adjacent beach huts, his pocket polygraph, his blood pressure kit, his jaundiced eye, curling lip, quivering bulbous nose and the nasty habit of looking at you as if you were Clint Eastwood trying to con the Army Recruiting Board into declaring you unfit for service. His trick questions, his sniffing of one's metaphysical BO, his jeering laugh at my outlandish exploits. "Come on, Joe, you can do better than that. What do you take me for, Simple Simon?" Or he would glaze over with sweat and disbelief, the veins pulsing in his neck, gritting his teeth and pounding the wall in frustration, switching off his tape and walking down to the sea, then returning to start all over again, from the top. He drew a map of my odyssey, from Upper West Side Manhattan to Jerusalem, Amiel, Ramallah, to Zion National Park, via the mystery "government facility" he had to grudgingly confirm did exist, to his knowledge, near Afula, in the Lower Galilee. But discreet probes, made by Lauterman to the Highest Authorities, had produced point-blank denials that I had ever been held there. A "maverick operation." By whom? Buttoned lips and closed mouths. Nor did my description of a "Melies moon" colonel ring any bells, except in my head.

"You were dreaming, Joe," Padan accused me.

I freely admitted that. "I was higher than a kite, Padan. They shot me full of God knows what. My old Reserves colleague, Avi Tsemach. Now there's a name you'd have no problem tracking down."

"That's what you think," he said sourly. "The records show he emigrated to the United States in 1981. His experiences with you on the Jordan River must have been the last straw. All contact addresses draw a blank, so far.

"Look, Joe," he said to me, settling down finally in a haze of rancid coffee breath, "what you're trying to tell me is the following: Our secret services have a deep penetration spy in the United States, who remained in place after the Pollard affair. An American Jewish *macher* and blacklister, Murray Waiskopf, seems to have found out this name. In an inconvenient coincidence, Waiskopf's name was used to bait you into a meeting so that this hundred-year-old other American *macher*, Schatz, would leak you details of an alleged conspiracy between Jewish settlers in the West Bank and a Christian Fundamentalist lunatic to blow up the Moslem mosques in Jerusalem. As a lever against our secret services, this lunatic Risegood also knows the spy's identity – through Waiskopf, or the other way around? We don't know. Certainly a lot of people in that ballpark. A whole fiendish dance is then danced between the Reverend, the settler underground, our own services, and the FBI, all over Joseph Dekel's poor corpus.

"So far I've got a reasonable embryonic script for a Benny Hill comedy, minus the blondes. Everybody is coming in and out of doors, like a Lubitsch film, whacking you over the head, like a Raymond Chandler story. You dive into an inky pool. Why should I dive after you? There's no substance here, Dekel. Just hearsay and innuendo. I couldn't negotiate a dog's license with this material."

"It's all I have. Take it or leave it."

"I think I'll resign, and write pornographic novels. Do you know translations are made in ninety languages? One good bondage and domination contract can set you up for life. You can shoot the video in three days. It's a growing market, in this day of AIDS. No one can risk the real thing any more. We live an ersatz existence, and now life is imitating bad Frederick Forsyth thrillers. At least the books have a coherent plot line. With this, all you can do is cry in the dark.

"OK. So we know our secret services are infected by the same schizoid nature of our people. Our double-headed government. The Pushmepullyou. You wrote your book about that. Whatsisname, Moishe-Ganef? Schism in the Intelligence Family. Some think we're going to end up with the two-state solution and the sooner the better for our sanity. Others believe that's one step to destruction and will do anything to stop that outcome. Some believe Arafat is the true partner for negotiation. Others want his head on a pole. Extremists might shield the settler underground, support its policy of provocations. We have them all in our bosom, the meat, the milk and the neutral. The Good, the Bad and the Ugly. We live in a state of limbo, after the death of all our certainties and iron convictions. The Palestinian Enemy confronts us with an unexpected resolve to sacrifice in an intense unity. Our right-wingers are full of rage and envy: Why can't we show the same resolve? Where has our much vaunted, famous unity against adversity vanished to? Some cry in newspaper columns, others whip up political passions, and others, without a doubt, plan more effective acts. The closing of ranks in War and Siege. The Good Old Days of No Choice.

Bring back the Enemy with the familiar fortress face of bloodlust and no compromise. Eventually, someone will light the old match under the gunpowder barrel. So who are we to stick our bare fingers in the dike, Yosseleh, and expect it not to crumble?"

"It may be better than sucking our thumbs."

At the end of the day, Padan's stone heart, like the rest of us, bleeds profusely. We sit in the dark, Anat, Lauterman and I, after his departure, watching the flickering dots into images of our television broadcasting service. The set is an old one, and constantly splutters into incoherence, having to be thumped with a fist to restart. The routine body count of our counter-insurrection: Three local inhabitants killed in "Judea and Samaria." The army is investigating. A petrol bomb was thrown at a settler vehicle, but no one injured, thank God. "Disturbances of law and order" in several places. Our Prime Minister's proposals for elections in the disputed territories excludes the PLO and rules out the two-state solution. Across the world, in China, a new *intifada* is gathering pace, hundreds of thousands of students and workers, filling the main square of Peking. Army trucks, called in, are stalled by human barricades. Ordinary people climb on the trucks, bringing cups of tea, talking to the soldiers who look bemused, wretched and depressed. The People's Army cannot act against the People. Or can it? Experts hold differing opinions.

Bizarre thoughts. As I sit here in Ashkelon, the world eddies, swirls and changes. Gorbachev in Russia, Peking, Angola, Chile, Argentina. Only in our pisspot corner of the globe nothing can advance, nothing pulls out of the mud. The Ayatollah is ailing in Iran. Lebanon burns. Iraq and Syria simmer, the low flame, the lid held down. We wished to be Europeans, but we are tied to our region. A common fate, whether we like it or not.

Later at night, Lauterman snoring in the adjoining room, we lie together, Anat and I, in the damp May heat, listening to the waves and the creaking walls. It's like being on board an old sailing ship, becalmed in the middle of the ocean, going nowhere, perhaps with nowhere to go. Again the thought that crept in to haunt us in the last two or three years, after almost two decades of contraception: Conception or not? Department of last chances, before old age takes its toll. To get it up against a sea of troubles . . . Is there a future? Can we make decisions for a being not yet here? Another soul to be trapped in the time machine of Spartan vigilance without end? In eighteen years and nine months, will we still be reading of the Christians and the Moslems smashing Lebanon, of our Deterrent Capability, of Disturbances in Judea, Samaria, Jerusalem, Ashkelon, Tel Aviv? Or will it all have been swept under by our self-destructive death wish, our Holocaust paranoia and our soured Revolution that turned its back on the world? Or will reason and hope prevail in the end, will he or she sip coffee at The Hut, smoodge about the Cinémathèque and piss on the trembling, psychotic parents with nerves still twanging from redundant fears? Will we even survive the next week, let alone these two decades in which we might wait to see if history is a line or a loop?

Padan returned the next day, and the day after. Turning me inside out, going over the same material, checking facts and possible fictions, filleting my soul. On the fourth day he turned up with a look of greater respect than I would give him credit for, and tossed a manilla envelope into my lap. I opened it. It was the blacklist file I had seen in my "dream," under the influence of Avi Tsemach's hallucinogenic painkillers, in the light of the Melies moon. But here it was, solid in the sober light of day:

ANTI-SLANDER LEAGUE
MEMORANDUM: MEDIA WATCH

To: ASL Regional Offices **For Your Information:**
From: M. Waiskopf ASL National Commission

THE SILENCER

Date: September 1986   Affiliated Federations
Subject: Joseph Dekel   Board of Governors

The subject of the present Media Watch program Memorandum is an Israeli journalist and author currently offering his recently published Hebrew novel for publication in translation in the USA.

The novel, THE DEATH OF MOISHE-GANEF, presents a familiar stereotyped view of the Israeli-Arab conflict as one between a manipulative, evil-minded Israeli secret service and a Palestinian resistance movement with which the author has much sympathy, and which he treats with an understanding and compassion not evident in his treatment of "his own side." As the *Jerusalem Post* reviewer pointed out:

> Joseph Dekel presents his country as utterly corrupt, irredeemable and seemingly abandoned by God. Dekel is a malcontent. He snipes at and condemns almost indiscriminately whatever he sees, though often with some humor. Modern Israel could provide any novelist with plenty of good material for satire, but Dekel presents a country almost unrelievedly malignant, frenzied and unbalanced. As a spoof spy story, THE DEATH OF MOISHE-GANEF could be amusing and funny, but the constant jibes leave a somewhat bitter taste.

And they say reviews don't count. For my sins, there were several more pages: An analysis by Murray Waiskopf of my literary shortcomings, a list of alleged errors of fact, including a street in Tel Aviv I had invented so as not to finger one of my characters, and a conclusion stating that my book would do nothing to achieve a meaningful Arab-Israel peace. "We are not helped," wrote Murray Waiskopf, "by texts written purely for commercial exploitation, harmless enough in the Israeli context, but which would only serve to give Arab propagandists fuel

by pointing out our 'shortcomings' from 'the horse's mouth.'
Although there is little likelihood of Dekel's book being accepted for U.S. publication, our members should be aware of
the above background information so that they can adequately
respond to any problems which might arise."

'*Chob nischt tsoris*. "Where did you get this?" I asked Padan.
He shrugged. "People find things lying about. If you press in the
right place, the boil pops open."

"We'll publish this too," said Lauterman. "What the hell. In
for a penny, in for a pound. From the sublime to the ridiculous.
Let's throw everything in the pot. Eye of newt and toe of frog,
wool of bat and tongue of dog. I'm tired of being a newspaper
editor, anyway. I think I will take up angling. Killing fish, that's
safe enough. Quiet beasts, they just float along, waiting for the
hook to pierce their lip. What do you say, Padan, do we have lift
off?"

"I'll write the story," said Padan. "The rest is up to the Gods.
What we have, we have. We'll leave the gaps in, like a connect-
the-dots drawing. *Morituri te salutant*."

"*Ego te absolvo*," said Lauterman. "And remember to wash
your mouth with soap."

We abandoned the Ashkelon beach. An eerie hot afternoon,
Lauterman and Padan decamping in their two cars up north,
Anat and I climbing into Alexander and turning its battered
hood towards Jerusalem, past the parched swathe of the Lachish
lowlands, turning at the junction by Yesodot to follow the old
main road from the coast to Jerusalem, via Har'el and Eshtaol.
The narrow winding highway on which one used to get stuck
behind heavy trucks, honking and sweating, before the Six-Day
War which liberated us from our provinciality and made us
players on the world stage. Losers, perhaps, but, nevertheless,
players. One has a seat at the table. I prefer the empty seat left
for Elijah the Prophet at the Passover feast. An open door to
another moral plane. But who wants to waste a seat nowadays?

The City, rising from the hills and terraces again, the lump in the throat, hopefully not a tumor. My mind turned back to Murray Waiskopf, his last words and accusation. *Soneh Amcho*. No, I'm sure he got it wrong. The people, my people, are just a microcosm of the squabbling heap of humanity. Nothing makes us stand out from the rest. Our arrogance, our terrors, our insecurity, our boycotts and excommunications, are not, at the end of the day, an ethnic inheritance. The global state. *La condition humaine*. We are fucked up, therefore we exist. There is nothing inherently Jewish about this. It is a bipedal problem. Even chimpanzees go crazy, commit murder and suicide. I saw that on a BBC program once, so it must be true.

Our home still stands. Luckily no immediate phone call. An ominous silence from that quarter, the gorilla having vanished into his sea. Didn't he tell me in Amiel he had a wife and two children? Maybe he, too, sank back into his microcosm, hidden from macrocosmic madness? We return to a tempting patina of tranquillity, everything as if waiting for us to pick up where we left off, three months ago, before I gallivanted off to Noo Yok to talk peace with the PLO. Perhaps I can forget it all, telephone Lauterman, tell him it was all a big mistake, nothing happened, it was all in my head. I love Big Brother. Unpublish and be blessed. Just give me my TV and computer, I shall be happy in my own four walls. There was a new video game I'd received just before my trip but hadn't had time to study its manual: Space Station Construction Simulator. It puts Jumbo Jet in the shade. You ferry your orbiting components in the Space Shuttle, build them in space and then you have to maintain your station, to strict NASA specifications. One slip, and you plunge back with your entire crew in flames towards the planet. Just forget the earth, and aim for the stars! I step out to the grocer's, stock up on comestibles, stack the fridge, boot up and try to sink into the electronic ooze, while, in the depths, Lauterman's gnomes toil, mining God knows what fool's gold . . .

222

Could it possibly just fade away, truly? The Silence, willed, not imposed . . . A detective story without an ending: The detective gives up, retires, thumbs his nose at all attempted solutions and lets the murderer get away. The book ends, before its final chapter: no denouement, no unmasking solution. *Caveat emptor.*

The soul of the Rabbi of Lublin, it was said, could see from one end of the world to the other. Gazing on the great evil present, it begged God to be relieved of this gift. The power was limited to four miles. So when the Rabbi looked at anyone's face, he could see into the depths of the soul. The Rabbi, terrified at what he so often saw, begged again to be relieved of this gift. But he was reminded of the words of the Gemara: God gives, but He does not take back.

I ought to be glad then that God made me practically blind, and stopped my powers at the tip of my nose.

The weekened. My atavisms. Familiar rituals can be soothing. Eve of Sabbath, trawling through the newspapers piled up during my hiatus. Military Intelligence, a leak reveals, believes there can only be a political, not a military solution to the *intifada*. The Mossad disagrees (from the people who gave you the Israel-Phalange axis). A religious Cabinet Minister used the words "dirty Arab" in a Knesset debate. Arab members protested. A mini-*intifada* in Jordan as people rioted against rising prices. Rabbi Wars escalating, between rival guardians of the Fundamental Truth. Israel has been denounced in the Security Council. The Americans support Prime Minister Shamir's "peace plan." A well-liked and eccentric writer and satirist has held a "Closing Down" party for his own life, which is soon to be terminated by cancer. A brave laugh and cry in the face of oblivion.

Can I regain my cocoon? On Sabbath morning, inevitably, an interruption. Our well-known interdiction on Saturday calls is shattered by a colleague from Anat's office, Yolanda, the terribly nice Venezuelan who lives just down the road, bringing her a full-blown crisis: Someone has broken into the Jerusalem in Miniature exhibit at the "Abode of the Tranquil" and smashed it to smithereens. Yolanda, who usually deals with collagists and vegetarians, has come to carry my wife off to the scene of the crime. "The police claim it's an Arab on an *intifada* kick, but whoever it was also tore up the *peshkvilim*." Anat's collection of religious tracts and wall posters. It's a case of choose your zealot. Some of my more extreme brethren would sanction acts like this on the Sabbath in "Sanctification of the Lord." Or some secular vandal? In this City, if you rounded up the usual suspects, half the inhabitants would be in jail.

In the evening, I joined Anat at the "Abode of the Tranquil." It was a quite impressive sight. The intruder, like a modern Titus, had done the job thoroughly, starting with the obliteration of the Canaanite level and then working his way up history: The City of David lay in little plaster shardlets like the real thing outside the City walls. The Second Temple – yok. Aelia Capitolina had been pulverized practically into powder. Tiny remnants of towers of David, battlements, cupolas, spires, still lay on the floors, where they were just being swept by Anat and her colleagues into neat piles, after the police photographers had come to record the devastation. Old Sandpaper, the Mayor, was standing over the ruins with a barely repressed fury. "I give up. For every person who wants to create something in this City, we find ten willing to destroy." The craftsman himself was, luckily, in Los Angeles, so was not present to wail at his Wall.

"Maybe they'll stop short at the representation," I said. No one thought this very funny.

I drove Anat home. There was nothing much to say. Every cud already chewed. We watched television, a mediocre French policier, a mediocre news, a worse alternative on Jordan. I ought to reposition the aerial on the roof, so we can get mediocre programs from Egypt. The boondocks. The provinces. And, in six days' time, the Joe Dekel smidge of Fame. It's too late to stop it now. *Que sera sera.*

Sunday morning. My wife returns to what's left of the Jerusalem Arts. I return to Space Max. I manage to get my crew safely on board the Space Station, but I keep losing them within a few minutes to decompression, loss of power, fire and explosion. I am running through astronauts like Malinovski's Army through Tatars. I shall certainly never get to the moon, let alone the stars. The earth is all I can hope for.

A break for lunch. Sandwich, yogurt. Siesta. Then back to the more familiar hazards of Jumbo Jet. By five-thirty p.m. I have managed to bring myself to the brink of a successful landing at Frankfurt Airport. All that would be left is Passport Control, Customs, bratwurst and irascible taxi drivers. Eureka! I shall at least have accomplished something in life, even if it is wiped off a machine's memory with the touch of a key. The phone rings.

"Is Anat there?" It is the secretary from the office, Gila. A spectacular blonde who makes love to the sun as if it is the last male on earth. And what about me? Nada. "Oh, I thought she was going home. She should be there soon. Can you ask her about this Sunny Amko business?"

This what? Alarm bells ring in my head. My brain feels as if something, deep in the gray cells, is rattling microscopic bars.

"Say that again?"

"It's nothing important, Joe. These people from Texas who have a helicopter and are taking aerial photographs of the City. The Mayor's office wants to know if we're going to use them for an exhibition later this year. Don't worry, it can wait till tomorrow."

"Wait a minute." I held on to the telephone as if it were an umbilical cord. "You mentioned some name, some Sunny something. Tell me again. What's this about aerial photographs?"

"The Sunny Amko Company of Dallas Texas. Some big shot who's hired a chopper to photograph Jerusalem from above.

225

Apparently they're going to be up there, tomorrow morning, taking pictures of the Old City, the Walls, the battlements, the Holy Places. You know the sort of thing."

"The Temple Mount, and the mosques?"

"Yes, Joe. It's nothing urgent. You sound odd. Are you all right?"

Definitely not. Coincidences are crawling up my belly button. My brain is boiling. My skin is coming off my bones. My eyes are melting like soft fried eggs. The tinnitus in my ears is like thunder.

"Don't move! I'm coming right over!"

"What, Joe?" Her voice faded. "Oh, it's OK, Anat's just walked in. I thought you'd gone home . . ."

"Give me my wife!" I shouted. She came on, puzzled but not surprised at my panic. The weary voice: "Joe, I have to do some late work here. What is it now?"

"Stay there!" I shouted. "Don't move! Find out what time they're starting! Who's in that chopper? Where are they taking off from? That fucking bastard! Sunny Amko, Goddamnit! The son of a bitch wasn't cursing me after all! He *was* giving me The Name!"

"Joseph," the long-suffering spouse, who can blame her? "It's five-thirty. Most of the offices are closed. What are you raving about? What's got into you?"

Enlightenment. The Moment of Truth. Revelation. The final ironic breakthrough. *Deus ex machina!* Who would possibly have believed it?

"SUNNY AMKO," not "*SONEH AMCHO.*"

Murray Waiskopf didn't hate me after all. That much. It was me. My triggered feelings of ethnic guilt, my bias, my own predilection, my expectations of fanatic hostility . . .

The Name of the Beast, not the final insult . . . Not at all "hater of your people" . . .

I had misheard the code.

226

Murray Waiskopf had confided in me, in his last breath, just as my enemies had assumed. Not about the spy, but about the central intrigue . . .

My ears! My brain! My battered soul!

What do you do, at five-forty-five p.m., when all bureaucratic offices are closed and you have just discovered that the world you know might well come to an end tomorrow morning?

Personally, I panic. I rushed over in Alexander, pushing the poor beast to its limits, from Rehavia to Anat's office in the Municipality Annex at the back of Mamilla Square. Today it's called Israel Defense Forces Square. What's in a name? The usual misconception. But all Anat had for me was a scribbled note from the Mayor's office on photographic exhibitions.

The City, in miniature, in representation, in image, in sculpted brick, bronze, silver halides. Mount Moriah and all its spin-offs, down the benchmarks of history. Old Abe and Isaac, the boy-king David, the Prophets biting at the ankles of monarchs, the First Fall, and then the Second. Greeks, Roman bulldozers, the Caliph Omar, the builder, Abd el-Malik. The Golden and the Silver domes. The Rock. Al-Aqsa. Later on, the Ottoman's Walls. The skyline we enjoy today . . .

In 1951, King Abdullah of Transjordan was assassinated on the steps of al-Aqsa by a Moslem gunman for ceding half of Palestine to the Jews. In 1969 a mad Australian Christian tried to burn al-Aqsa down and was hauled off to the lunatic asylum. In 1982 a fanatic Jewish American immigrant opened fire with a rifle in the Dome of the Rock and outside it, killing a guard. Two separate attempts by Jewish zealots to blow up the mosques have been noted. The Sons of Judah, an eccentric, vegetarian, dope-smoking sect whose members stockpiled weapons in the ruins of the Arab village of Lifta, were caught in the conception stage. The Jewish Settlers' Underground, however, got two of its members, disguised in Arab kafiyas, into the Temple compound with explosives. Various "Loyalists" of the Temple Mount have been campaigning for years for the enforcement of Jewish hegemony over the entire complex. Moslem Friday prayers here often spark off nationalist demonstrations, met by the police with baton charges and tear gas.

Everyone wants a piece of the action.

Anat and I were alone in the office. The secretary, Gila, had gone home, more than ever convinced I was insane. It was six-fifteen and we would have enough time to catch the first performances of the cinemas. Not that I could remember what was on. Was it *The Unbearable Lightness of Being*? Or *Dangerous Liaisons*? Is there a rollicking Israeli comedy anywhere. Not a very likely option.

Lauterman was unavailable at home or office. Presumably he was burrowing underground, putting together the mad annals of Joe Dekel. Would he welcome the peroration? Or just throw up his hands in despair? Sunny Amko, *Soneh Amcho*. Was it all in my mind? An aerial raid, the best means to bypass the mosque guards' surveillance and deliver – what lethal cargo? Imagination runs riot. But if not Lauterman, who could I contact and tell, if I thought I knew what was coming? Police? SHABAK, already up to their ears in Dekelmania? Amnon E— or Milek Stuckman? Who could I trust, and who would believe my ramblings?

There was only one effective option. Anat sat down and dialled the private, ex-directory number of her boss, the Mayor, Old Sandpaper. The man whose building plans I had impugned, the butt of a hundred of my columns. The fund raiser, the wheeler-dealer, the negotiator, Mr. Carrot and Stick, the City's guardian and nemesis, who had welded the two parts of the City together after the Six-Day War by *force majeure*, cajolery and threats of direr times to come if anyone dared vote in his adversaries, the right-wing and religious zealots.

It was not an easy confrontation.

"I'm sure your first impression was correct," he told me

sourly, after hearing my mad explanation. We had finally been granted an audience at the close of an At Home reception for the Mayor of Leuven, Belgium. The Mayor of Leuven had his own ethnic schisms between Flemish and Walloons. But so far his casualty list was lower than ours. He commiserated and sympathized, but was in favor of the two-state solution, if not for Belgium. A spirited debate over the chopped liver morsels. By the time we got to Old Sandpaper it was eleven p.m. We had already lost four hours. It was lucky he had a soft spot for Anat, or I'd have been shown the door in one minute.

"You were right. The man was cursing you properly. You are a pain in the neck, Dekel. You are one of nature's human mosquitoes. You bite, you draw blood, and you buzz. I'm sitting here because your wife is an asset to the City, whereas you are just a liability. She builds. You draw disfiguring graffiti all over other people's work. So you got involved in spy-counterspy stuff. Who asked you to meddle? Just stop buzzing for ten seconds."

He sighed, passing his pudgy old hand through his thatch of white hair. His face looked as if it had been camped in by countless hordes of refugees.

"So let me get you straight," he said, "if anything as bent as this can be straightened. Your adventures have led you to suspect that the Security Services are infiltrated by supporters of religious maniacs who are ready to blow up the mosques, with all that that entails. The Prime Minister, the chiefs of the police, of SHABAK itself, are powerless. Someone on the inside is committing treason. If you inform them of your suspicions, they might warn off the perpetrators. But if you don't inform them, this terrible act might proceed. It doesn't seem to me there is a choice.

"I'll have the police check the details and stop the overflight. We'll locate the helicopter and its crew. We'll find out who these people are and check them out. My cops are reliable. You give them a job to do and they do it. They work in daylight, not in shadows. If you're wrong, my dear, don't ask me for a rise in pay this year. On second thoughts, don't ask me for a raise regardless. And as for you . . ." He looked at me as if I was a cat he'd like to strangle, then waved a weary hand. "I'm too old for this nervousness and paranoia. I'm a practical man. I build houses, offices, industries, galleries, shops, museums. Things that people want and use in their daily life. I don't deal in ideology. That is a putrid corpse. I always suspect people who say they loathe money, that have contempt for the shekels. Right or left. Money is life for this city. Money makes things happen. All your high ideals and dreams – just stick them up your ass."

He made his calls. We sat in his kitchen, finishing off the reception's leftovers. It was out of my hands now. I could not phone Lauterman, the old man fearing the press like an ant the aardvark. They are not the asses he desires to kiss. Nahum would not thank me for this, nor Padan, deprived of a potential scoop, but the baton had passed on . . .

One a.m. Two police vans arrived. Anat and I were ushered out of the kitchen, into the back of the Mayor's limousine and off into the city night. The streets, under a blue-black sky, deserted apart from a few indeterminate shufflers, night owls heading home, insomniacs, post-disco stragglers kicking a tin can, an orthodox old man who perhaps can't wait for early morning prayers. The police jeeps, whisping to and fro. We curled, in a convoy, up by the dark, still battlements of the Old City, along the Tribes of Israel Road, past the American Colony and Sheikh Jarrakh, towards the police headquarters on Ammunition Hill. A great battle was fought here during the Six-Day War between ourselves and the Jordanian Army over control of the heights commanding the City. A memorial plaque honors the dead of both sides. It's only the living who are degraded here.

Briefing, in the Superintendent's office. Mahogany desk, hard-backed chairs, maps on walls with colored pins. The *intifada* battlefield. An immense aerial collage of the City and environs stuck up on a board. Men with shoulder pips and fifteen o'clock shadow bustling about, looking grim. A petite raven-haired Yemeni Sergeant caught my eye, but Anat's hand held firmly to my arm. Old Sandpaper, dressed in a khaki jacket which looked as if it dated from the Siege of the City in 1948, sipped a black coffee. We were not offered a cup. Senior policemen whispered in his ear. Finally he motioned us over.

"An American pilot and two photographers were booked at the Hilton," he said, "but they checked out suddenly just one hour ago with no forwarding address. Know these names?" On a piece of paper: James Coelecanth. Ambrose Deedes. Nada. "Aliases. What can we expect? Their company helicopter was parked at Kalandiya Airport, but it is not there now. An Arab guard heard a helicopter take off. We are calling in the army. Looks like you might get your raise, Anat. Something unkosher is going on."

We walked out after him, into the open yard, overlooking the black glutinous mass of the City, sullenly etched against the moonlit sky.

"Somebody leaked, didn't they?" he said. "Communications. Sometimes I wonder what that word means. Truth or lies, traveling along the same paths. Yes, there is some thing, some-one out there. I can feel it in my bones. Or is it just old age, grinding me down at last. I feel like that King, Canute, who tried to hold back the waves. They want me to go home to bed to let them handle it. The forces of Law and Order. I have to trust them. Any other way is anarchy, disintegration and despair. Maybe I should go to bed, and, like King David, let them bring me a young virgin to warm me up. An attractive lie, to give me warmth. But what does The Book say? The king knew her not . . . Then the king's son, Adoniah, and Zadok the priest, and others, sought to proclaim themselves his heirs. But Bathsheba persuaded him to crown Solomon. Who is my Solomon, Anat? Certainly not this man here."

No, I lack that ambition. Though there are perks to power . . .
But no, I still have my club feet . . .

"I've called for a helicopter," said the Mayor. "Unless they
find that Amko chopper quick, at the first light we'll go up and
look over the City. Two hours from now. There isn't that much
time."

Dawn, over the City. The red glow spreads, flares into gold. The sun rises behind us, over the Mountains of Moab, over Jericho. Armies with trumpets, marching round the walls of the City, willing it to fall. These days you need stronger methods. The stones have become immune to shouting and cacophony, cursing, blessings, incantations.

Dawn, over the City. If you have a good vantage point, on one of the surrounding hills, the slow creeping of the glow over the battlements, the cupolas, spires, television aerials has a formal beauty hard to describe. The architectural perfection of the walled City stands out in a bold and jagged relief. People are not seen. The messy, murderous squabbling of humanity appears to have subsided in a magical moment of truce. Frozen in time, the City appears to have found its metaphysical, aspiring, still center. All the more so if you rise, in a light aircraft or helicopter, from any of the hills surrounding the City, looking down on it like a bird on the wing, as the gold spreads over the pores of its skin.

The City at your feet. The City at your mercy. Anat, and I, and Old Sandpaper. Tearing our eyes from the panorama, searching the brightening sky. Another police helicopter has taken off, buzzing low over the landscape around the City, searching its seven hills, its nooks and crannies, its valleys and clefts and shadows. The true National Park of Zion, with its real cathedrals, angels' landings, patriarchs' courts, virgins and sentinels and streaked walls. No canyons, except in the mind.

We spread our arms, embracing the City. It's in our blood, our genes, our hopes and fears. Vibrating in our childhood, that provinciality, enclosure, the sense of mystery and siege. The split, schizoid, schizophrenic town, vibrating with its *mélange* of religions, ethnic groups, creeds. The living embodiment of that impossible inevitability which we played out in pantomime on the New York University stage: The coexistence of apparent opposites which are, in temperament, the same: Jews and Moslems and Christians, Armenians, Copts, Greeks, Ethiopians, Israelis and Palestinians. Hatem Abu-Riads and Yochai Magen-Davids and Eliyahu Saltsmans and Akram Ibn Ghallalahs. Even Dorothy Morgenthals and Yassir Arafats. Bleeding hearts, chairmen, professors of human ecology and deposed mayors, freedom fighters-cum-terrorists of either side, and all the waiters, taxi drivers, shop owners, garageniks, mechanics, café loungers, mixers, fixers, piss artists, shit kickers and shabab of all sizes, genders, creeds and colors who are waking up to a new day below us. This is what it's all about. Live together or die together. Of course, we could all emigrate, leaving the City to orbit on its own, its buildings crumbling, its alleyways cracking, its ambience decaying, its glories sinking in mounds of squashed cartons and donkey turds.

Our helicopter hovers over the stones and terraces. To our right I can see the blip of an army Huey which has risen from its base to join the search. Static crackles around our police pilot's head. Old Sandpaper's wispy white hairs are enclasped in earphones, which crackle in his ears. Anat and I sit hunched up like a couple of punctured spare tires.

Our microcosm and our macrocosm. Anat and Joe, versus The World. Eventually the world took up the challenge, slipped a lead weight into its gloves, and slugged us. Evidently we had not hidden deep enough. We were not sunk enough in our cozy consensus of Art, Television, video games and home cooking. We poked our heads above the parapet. In Beirut, we hear, there are families which have lived for months in the cellars of their own homes, with months of supplies of tin cans, a forced embodiment of those parodic survivalists who stockpile their nuclear bunkers. They are already living in a post-Holocaust world, and perhaps that should have been our own strategy. Brick up the windows, cut off the phone, stack the freezer, buy a personal generator to power the fridge and PC. I could not live without the PC. I wonder what happens next with the Space Station Simulator? How does one keep the crew from perishing constantly from decompression, gas leakage, loss of power, fire, radiation, meteorite collision and lack of access to the escape hatch?

I am falling asleep. Dreaming again, briefly, of satellites, moons, valleys of death, infernos, and blacklists expunging my name from history. Falling, down the rabbit holes of memory. Storytelling Rabbis, floating on clouds. The undoing and creation of worlds. Rabbi Shlomo Hayim of Kaidanov used to interpret the third verse of Genesis thus: "And God said: Let there be light" – and he said: "God, let there be light" – this is the call of the man who prays with true fervor, that God should show him the light, and he will see it . . .

The helicopter, turning, brings the rising sun into my eyes, waking and blinding me at the same time. Old Sandpaper's hand is on my arm.

"End of story," he shouts in my ear. "I've just had a report that the target has been located. The fugitive chopper has been grounded and its crew have been held. The army is calling off the search. We can go home."

He waves at the pilot and the helicopter turns further, accelerating over the hills. I can see that we have been scouring the folds south of the Old City, over the Hill of Evil Counsel, the old UN Government House, the Mount of Offense, Abu Tor and Silwan. The sun is now rising in full yellow-gold over the two grand mosques, the silver of al-Aqsa and the majestic gold of the Dome of the Rock. Everything stands out in stark relief, the battlements, the ancient stones, the Western Wall, Mount Zion with the Dormition Abbey. All the turrets, bumps, twiddles and curves. The other army and police helicopters have vanished from the sky. Or have they?

Something is coming out of the sun, out of the east.

"Which one is that, then?"

"Which one is what?"

A small light helicopter is approaching the Walled City from the direction of the Intercontinental Hotel.

Anat has better eyes than either of us: "That's not a police helicopter. That's a private craft."

"You haven't heard me," shouts Old Sandpaper. "It's over. It's in the hands of the authorities."

"So was the war in Lebanon," I shout back at him. "And the SHABAK bus scandal. And the *intifada*, too."

"What do you want from me?" he shouts back. "Blood?"

Anat grabs the binoculars that are slung round the old man's head, deftly expropriating them, leaning forward dangerously at the open space in the glass bubble as I grab the belt of her pants.

"Sunny Amko," she cries out. "I can see the name clearly."

"That's ridiculous," cries the Mayor, "I received a categorical assurance, over the radio."

One should never believe what one hears on the airwaves.

The small private chopper hovers over the Temple Mount.

"Call that son of a bitch up!" Old Sandpaper shouts to the pilot. "Ask him what the hell he thinks he's doing! Tell him to get the fuck out of there!"

The police pilot draws us closer to the hovering craft. We don't need binoculars now. Even with my half-assed eyesight, I can make out the massive shape of Didi Schaeffer, beard and *kippa*, curled up beside a tall, silver-haired man in a sober gray suit whom I had last seen sending me forth on a final journey half the planet Earth away.

The Reverend Risegood saw me just as I saw him, and waved, as if we were old friends who had just crossed each other's paths at a beach resort in Natanya.

"Is that them?" the Mayor shouts in my ear. I nod at him. "I've been lied to!" he bellows up in the air. "The bastards lied to me, God damn their souls!"

God will have a busy day ahead of Him with many souls today if what I think is meant to happen takes place.

Doomsday hovers over the ancient, bloodscarred hub of Faith and Fanaticism, a plastic bubble waiting to deposit its literally cosmic egg.

"I have radio contact," says the pilot.

Didi Schaeffer's voice crackles over the airwaves.

"I told you you'd see Messiah's birth pangs, Dekel. Welcome to the maternity ward."

You can't make an omelette without breaking the eggs. But I only asked for a hummus and tahina.

"You are in restricted airspace," the police pilot speaks calmly into his intercom. "Leave the area immediately and land at the police landing pad on Ammunition Hill. I will guide you down. Respond, over."

We could now see the face of the private chopper's pilot as we matched speed, came parallel and hovered. A familiar jeer, turned towards us. Whadaya know – the thuggish keister of the Ampule Man, Dorothy Morgenthal's nunchaku victim. So he can drive, too. Life is full of expected surprises.

Schaeffer ignored the voice of Authority and addressed me: "What do you think, Joe? It's a coincidence that we keep meeting in bizarre circumstances? Two men, with the same, but apparently different God? It's no coincidence. God tests our resolve, every day, to do His bidding or to turn away and hide. Happy is the man whom thou chastens, O Lord, whom thy teacheth out of thy Law. That thou may give him rest from days of adversity, until the pit be digged for the wicked. For the Lord will not cast off His people, nor will He forsake His inheritance. But judgement shall return unto righteousness, and all the upright in heart shall follow it. Who will rise up for me against

the wicked? Who will stand up for me against the workers of
iniquity? Someone has to answer the call, Dekel. It certainly
won't be you."

"What is he babbling about?" cried the Mayor, squinting. "I
know that other man there, good God. That's the Christian
priest, Risegood. What the hell . . . I had that man to dinner
once . . ."

The Reverend Risegood waved at him too. Didi Schaeffer
was maneuvering a large metal box towards the door of his
bubble. Their chopper was hovering directly over the dome of
al-Aqsa. A worried crowd had already gathered down below.
Men in robes and jalabiyas, suits and kafiyas, gesticulating
wildly. I saw a group of Border Policemen, with *waqf* armed
guards rushing up, pointing guns. A strange pantomime of
silence, all other sound drowned by chopper drone and radio
hiss.

"Oh my God!" shouted the Mayor. "Oh my God!"

But Anat nudged me in the ribs. Rising, on our other side, the
army Huey, with the ugly muzzle of a machine-gun poking out
its open door. Beside it, the squatting shape of a rifleman with
sniperscope sights. Our pilot saw him and lifted our machine,
sharply. I turned my head. The two machines were below us.
The dull crack of a rifleshot snapped through the chopper buzz.
Then a second and a third. The bulky shape of the zealot giant,
Didi Schaeffer, appeared, empty-handed, at the bubble opening. He tottered, pitched forward and fell, almost immediately
below me, plunging, just missing the crescent spire of al-Aqsa
and slithering, rolling down the silver dome, striking the parapet, and tumbling to the flat roof just beneath. The crowd
waved, eddied, swirled, leapt. The guards and policemen
opened fire.

"Idiots! Idiots!" the Mayor shouted.

Bullet holes ripped the glass bubble. A burst just clipped our
own flanks. We rose, and Sunny Amko rose beside us, the

Ampule Man fighting desperately for control. I could clearly see the body of the Reverend Risegood, sprawled over his seat, held in place by his seat belt, a jagged wound in the silvery head. Our pilot yanked us further up, sharp right, out of the line of fire. Anat, Old Sandpaper and I held on to each other like stranded sailors on a barrel. The City turned, twisted, standing at an angle, the flanks of walls looking up to heaven. The angle softened, straightened out. Again, we saw the Amko chopper. Smoke was curling up from its side. There was something wrong with its rotors. It veered, rising for a brief moment over the compound wall, clearing the Western Wailing Wall, the half-excavated site of David's City, the Ophel and the Kidron Valley, then spiraling and plunging out of control over the houses of Silwan. It cleared the houses, then was ripped apart by a massive explosion. A vast ball of fire scoured through the morning sky. Our little craft was buffeted by its heat wave. We were flying through a sudden bank of black smoke. We gained height again, rising above it. A second explosion wracked the hills. The fallen chopper, or what was left of it, had impacted, beyond the village houses, upon the northwest face of the Mount of Offense. King Solomon raised his altars here to the Pagan Gods of his thousand wives. The Reverend Risegood would not have chosen it as his final stop on Earth. But he must have experienced The Rapture, because nothing was ever found of his corpse.

The City sits, waits, contemplates its navel, sighs. Another day, another dolor. Another commercial strike, another day of disturbances of Law and Order. Little plumes of the white smoke of tear gas grenades wafting over the hills and valleys. Some people go to work normally, earning a living, pursuing a career, or a mate for the night or for life, worshipping God in various peculiar ways, drawing water from their own wells. Others seethe under curfew, plot, plan, meet in secret committees, brief the press on violations of human rights, mourn dead relatives and friends, grieve over jailed fathers, sons, mothers, daughters, sisters, brothers. They dream of walking freely down their own streets some day, while others curl up in fear of the disappearance of their own fragile freedoms. In smaller groups, more dangerous dreams and nightmares hatch, nurture, incubate.

Who am I to judge? At last, I do fall silent, awed by the inertial mass of it all. Palls of smoke, scattering from so many explosions. It's a wonder I have one gallstone left standing on another. It's a wonder anyone comes near me now without a mine detector. It's a wonder my wife isn't off to the divorce courts. It's a wonder I haven't hightailed it myself, to the American Embassy, for an emigrant's visa . . .

And yet . . . And yet . . .

Denunciations from Nahum Lauterman, alerted not by me but by His Own Correspondents. Padan breathing fire and brimstone from the secret hiding place he had arranged to design and write the pirate edition. "He thinks you've let us down, Joe, and welshed on our deal. Why couldn't you trust me just once, Joe?" But this was said more in sorrow than in anger, he knows the rules of confusion. The awful truth: We had not been paranoid enough. We should have set up a secure emergency line. Now he would have to rush to integrate this last chapter into the weekend's splurge, and gnash his teeth as the other gladrags scrummed *en masse* to the story. The hacks had dug out my presence with Anat and Old Sandpaper in the search helicopter. Linkages made with my earlier stun grenade disappearance, *sicarii* rumors and all. Is this some Lautermanish stunt? his rivals clamored, besieging Anat and myself in the manner of British tabloid hounds closing in on the Queen's dying corgi. My neighbor Bardak hosed them down from his garden, provoking several civil lawsuits.

Today's scandal, tomorrow's old hat. The Mayor stood his ground at a press conference. He had worked out the official version with his police chiefs and SHABAK. It was a dumb story, hinging on an undercover surveillance operation which went awry at the last moment due to technical communication errors. Despite it all, at the crunch, the Security Services foiled another dangerous plot by fanatics to "take the law into their own hands." As if a legal bomb dropped on the mosques might be, in theory, OK. Anat and I had been present due to the marginal involvement of the Department of Arts and Exhibits in the Sunny Amko cover ploy. It was regrettable that one journalist had received preferential treatment. That's what they call putting my life on the line. But what are you complaining about, gentlemen? An unthinkable crime has been foiled. Three cheers for SHABAK, the Municipality and the sane forces in the State of Israel.

Sitting at home watching the whole farce on television. Feeling sorry and not a little anxious about Old Sandpaper when he opens his coming weekend supplements and discovers what rough beast has slouched forth from my loins, in Tel Aviv, to be born.

"I'll show them," said Lauterman, addressing us again at The Hut, over a Bombe Jerusalem cocktail: "This time heads will really roll. The PM wants to know who knew and who didn't know and why about the Sunny Amko operation. Who protected Schaeffer and his group and let them get so close to success? Why was the mosque plot allowed to get so far? Who authorized protection of the Risegood-Schaeffer axis to the point of collusion? Who sabotaged the Mayor's intervention and gave the police the false all-clear? Who allowed official facilities to be used by Risegood and how did the good Reverend come to have the information that gave him a hold over whoever it gave him a hold over? Don't forget nobody's mentioning our alleged U.S. spy, who doesn't exist, of course. When that shit hits the fan . . . Oh boy. Well, all these and many other questions will not be answered in next week's episode of 'Soap.' The miracle ingredient, which cleans as it scrubs as it whitewashes. All we can do is fling a little grit in the works . . ."

And other unsolved riddles, enunciated by Anat, who is always in search of the rational: Why was Risegood himself on board the lethal chopper? Why did the plotters not abort when found out? Why go ahead with practically a suicide mission? Perhaps we are learning from our adversaries. We ape their worst. They strive towards ours. The violent spiral twists upwards. Later on I discovered from Dorothy Morgenthal some tidbits dropped by Agent Kool, via Nederlander Schatz, who returned from the Virgin Islands to be briefed by the FBI: "It seems your Colonel O'Donnell handed the Bureau enough evidence to charge Risegood with ordering Waiskopf's murder, and your Ampule Man with the actual deed. Risegood's Mossad protectors were showing him their dust. So I suppose he thought What the hell, let my soul die with the Philistines . . . well, they can bury that story now . . ." The crackle of her sigh over the oceans, from Manhattan to Man Hat On . . . Samsons beware, you have nothing to lose but your eyes. But by then . . .

"How should I know all the answers?" quoth Lauterman. "I'm only a simple Jewish hack, my honeys, my grandfather sold bread in Wurzburg. My father ran errands for *Die Deutsche Zeitung*. Then he slaved in the engine room of Ma'ariv. Shop-keepers, laborers and refugees. That's what we are. It was an honorable living."

This from a man who owns a six-bedroom villa in Tsahala, two cars, a share portfolio kept in his underwear, and a salary closing on six figures annually, dollars U.S., no pesos or Italian lire.

"Well, in three days' time, we'll see if we set fire to the world." He slapped me on the back and motored back to the coastline, to coax Padan and his printers into action. I took reluctant leave of Anat, who walked back to the Municipality, to see if she could put together Humpty Dumpty Jerusalem.

I walked out among the shards. Zion Square, the dusty traffic of the Jaffa Road, its souvenir shops, bagel kiosks, ice-cream shops, news-stands, bookshops, electrical stores, schmutter venues, a time warp going back to the 1950s but no further, no dead weight of history here, just choking exhaust fumes, car honking and lazy pedestrians waiting for all the lights at the King George junction to change at once, the crisscross free for all. Up Jaffa Road towards the jostling street market of Mahaneh Yehuda, the Camp of Judah, tomatoes, lady, apples of my eye, cucumbers at one-tenth the price, best halva, fresh meat slaughtered under your nose, madam, dust and grit from the crowd.

An honorable living. *Soneh Amcho*. It was I who read it in the contorted features of the dying recalcitrant Jew in his dingy letter-drop Manhattan office, with its cobwebbed desk and empty files. The revulsion that can't be denied for the direction my people have taken in these four decades. The headlong rush into fear and loathing, the soured compassion, the blindfolds, the suspicion and terror, the trickledown greed of the political classes. *Pour quoi, mes amis? Quo vadis?* A stiff-necked people, afflicted with a spiritual lumbago, crying our aches and pains to the world. Mistrustful of all doctors, soothsayers, soothers, reassurers and healers. Slamming the door to the enemy-cum-suitor on our stoop, holding up a placard to the reinforced steel bars and mesh-protected windows: LET ME IN, I ONLY WANT TO TALK. Oh Yeah? Piss off, shmendrick sons of bitches! We know your sort. We've buried enough dead. So what if we have to bury a few more? We have no fucking choice. We can trust absolutely no one.

The brainstruck generals, the veteran ex-terrorists, the venal politicians, the mad Rabbis who argue whether War or Peace is God's true commandment, who anathemize each other and everyone else. Does the Divine Law permit us to return land for peace, in order to preserve the sanctity of life, or does the commandment of Deuteronomy hold: "And when God delivers them to you, and you defeat them, then shall you utterly destroy them." Is that where we are heading? A religious sanction for genocide? Or will the God of Mercy, Compassion and Common Sense somehow wrest forth the last word?

Was Murray Waiskopf a turncoat? Did he rebel at the last moment, against the dark alliance of ecumenical zealotry? Before the blunt instrument of my Ampule Man, the Jew-hater, finally delivering a Jew, sent him out as a harbinger of The Rapture . . . Certainly he was not glad to see me: "Joe Dekel? You should be ashamed. You traitor." Those words were definitely uttered. But in his last breath, that final decision to give me the key to foil his ex-friends . . . Sunny Amko. A jolly banality masking a stern Revelation. In his last breath he tied us together. Was it an absolution, a forgiveness, or an ironic expedience? I don't think we'll meet again to find out. Even up above, as below, our brethren may well maintain their separate synagogues: My synagogue, his synagogue, and that one in which neither of us will set foot. Scratching each other's eyes out into eternity . . .

My Silencer. Whispering his blacklist files. Protecting us

from ourselves. "The Jewish Conspiracy," beloved of anti-Semites, is only directed against the Jews, ourselves. Old exclusions, the authoritarian cover-up of the cracks, all schisms denied, on pain of schism. There is the One God, and only One Path to Him. Never mind the diverse paths of reality. We prefer to construct and live in our fantasy. The terror of infiltration and pollution. And yet we swim in the muck of the world's reality, its disparate, incongruous, manifold complexities, its promiscuous jumble of perspectives. If God exists, then it is this He created. A function of sin? Or simply because it's more interesting this way? Should theology be left to the theologians? And of which sect, which splinter?

"Dekel is a malcontent. He snipes at and condemns almost indiscriminately . . . the constant jibes leave a somewhat bitter taste . . ." You should be in the inside of my mouth, baby. Dust and ashes. Is there a phoenix in the house? Preferably without a Boojum Tree. I see what I see, I taste what I taste. Feed me shit, I can't pretend it's chocolate. I have to report accurately, to the best of my knowledge and abilities. Of course, I can accept the judgement of my superiors: Shut up, and eat your spinach. But even if I shut up, others will shry: Dorothy Morgenthals, Peaceniks, Justiceniks, bleeding hearts with big mouths. The voice of witnesses, and of victims. We can't live on our own past pain for ever . . .

Evening, quiet, with Anat. I cook up a vegetarian stew. Not from principle, just because it's easy. Television again. The usual tumbrils: Two Palestinian teenagers shot dead in the West Bank. A Palestinian woman shot in Gaza. A petrol bomb thrown at a Jewish settler's car near Nablus. The aftermath of the Temple Mount plot, among the settlers. A majority disavow the attempt. Didi Schaeffer's wife is interviewed. A handsome young woman of barely twenty, traditionally headscarved, with two tots hanging on to her arms. Their faces are blank and bewildered. *The fathers have eaten sour grapes and the children's teeth are blunted.* She claims her husband was innocent. He was a gallant man, a Good Jew. If he acted rashly, it was out of love of his people, his country and his family.

What can I say to her grief? Nothing. But experts worry the affair, as usual, to shreds. A liberal specialist on the territories declares: The Occupation has been catastrophic for Israel. Our society has become torn and wounded. The *intifada* has broadened the trauma and brought it back to its primeval origins: Jew against Arab, to the death, with bows and arrows. But the alternative, peace with the Palestinians, is a chimera. Returning the territories would be an admission of weakness, a goad to further action by the Arab World. We can neither fight the war nor wage the peace. A pretty pickle. The counsel of despair, decay, endless turmoil. With such liberals, who needs reactionaries? Perhaps like moles we simply detest the light. Like the bewildered children, we cling to the apron strings of our fears . . .

Me, I still believe in the dialogue, the muddled fumbling through the swamp towards peace. Ex-terrorists gobbling Dorothy Morgenthal's gefilte fish. Mind-numbing speeches on wispy wraiths of friendships. The reconciliation of opposites which have turned out to be mirror images. The birthday party of the Siamese twins.

If there's no light at the end of the tunnel, then we should bloody well go and switch it on. For the world it is a-changing. The electronic window charts the flow: More Chinese students massing in Tiananmen Square. The new Russian Parliament lifting rocks, disturbing maggots of a slimy past. The Poles allowing semi-free elections. Can it last? Or will the darkness close in again?

You shouldn't knock it till you try it. Thursday. Anat goes to work on the Arts. The model-miniaturist will rebuild the shattered City, particle by particle. I stay at home with Space Max, managing to get my crew aboard the Space Station safely. I have managed to avoid decompression, loss of power, explosions and fire. Incredible. I save the program, freezing it at the peak of its optimism. For forty-eight hours now, no word from Lauterman. Better this way. The presses must be rolling, the weekend edition, with its sixty-page supplement, should be belting out in dozens of delivery vans around the country, bearing the secret edition, as the dummy run goes to the pulper. Panic again: Do I need this? What was wrong with being my own Silencer? The quiet life. Why volunteer? Just keep the crew orbiting up there, above the earth, safely cocooned . . .

I cling to Anat in the night. Her warmth, her strength, her acceptance of obligation and responsibility. Me? It's not my fault the world is fucked up. Do I look like the repairman?

Friday morning. Like any other day. The summer sun, streaming in the window. Bird chirps. A morning breeze.

Thump! A familiar thud at the letter box. "I'll get it!" says Anat. Climbing out of bed. An angelic sight, popping on the knee-length T-shirt with the *Peace Now* logo. She unlocks the door, scrabbles outside, comes in with the heavy folded edition, extracts the weekend supplement, opens it and riffles through. I examine the cracks on the ceiling. Redecorating is long overdue.

"Joe," she says quietly, "I have to tell you something."

"What might that be, light of my life?"

"There's nothing here. No Joe Dekel opus."

I snatch the supplement from her and crackle through. Police investigate murders of old age pensioners. An ex-bank manager who claims he was framed. Football scandals, an in-depth exposé. The new biography of a cocaine celebrity. Glasnost, a major report from Moscow.

Riffle through the main sections. Acres of newsprint, but no Dekel. No Christian-Jewish plot against the Temple Mount. No blacklist dossier revealed. No Waiskopf. No Didi Schaeffer. No Risegood. No Spy Who Never Was. Nada.

An enormous, overwhelming sense of relief, mixed with an

abyss of betrayal. I lunge for the telephone. They chase Lauterman for me, down corridors, up stairs, round bends, in broom cupboards. After thirty minutes his tentative voice on the line.

"OK, Joe. We had a try."

"So what happened?"

"They came at ten p.m. last night, in force. They stopped the presses and carted the lot away. The owner and the publisher were there, in their limousines. They ordered me to print the dummy copy. They sympathized. The lawyers would weigh our chances in the High Court. Given our secrecy and subterfuge they'd probably come down against us. It's a setback, Joe, but not the end of the story. The Spy, that's what got up their nose. An unfounded, unsubstantiated allegation that would seriously damage State Security. Mr. SHABAK came and wept in my office. What did we think we were doing? How could we jeopardize the entire U.S. relationship on a shaggy-dog story? American Jews would throw themselves from high windows. Funds would dry up. Strategic support disappear. I don't have a choice, Joe. But I'm not letting go. Padan will go to the States to dig for more pay dirt. At the least, we'll run the Risegood-Settler axis. That's safe enough, to bite the ass of extremists. Going for the mainstream: That's beyond my powers. They tagged us all the way, Joe. Ashkelon, my hide-out. I think they just wanted to know what we knew. Now they know we know nothing, they've come down on us. The PM phoned me at three in the morning. 'Nice try,' he said, 'but I'll have *your* balls in the wringer one day.' The fox still rules the roosters, when all's said and done. Sorry Joe. We tried. How do you feel?"

Like a pricked balloon. "What about the blacklist dossier?"

"It's pathetic. We had to ask the Anti-Slander League for a response. They said it was a forgery. Like the invisible spy, it does not exist. Nobody hates you, Joe, it's just your own paranoia. The Self-Hating Jew. You've been elected. It's all in your own head. The planets revolve in their orbits, the earth goes around the sun, the moon is made of green cheese. Everything in its place, in the best of a bad world. Don't meddle. Just leave it to those in the know."

The three wise monkeys. Blind, Deaf and Dumb. By choice. Well, it takes all sorts to make a world. If God had wanted it otherwise, he might have rewritten the program. As the Bible says he did, with Noah. But I can't see the difference between Mankind before and after the Flood. Both kinds seem pretty mean sons of bitches. Leavened by kindness, beauty, truth. What do I know? Am I a Prophet? Thank God, not any more.

There are no neat endings. Uncertainty, anxieties, will continue. All the Snarks who'll turn out to be Boojums. What was the G-Man's final hint here, about the Spy Who Never Is? The Name, which the Reverend Risegood took to his Rapture, the secret presumably kept, deep in the heart of Texas, by the Untouchable E. Dermott King – the Rich Man, slipping and sliding through the eye of the needle, who tried to help God Rise Again (though Sunny Amko can't be traced to him, another lead snapped by the wind) . . . The Name, still chased through the shadows by all the Agent Kools and kool agents, the Colonel O'Donnells, Jew-hating, Jew-loving, reformed CIA assassins . . . The Name, which everyone tried to shake out of me and which I shall probably never know: The Invisible Man, minus his bandages, still at his desk at some Pentagon locus, beaming his country's "secrets" towards us. Forbidden knowledge. The *prima materia* of inter-governmental blackmail. The manure pile of state security. While down here we sullen mortals will continue to be as secure as snowflakes in July, pretzels in a mixer, quarks in a cyclotron, hoping to exist for one instant.

Remember us unto life, O king who desires life, and write us in the book of life, for thine own sake, living God . . .

The instants pass. The quarks dance on. Time oozes. Nevertheless, things happen. You don't believe it till you see it, and even then you're only seeing it in light beams on the magic tube . . . Remembering that morning of pain and pique, sunk in the whirlpool of amazing days . . . That mad bad Friday, eve of Sabbath, as I sagged into my atavisms. *Blessed, glorified and extolled be the Name of the Supreme King of Kings . . . the First and the Last* . . . At least there's one Name to look up to. Saturday night I emerged from my contemplations. Another quiet evening at home with Anat. Both feeling we had to make a decision. One way or another. Either there is a future, or there isn't.

"I'll skip the diaphragm tonight, Joe," she declared.

Who am I to argue with my beloved?

The Rabbis say one should think holy thoughts on such occasions, and consider the sayings of the Wise, and so on. I failed to observe this commandment. I just enjoyed, and shot my seed, regardless.

In the morning, the world brought back its fears. The students of Tiananmen Square, massacred. Thousands shot, burned, crushed by tanks. The world watching the entire horror on television, as one, in terror and pain.

In Iran, the death of the Ayatollah Khomeini. Frenzied millions mourning about his bier. Will Faith continue to burn, with the quick fuel of martyrs? We held our breath, and hoped not to choke.

In Poland, the ballot box, speaking of hope against all odds. A dawn sighted, after a long, frozen night, in at least one corner of the globe?

But in the Middle East, *plus ça change*, et cetera. The old wheel continuing to revolve. The killing resumed, in Israel-Palestine, after a relatively quiet weekend. To which station are we headed, on our runaway train? To Warsaw, or to Tiananmen Square?

The weeks, the months slide by, as we wait to find out if there is a continuation of the Joe-Anat saga. Medical science confirming procreation. A surge of delight and panic washing over us, as the rest of the world sinks into the mush of background –

astounding events and tumults, elsewhere . . . Hungarians tearing down their Iron Curtain, East Germans flooding West in droves. A Solidarity government in Poland. Old hard men shattering in East Berlin. Anat pukes all over the bathroom sink, while Berliners pour through their shattered Wall, crying and reveling, tearing the concrete blocks with picks and shovels. The world seems with child. A fair or foul countenance? Massed crowds joyously demanding Freedom. The chiming keyrings of Prague. The Bulgarian Communist Party pledges reform! Anat waddles, in taut clothes, my own belly swells in empathy. We raid the icebox in relays, growling strangely. In Romania, of all places, the pressure bursts like a bomb, sweeping a tyrant into the dustbin of history. My wife's stomach is warm with the presence. Was that a kick? A premature pulse. In Jerusalem, Peace Now demonstrate again. A day of rubber bullets and police hoses. Arabs and Jews, tear gassed together. At least that might be some advance.

February, Nelson Mandela walks free from jail, and my wife is like a barrage balloon. South Africa to be free? Who could believe it? But on our terrain, business as usual . . . Will we talk peace? And with whom? And over what? Will we find a way out of the cycle of violence, or will we be caught out again? What sort of government will we end up with, one-faced, two-faced, six-faced? The world fiddles while we burn. Till when, O Lord? A million Jews are expected to flood in from the old broken Russian Empire. The Nation, still besieged, yet determined to multiply. But I will reproduce in a more personal way.

We have opted for a natural birth. The child will emerge from the mother, not the other way around. I don the white coat, the gauze mask. Again, a mere observer of the scene, gibbering, sweating and perplexed. In a short while, God bless, there will be a new voice, asking questions, probing, protesting, grumbling, griping, nagging, noodging, carping, complaining and criticizing, refusing to take no for an answer.

MOUNT, ZION

Yes, let all the pain, anguish, frustration, anger and burning dreams of the fucked-up human race flood in, pervade, transfuse, and soften our iron carapace. Unplug your ears, and let the cries all echo. Just let them know you're not having it. Don't ever let time run out!

> Come out, come out, whoever you are!
> The more of us malcontents, the better.
> Replenish the earth. Amen. Selah.
> So what do you expect, a medal?
> Get on with it, for God's sake!

A NOTE ON THE AUTHOR

Simon Louvish was born in Glasgow, Scotland, in 1947, and lived in Jerusalem, Israel, between 1949 and 1968. He served in the Israeli army between 1965 and 1967 as a military cameraman, including the period of the Six-Day War of June 1967. From 1968 to 1970 he studied film making at the London School of Film Technique, and from 1970 to 1975 co-produced a series of controversial independent documentary films on South Africa, Greece and Israel. In 1979 he published in Great Britain an account of his Israeli experiences in *A Moment of Silence*. He has since written five acclaimed novels, including the anarchic *Blok* Trilogy, a massive satirical saga of the Middle East. He has been involved for many years in advocating Israeli-Palestinian peace, supporting those campaigning to promote a political settlement against the tidal waves of conflict and war. He is married and lives in London and also teaches part-time at the London International Film School.